MW00355929

THE MOMENT
of
MENACE

A Novel

JOE ROTHSTEIN

JOE ROTHSTEIN

Printed in the United States of America
First Printing 2022
First Edition 2022

ISBN: 978-0-9976999-5-1
Library of Congress Control Number: 2019902936

For information about this title or to order other books by Joe Rothstein:

The Latina President and the Conspiracy to Destroy Her
The Salvation Project

www.joerothstein.net
jrothstein@rothstein.net

For my family, and yours

FEBRUARY

CHAPTER 1

For most of the year, Ohio's governor, Lester Bowles, followed the same morning routine: awake at 5:00 a.m., mount his Trek Domane and bike the predawn streets from the governor's residence to nearby Alum Creek Trail, then follow the trail south five miles, where a waiting staff member would drive him back to the governor's residence; shower, dress, breakfast at six thirty, begin his work at his residence office at seven thirty.

Occasionally a state legislator or a political ally or an enterprising lobbyist or a resourceful reporter would join him on his ride. The paved trail ran easily, conducive to private conversation. When snow or other severe weather became an obstacle, Bowles remained in the governor's residence, utilizing its well-equipped gym to focus on strength training.

This routine was severely constricted during the six months he was the Republican Party's nominee for vice president of the United States. Six horrible, embarrassing, forgettable months. Now it was over, the unwanted notoriety mercifully receding. The comfortable, organized, productive life he never really wanted to give up was slowly returning to routine.

This winter had been exceptionally mild for Ohio. By early February only patches of snow remained. They were shaded by beds of Indian grass that lined portions of the bike path. Winter chill required layering up a bit, but for Bowles, a fifth-generation Ohioan, the crisp air washing over him felt like a pleasant wake-up shower.

The remainder of this day would not be his own. The legislature was in session. A full calendar would demand his time. But now, on the trail alone, Governor Bowles could just be Les, free to converse with himself, often a productive partner. Solitude was welcome for a man who enjoyed his own company.

When Bowles reached the southern section of the Alum Creek trailhead this morning, however, much to his annoyance he could see he would not be alone. Another rider already was there in semidarkness, silhouetted against the bare branches of the red maples that lined that portion of the path.

"Les."

It was a half-whispered call.

Les? Supplicants who arrived for these morning rides almost always deferred to him as "governor."

And then a bit louder: "Les."

This time loud enough for him to recognize and be startled by the source.

"Gil?"

"Yes."

The apparition moved closer.

"My God," said Bowles. "Gil! Where have you been?"

"Here, near the trees, where it's darker," the voice summoned him.

The generally undemonstrative Bowles wrapped his arms around the shadowy figure. For the past few months, Bowles had been quietly searching for Gil Adonis.

Gil eased out of Lester Bowles's grasp.

"We have to be very careful," said Gil. "If anyone sees us, this needs to look like two friends out for a casual early morning ride. Nothing unusual."

"Gil, if you're in trouble, I've got a state police car waiting nearby. They monitor me just in case," said Bowles. "I'll call them. Let's take it back to my place."

"No," said Gil. "Someone wants me dead, Les. I don't know who. It could be the president herself. I can't be seen with the law, even yours. Let's just ride and talk. I'll explain."

"How did you know I'd be here?" asked Bowles.

They started biking slowly together.

"Do you think there's anything I don't know about you after all these years?" said Gil. "Unless the snow's waist-deep, I knew you'd come. I just thought you'd come sooner. I've been here every morning for about a week waiting for you."

Gil Adonis and Lester Bowles had grown up together in a wealthy Columbus neighborhood. Bowles, scion of a political family, was ordained to follow his father, grandfather, and uncles into government. Gil set out to make millions managing his own hedge fund and instead made billions. Last year, Gil had engineered the nomination of Zach Bowman as the Republican Party's presidential candidate; then he had talked a reluctant Lester Bowles into serving as Bowman's vice presidential running mate. A Bowman scandal late in the campaign blew up the team's election chances. After the election, Bowles, embarrassed by his association with Bowman and in a bid to minimize media contact, went to Europe with his wife for an extended vacation. When he returned, Gil had disappeared.

There was barely enough light to see, but the trail was well maintained with few ruts or obstacles. Gil and Les were alone on the trail, riding at an easy pace.

"I need your help, Les," said Gil. "Someone tried to kill me. I don't know who. Most likely my old friends at the Salvation Project put out a contract on me because I failed to elect you and Bowman. I knew when I signed up with them that they were a 'take no prisoners' crowd. And since I didn't deliver a president for them in the election, that's probably a capital offense in their eyes."

"Who else could it be? A jealous husband or someone you screwed in a stock deal?"

"I wish," said Gil. "I could get out of that easily. No. If it wasn't the Salvation Project guys, it was the president."

Les stopped biking and turned to look at Gil.

"You can't be serious. Tenny won the election. She beat you. Why would she want to kill you?

"Because I tried to kill her."

Lester Bowles shook his head in disbelief. "I can't believe that!"

"It's true, Les. I was on a mission to save the world. That meant getting rid of her and electing that idiot Bowman, with you as vice president. Then, maneuvering you into the White House. I'm not a killer, but most people who fire weapons in war aren't killers either. They fight for a cause they think is worth killing for. That was my mindset."

The sun was a bit higher now, the trail much easier to see.

They resumed biking.

"That was your mindset, or still is?" Bowles asked.

"The most unbelievable thing happened a few days after the election," said Gil. "The president invited me to have dinner with her at the White House. Her intelligence people had found out about our project. They arrested some of our key people. I was sure they knew about my role in all of it, and damned if she doesn't ask me to come and have dinner with her."

"Likely a trap to arrest you."

"That's what I thought. But I figured that if I didn't accept her invitation they'd find me anyway. No point running away from a president of the United States who might be stalking you. So I went. It was just her and me, having dinner together like we were old friends. And yes, she knew all about the Project and where I fit in. Tenny even knew I tried to have her killed. She wanted to know why."

"That was pretty gutsy of her."

"Not just gutsy, but she really wanted to know why someone like me, stinking rich, powerful in my own world, would get involved with a conspiracy like the Salvation Project. And why other successful people would be part of it too. So I told her. We spent nearly three hours alone together."

"How'd she react?"

"She pretty much agreed with me about what needed to be done to save the country, but she disagreed about our plan for doing it."

Bowles biked in silence for a moment. "It sounds like you should have talked with her long before the election. It would have saved you a lot of money and trouble. Why do you suspect she might have set you up to be murdered?"

"Les, after our dinner I got into my car, parked right outside the White House. It was a driving rainstorm. I jumped into the back seat not realizing that the driver wasn't Hughes, my regular guy. Whoever was in the driver's seat turned around and smashed a towel against my face. I don't know what was on it, but it knocked me out before I knew what was happening. When I woke up, I was in a doctor's office. Luckily, my security guys were parked nearby and realized I was in trouble. They tracked the sensors in my car and chased off the fucker who gassed me. Then they took me to one of the docs on my medical team. If my guys hadn't been sharp enough, whoever was behind it would have killed me and dumped my body somewhere."

"And you think your meeting with Tenny was set up so she could do that to you?"

"That was my first guess. Who else would know I was there? So after I left the doc's office, I found a place to hide. I needed time to think, time to stay out of sight. Let whoever tried to kill me think I might be dead from that shit they shoved up my nose. I didn't want the FBI or CIA looking for me."

"So now what will you do?"

"Since the election, the president's been doing what she told me she'd do. I've been following it in the news. She's saying the right things, putting together people to study the problems we talked about. I'm less inclined to think she was behind what happened to me. If it wasn't her, it must have been the Salvation Project people. In that case, I need her help to get them off my back."

"How?"

"I can give her more information so they can break up the Project. As long as they're operational, I'm not safe, and she's not safe either. They're a ruthless crowd, Les. I didn't realize that until late in last year's campaign. When I got involved, I thought I was dealing with people like me who think humanity's at risk and that we need to change things pretty fast to save it. Toward the end of the campaign, that's not what I was seeing. What I saw was a bunch of murderous people who would do anything to get power. They've taken control of the Project. It's the real threat now."

"And what if you're wrong about who tried to kill you? You'd be signing your own death warrant if you contact Tenny and she's the one who set you up. She's one tough lady, and I'm sure she holds grudges like the rest of us. Finding out you tried to kill her makes for one helluva grudge."

"It's a gamble. But I need to find out. I can't hide forever. I need to make contact with Tenny. And I need to do it in a way the Project doesn't find out. That means I can't just pick up the phone and call her directly. That's why I've come to you. I need your help."

Bowles stopped riding.

"I'll do anything to help you, Gil. You know that. Let's go back to house. The place is guarded like Fort Knox. You'd be safe there." He reached for a small box attached to his belt. "All I need to do is press this button and my security guys will be here in a minute."

Gil shook his head. "No good, Les. I've thought this through. There's no place to hide. How long could I stay with you without people raising questions? Word would get out. You and your whole family would be in danger. All my life, when I've had a problem, I've dealt with it, not ducked it. This is the biggest problem I've ever had. A real life-and-death problem."

"How can I help, then?"

"Let's ride and keep talking," said Gil.

Morning light spilled through the lowest branches of a grove of pines. Gil's forehead became a ruddy image behind a protective riding mask and gray wool cap. Only his eyes seemed to speak.

"Les, I need to meet with Tenny again. Find the safest way for me to get that message to her without calling her yourself or contacting her directly. That would tip off someone in the White House who might monitor her calls."

"The Project has someone in the White House?" asked Bowles incredulously. "With all that security?"

"I'm sure," said Gil. "That's the only way they could have known I was meeting her for dinner. And they may be monitoring your contacts too. You need to go through a third party."

They biked in silence to the point along the trail where Lester Bowles's car and driver were waiting.

Gil reached into his pocket and pulled out a three-by-five card.

"Here's my new cell number. When you've got a plan, get someone, not you, to call that number. Let it ring twice and then hang up. I'll meet you the next morning just like this, for a ride down this trail. You'll do it?"

Bowles removed his riding helmet and lightly tapped his friend's with it. "And now where are you going?"

"I've got a place, safe for a while," said Gil Adonis. "Remember, I grew up in Columbus, same as you. And I've got my own security guys waiting for me, same as you."

CHAPTER 2

Library board meetings generally are congenial gatherings of public-service-minded locals discussing ways to expand resources and increase community engagement. But not tonight. Tonight, two hours of mostly angry testimony crowded out other matters on the agenda. Two hours of taunts for some speakers, applause for others. The small meeting room grew increasingly uncomfortable with the presence of a standing-room-only crowd and overheated arguments.

The issue of the moment was Captain Underpants. A citizens' group had petitioned to ban the popular children's series from the library's shelves. Too offensive. Too potty-mouthed. Too many of the wrong messages for impressionable young children. Others felt just as strongly that the series should remain available. They argued that the books contained no sexual references; no profanity; no more violence than in TV cartoons, video games, or comic books. And the kids loved them. The Captain Underpants battle had been fought at library board meetings in many states and localities. Tonight, the fight had arrived at Kitsap County in Washington State.

Ben Sage, reporter for the *Poulsbo Monitor*, loved it. This debate, the tension between children's interests and free speech, was what he had been missing on the larger political stage where he had lived the past few decades. Tonight, Ben was the *Monitor's* local government reporter. He also was the

Monitor's editor and publisher. A new role, a new life, and Ben was reveling in it. His goal had been to escape the grasp of national politics. Here he had done it.

Ben Sage had managed the political campaigns of countless members of Congress, state governors, and candidates on all rungs of the political ladder. He was widely recognized as a master strategist and image maker. Months earlier he had guided the reelection campaign for the president of the United States, a charismatic Mexican American heiress known to the world as "Tenny." President Isabel Aragon Tennyson was Ben's political creation. Many years ago he had recognized that she had a rare combination of charisma, social purpose, and the wealth to underwrite her own campaigns. With Ben's guidance, she won a congressional seat in Los Angeles. Then she became a US senator from California. Four years ago, Ben had managed Tenny's successful campaign for president. In November, she had won a second term in the White House.

That reelection campaign had been unlike any in Ben's experience. During the Democratic Party's national convention, Tenny's longtime friend Carmen Sanchez was poisoned and nearly died. The opposition inferred that Ben committed the crime, suggesting that Ben, Tenny, and Sanchez were involved in a love triangle, and the motive was jealousy. Authorities quickly debunked that rumor, but Tenny's image, and her poll numbers, had been seriously damaged. The notoriety forced Ben to resign from the campaign at a critical time.

Ben was a backstage guy. A noncelebrity. One who wrote the script and directed the show while others were in the spotlight. But the scandal manufactured by the opposition had dragged Ben to center stage. Ultimately, Ben had returned to manage the campaign's final weeks. Tenny was narrowly reelected, but by then Ben decided he had had enough. He said goodbye to Tenny, to politics, and to political image-making. He turned over his consulting and media company to his longtime partner, Lee

Searer, and accepted a friend's offer to manage a small newspaper in the picturesque port community of Poulsbo, Washington.

Tonight, Ben's most significant concern as he walked to his car after the meeting was how he could do justice to both sides when writing the story of the Captain Underpants debate, three thousand miles and a world away from the turbulence of national government and politics.

Engrossed in thought, Ben was not immediately aware of the footsteps directly behind him until a voice quietly whispered, "Ben Sage?"

Ben turned to respond, surprised that anyone in his new community recognized him.

It was a tall man dressed entirely in black, the hood on his down jacket pulled so low only his eyes and lips were visible. The man held out his right hand in greeting and pushed back the hood from his face with his left. Ben was startled to see a face that was all too familiar and all too out of place in Poulsbo. It was Lester Bowles, Ohio's governor, the Republican Party's candidate for vice president in last year's campaign.

"Please don't say anything," said Bowles.

Ben, disoriented by this odd encounter, simply nodded.

"Is this your car?" Bowles asked.

Ben nodded again.

"Do you mind if I join you in it for a few moments of conversation?"

"Of course not," said Ben, finally able to find his voice.

Bowles was six feet three with graying, close-cropped hair. Poster perfect for political media. Ben's car was a Toyota Prius, not ideal for large people, and Bowles had to bend carefully to settle into the front passenger seat.

"You're probably surprised to see me here," said Bowles.

"Surprise is hardly the word," said Ben.

Bowles could not suppress a chuckle. "Me too," he replied. "After the fiasco of that campaign, I've been embarrassed to be seen anywhere by anyone. I made such a damned fool of myself."

"You weren't the fool," said Ben. "Zach Bowman was."

Bowman, the presidential candidate, had been caught in a sex scandal that destroyed his credibility. Bowles resigned from the ticket in disgust. The combination of the scandal and Bowles's resignation was enough to ensure Tenny's reelection.

"No surprise there," said Bowles. "Zach always was an unpredictable clown."

"Why did you run with him then?" asked Ben.

"Long story. Can't tell you."

"Okay, but you're here now because you want to tell me something."

"No, I want to ask you for something." Bowles hesitated, momentarily unsure of how to begin. Finally, he said, "I'm sure you're familiar with the name Gil Adonis."

"Of course. One of your richest financial backers."

"He's that, but not only that. He's my closest friend. We grew up together in Columbus. We're like brothers. It has nothing to do with money or politics."

"That I didn't know."

"Few people do. And he's the reason I'm here. Gil's in serious trouble. Serious as in some people are out to kill him. He needs to meet with President Tennyson, and he needs a place to hide while he's waiting to do it. I'm here to ask you to make the contact with Tenny and to hide him until they can get together."

Ben looked at Bowles as if he were insane. He tried to say, "You can't be serious," but the words didn't form. All he could do was stare.

"I can't tell you everything," said Bowles, "but let's start here. You know for a fact who I am, don't you?"

"Of course," said Ben.

"And you know I'm not a frivolous person. In fact, my reputation is that I'm downright stodgy."

Ben smiled at the self-deprecation. "I'd agree with that."

"Now, let me tell you something you don't know. The president invited Gil Adonis to the White House a few days after the election. Just the two of them. For dinner. They agreed to get together again right after her State of the Union speech. That was about ten days ago. She's likely wondering why Gil hasn't responded to any of her attempts to contact him."

"You got this from Adonis?"

"Yes. It will be no surprise to her that he's ready for that meeting."

"Well, why can't you do it? You're a governor. They'll take your call."

"That's one of the things I can't tell you," Bowles said. "I can't make the call, but you can, and that call may save Gil's life."

Ben closed his eyes as the memory of the campaign's last few weeks of terror once again consumed him. The images from those weeks were still so real. The CIA director had approached him just like this. Ben was the only one the director said he could trust to deliver a package to the president. He couldn't say why, but it could mean the difference between the president's reelection and defeat. And, admitted the director, the mission could be dangerous. Dangerous? Ben had barely survived. On a moonless night, he was chased through the woods by assassins determined to kill him for that package. Ben was shot and nearly died, but he accomplished his mission. Tenny was reelected. Then he had moved three thousand miles away and given up a lucrative business so he would never again need to navigate the dangers and intrigue of high-wire politics. But he had not escaped his former life. Not with this man sitting next to him in the car's passenger seat.

Governor Lester Bowles was not a frivolous man. Coming to see him incognito with this request was a risk few people would take. The situation he described certainly must be real for him to be here. The danger must be imminent.

Without opening his eyes, Ben said, "Governor, I just can't do it. There are things I can't tell you either. Things that happened last year during the campaign. I can't talk about them. I don't even know what was behind them, but I do know I don't want to relive them."

"Ben, I don't want to be here. I have no business being mixed up in whatever this is. I won't know how to explain it if anyone finds out I'm here. I'm here to try to help my friend Gil. But this is about more than saving Gil Adonis. This is about saving Tenny too. Probably saving the country. I'm convinced of that. You have to do it."

A long pause filled the chilled February night air. If the car windows had been open, they might have admitted the sounds of waves gently caressing piers jutting into nearby Liberty Bay. Maybe the squawks of a few gulls, searching for food in the floodlit beam of the public walkway. Some chatter and laughs from a waterfront restaurant. A car's engine coming alive from the other end of the parking lot.

But the car windows were closed. All Ben could hear was the sound of danger.

Resignation forced an unintended sigh.

"I've got an extra bedroom in my apartment," said Ben. "But what do I do with him? He can't stay there all day."

"Then you'll do it?"

"I'll do it, and I'll try to get him in and out of here fast. How do I contact him?"

Bowles reached passed Ben toward the dashboard's hazard light switch. After a few quick blinks, he pressed it again to turn the hazard light off.

Almost immediately, a figure emerged from the darkness and walked quickly across the parking lot. He opened a back door and seated himself as if he were a taxi passenger, an ordinary fare, ready to tell the driver "where to."

"Ben," said Bowles, "meet Gil Adonis."

CHAPTER 3

Gil Adonis, one of the world's richest people, slept that night on a single bed in a room Ben had not yet fully furnished. In the room's small closet, Adonis hung a dark blue Armani suit, two pairs of tan chinos, and four shirts, one of them business white, the others casual. For outerwear, Gil had a Patagonia puff jacket. In a dresser drawer he placed a black turtleneck, one folded tie, three pairs of boxer-style shorts, three handkerchiefs, and three pairs of socks. All of this emerged from a Tumi shoulder garment bag. He carried a lockable leather valise as well, containing cash and other valuables. Gil Adonis was a man on the run, traveling light.

The next morning Ben pointed out the location of cereal, eggs, and coffee in his kitchen; On a tourist map he marked the location of an IHOP three blocks away. Then Ben hurried to his office to write the story of last night's library board meeting. He decided to be proactive about mentioning his houseguest to his staff. An old friend from DC, he said, down on his luck. If you see him, don't embarrass him with personal questions. It's just a short stay until things work out for him. Ben managed to keep from smiling at the irony of describing a billionaire as an out-of-work vagrant.

Ben spent the rest of the day obsessed with the puzzle of how to make Adonis's stay as short as possible. Governor Bowles seemed to think it was as easy for Ben as dialing into the White House and making an appointment. But once Ben took possession of Gil Adonis, he realized the potential complications. Yes, he could call Tenny's chief of staff, Henry Deacon. Deac would take his call. But what if the situation wasn't as Lester Bowles described it? What if seeing Adonis was not what Tenny wanted? Ben would be in the awkward position of antagonizing the president and having no path for getting rid of his new roommate. He could call Carmen Sanchez, Tenny's best friend, now also the US secretary of commerce. Ben, Tenny, and Carmie had shared many adventures through the years, but he was reluctant to involve Carmie if there was danger. Ben mentally speed-dialed through his many Washington, DC, contacts, failing to think of anyone who would have ready access to the president and who also could be trusted to maintain the secrecy the circumstances required. Gil Adonis was an important financial figure, an international personality. The fact that he was on the run was news. Washington was a town that leaked like a rusty downspout at the hint of such stories.

The workday ended. Ben stopped by the Poulsbo dock, bought a few fresh crab cakes and a six-pack of Alaskan Amber ale, and returned home to find Adonis reading his copy of *The Story of Philosophy* by Will Durant.

"You've read this?" asked Adonis.

Ben nodded. "In college. I've kept it around and now and then dip into it."

"Same here," said Adonis. "I have a hard time with philosophy, but Durant ties it all together. Like he says with the title, this reads like a story."

Adonis began the day searching the apartment to assure himself there were no hidden weapons or recording devices. It didn't take long. The apartment was one of six attached two-bedroom units on a single lot. Each of the bedrooms had its own bath. A twenty-by-twenty-foot space served as both a living room and dining area. The kitchen was just large enough to be serviceable for both food service and a washer-dryer combo. It was clear to Adonis from his search that Ben hadn't occupied the apartment long. Packing boxes still lined one wall of Ben's bedroom.

Just to be certain, Adonis summoned his security team, which had accompanied him and Bowles to Poulsbo and taken up posts nearby to keep the apartment under surveillance. Posing as a maintenance worker, a security man entered the apartment and swept it for hidden electronics. All clear. Adonis, at least for the moment, could relax.

"Beer?" Ben asked. He took the caps off two of the bottles and handed one to Adonis. "Crab cakes and beer for dinner," said Ben. "Hope that's okay with you."

"Fresh off the boat, I assume," said Adonis. "Thanks. Haven't had them in quite a while."

Ben had trouble deciding what to ask or say. So much of Adonis's financial life was a mystery, and his campaign to elect Zach Bowman was unfathomable. Such a smart, successful guy trying to make such a dunce president. And now Adonis was running from some force so menacing he couldn't talk about it, except to the president of the United States. Where do you start that conversation?

Adonis had no such problem. Over dinner, he focused entirely on Ben, his personal history, his political campaigns, his reasons for moving to Poulsbo and abandoning a national reputation and the political and financial power that came with it. Ben soon realized that Adonis's curiosity was behind much of his financial success. His mind was programmed to seek out and absorb information, whatever the source, even if it was in a small apartment like this with a total stranger like Ben.

After a few beers Ben felt enough at ease to ask his own questions, starting with the one that had nagged him for months. How had Gil Adonis become obsessed with electing Zach Bowman president?

Adonis picked up the copy of *The Story of Philosophy* that he had been reading earlier, flipped through a few pages, found what he was looking for, and handed the open book to Ben.

"Have you read this?" Gil asked.

"Plato?"

"Plato's *Republic*."

"I'm sure my college philosophy course covered it," said Ben. "If you're going to test me on Plato or philosophy here, I can guarantee you I'm going to fail. I've spent my life working in one of the least philosophical businesses there is—practical politics."

"If you think that, you don't know what business you've been in," said Adonis. "The question of how a society organizes itself has been central to philosophy since the Greeks. It's right there with questions of who we are, why we exist, what's the meaning of life. Philosophy is at the core of politics."

Adonis gestured to one of its pages.

"More than two thousand years ago, in Plato's *Republic*, he talked about the same problems we have right how. Should rich people rule because they're rich? Should the strongest rule because they're strong? Should the people rule because they're numerous? Should religion rule because that's God's plan? More than two thousand years later, after real-life experience with all these systems, we haven't figured it out yet."

"We have figured it out," Ben quickly responded. "That's what democracy's all about. It's what America's all about. I can't sit here and tell you I've worked with philosophers or political geniuses as candidates. A lot of lightweights run for office and get elected. A lot of bad decisions get made. But the system self-corrects. I think that's the strength of the system. It makes mistakes, learns from them, and self-corrects. Isn't that also the core of science? Try. Fail. Learn from your failure. Make progress from the experience."

"That *is* the core of the scientific method," Adonis replied. "But science is advancing while your system of politics is getting weaker. In fact, science is making politics weaker. Science knew about global warming decades ago. Your politics couldn't do much to respond until the planet was on fire. Science developed the communications system we call the internet. Your politics let it grow so wildly it's distorting democratic elections. Nuclear energy? It's more of a threat to destroy humanity than ever. Your politics seldom discusses it. The problem is that science is developing far faster than most people can understand. And if they don't understand it, how can they decide how to use it and control it? Hardly a member of Congress comes out of science. A few doctors and dentists maybe. What do they know? What do the people who elect them know? Politics is not self-correcting anywhere near fast enough to manage the consequences."

Ben sat back in his chair and looked at this man sitting across from him. Adonis's argument disturbed him. It had been a long time since he was in a political discussion that didn't deal with the practical questions of strategy and budget and training and presentation. He knew there had to be answers to Adonis's argument, but for the moment, he was at a loss. In fact, he was a refugee from the disaster of last year's political campaign. He had run away from the very system he was now trying to defend. Ben had counseled his political clients that when they found themselves in spots like this during debates and media interviews, they should try to change the subject. Now he tried to employ his own advice.

"Gil, I asked you why you supported Zach Bowman for president, a guy who is the worst example of a political ideal. And you answered by pointing me to Plato's *Republic* and talking about political philosophy. What's the connection? I can't imagine anything less related."

Adonis closed the book and didn't reply. He sat quietly for a moment, trying to frame his answer. "I can't tell you, Ben. Sorry, maybe someday, but not today. But it's why someone wants to kill me. Why I'm here."

CHAPTER 4

Plato and death threats? The puzzling association kept Ben's mind churning when he should have been blissfully asleep. He had made what he thought was a clean break from political power combat, moving three thousand miles to distance himself from that life. In Poulsbo, Ben's evenings ended early and without guilt that he was shortchanging a client or missing a deadline. He was reading books instead of political polls, making new friends instead of attending campaign fundraisers. He was looking forward to fishing when the salmon showed up in the coastal waters and to hiking the trails in the Olympic Peninsula. He no longer was living on the knife-edge of triumph or disaster. But tonight, anxiety once again was his bed partner. Worse, so was fear. Each night noise was open to sinister interpretation. How easy would it be to defeat his front door lock? Did he hear someone near his parked car? Would he get caught in the crossfire if Gil Adonis's pursuers found him? Did he need to fear Adonis himself since he, Ben Sage, now was one of the few people on earth who knew Adonis's whereabouts and might be considered a person who knew too much, therefore requiring removal? From what? Because of what?

And what did Plato have to do with it? What Ben did know, and knew with certainty, was that Gil Adonis had to go, and quickly.

The sun was just a dim suggestion when Ben conceded that he had lost all hope of sleeping. He quietly dressed and drove to the Poulsbo waterfront for breakfast at the Green Light Diner.

"Whoa, you almost beat me here," said DuWayne Green, the diner's owner. "I just unlocked five minutes ago."

"Big day ahead," Ben lied. "Get me ready for it with your Hungry Viking special."

DuWayne tilted his head quizzically. "You expecting company? That's a lot of food for one. Hash browns, buttermilk biscuit with sausage gravy, ham steak, bacon, and a fried egg with cheese. Sure you want all that?"

Ben looked more closely at the menu and then back at DuWayne and smiled. "Hold the cheese."

While he waited for his food, Ben scanned the morning edition of the *Seattle Times* and on page three found the answer to his Gil Adonis problem.

Beneath a photo of US Vice President Sheila Fishburne was the news that she would be in Seattle, staying overnight while returning to Washington from a trip to Japan. Sheila Fishburne. Perfect. Ben and Sheila were longtime friends from the political wars. "Fish," he and her friends called her. He had helped her win Alaska's lone seat in the US House. Now she was Tenny's vice president. From his new perch at the newspaper he could play reporter and interview her privately. While together, he could pass her the hot potato known as Gil Adonis. Fish would be returning to Washington the next day and could carry the message to Tenny.

Ben quickly summoned DuWayne, changed his order to a carryout, and raced to his still empty office. It was too early for his staff to arrive but midmorning in Washington, DC. Fish's appointment secretary would already be there. Making an appointment for a private meeting with Fish would require just one call to her with little explanation.

The burden of decision finally off his back, Ben rewarmed his food in the office microwave and ate hungrily, wishing he had not skipped the cheese topping for his egg.

CHAPTER 5

Gil Adonis did not seem surprised when Ben described the plan to him later in the day. He already had sized up Ben as a well-connected problem solver and had confidence that if his friend Lester Bowles considered Ben a reliable conduit, eventually Ben would find a way to connect him with the president.

"When will the vice president be in Seattle?" he asked.

"She gets here day after tomorrow. Then leaves for DC the next morning. I'd guess she'll meet with the president the day after that."

"That fast? That would be good for me, and I'm sure a big relief for you. Tell you what. To celebrate, let's go out to dinner," said Adonis.

"Is that a good idea?" asked Ben. "You're supposed to be hiding out. What if someone recognizes you?"

"Would you have recognized me if you'd seen me at a restaurant table?" asked Adonis. "No, you wouldn't. And it was your business in the campaign to know who I was. I've never tried to attract media attention. I learned early that most of that hype is crapola unless you're in politics or entertainment. My ego doesn't need it. I've made some of my best deals because people created their own mental images of me, usually larger and worse than I really am. Man of mystery--ha. No, nobody will recognize me."

"But what if they do?" Ben persisted, concerned about his own safety as well as Adonis.

Adonis reached for his down jacket and wool cap. "Ben, you don't know it, but my security guys have been watching us ever since you picked me up in the parking lot. Have you seen them when you left the apartment or when you've come home?"

Ben was startled. He had not seen a suspicious person or situation anywhere, even though while harboring Adonis he thought he had been on full alert.

"They're good," said Adonis without waiting for Ben to reply. "If there's trouble, they'll be there. Faster than you can imagine. Otherwise, they just fade into the background. So let's have a good meal somewhere. I'd like to see the town. The waterfront area."

Ben drove them down Viking Avenue to Lindvig Way, past the twelve-foot steel-and-concrete Viking statue that guarded the entrance to the old town. He turned onto Front Street, lined with Norwegian flags, past the Sons of Norway Hall, Sluys' Bakery, Thor's Hammer and Needle Tattoo, and Valholl Brewing. Front Street would pass muster as a Hollywood set designer's image of a small waterfront community in Norway. Poulsbo was settled in the nineteenth century by immigrants who found the area remarkably similar to the Nordic sea life they had left behind, with its navigable waterways and abundant catches. Now, Poulsbo was dependent on tourism more than fishing, and on the economic benefit flowing in from nearby US naval bases.

Ben turned into the waterfront parking lot adjoining The Loft, a seafood restaurant on pilings reaching out into Liberty Bay. In summer, The Loft and other restaurants on the waterfront struggled to serve the large influx of visiting crowds, but this was February, and Ben and Adonis had their choice of tables. Outdoor seating was closed, a sensible decision to escape the chill wind. Moving inside, Adonis selected a corner table whose window faced the marina.

"Should we be this exposed?" questioned Ben.

"That's what my security guys tell me," said Adonis. "They want me in their sights so they can watch me, while watching for anyone else who might be trying to watch me."

Ben strained to see signs of life outside on this chill night. The sun had set. Moonlight had not replaced it. The marina's lights showed little evidence of activity. A car was just leaving the parking lot. A couple was walking briskly away on the waterfront promenade.

"No use trying so hard," said Adonis. "You won't see them."

Ben turned his attention back to the menu, which offered clam chowder and freshly caught Dungeness crab. Someone was out there, someone he couldn't see, someone watching him read this menu and talk to Gil Adonis. Maybe even recording it all. When they returned home, someone would be watching the car pull into the driveway, the lights go on, and, a bit later, the lights go off. All night someone would be watching the doors, the windows, the property. It should have given him assurance, made him feel safe. Instead, he felt like a target, only one trigger pull from oblivion.

CHAPTER 6

During the years when Sheila Fishburne was Alaska's lone member of the House of Representatives, Sea-Tac airport was a standard layover. Whenever possible, she would decamp in Seattle for a day or more to meet with local power brokers or sit for interviews or buy drinks for reporters at her hotel's bar. While Alaska had only vote, hers, in the US House, Washington State had ten. Cultivating those ten votes as allies was central to her ongoing strategy, and important for the many successes Alaska scored during her years in the House.

Now, as vice president, Fish had the power to return past favors. She was an important ally for Washington State and the entire Pacific Northwest. Her press conference drew most of the area's media and many local and state leaders.

Unlike Fish, Ben didn't invite attention. He did his best to avoid it, always wary that he could become a problem, not an asset, for his candidate clients if stories suggested he was pulling their strings from behind a curtain. The scandals of last year's presidential campaign did just that: spotlight Ben and his role as ringmaster in the campaign's political circus. As he took a seat at today's press conference, many heads turned his way. Ben was a curiosity, still newsworthy himself, a former political rainmaker who, for whatever reason, had chosen self-exile. Ben nodded greetings to reporters he knew and avoided gawks from those he didn't. He planned to keep his presence insignificant to avoid becoming part of the day's story. He would ask no questions and sit in a rear row, away from the cameras.

Fish had other ideas. While greeting the media, cameras rolling, she pointed to Ben, asked him to stand, and referred to him as "my great friend and political mentor." Reluctantly, Ben stood, smiled as cameras swung around to him, and then he quickly returned to his seat.

"We miss you in Washington, Ben," said Fish. "You folks in the Seattle area are lucky to have him with you. Readers, subscribe to his newspaper, the *Poulsbo* . . . What's the name of the paper, Ben?"

"The *Poulsbo Monitor*," said Ben, once more dreading the attention.

"Poulsbo. Such a charming community. One of my favorite places— outside of Alaska, of course," said Fish. "And you advertisers, do the right thing too."

She turned to the other reporters. "Okay, if there are no other questions . . . "

That prompted a round of laughter, and then a dozen hands shot into the air. The press conference lasted another half hour before Fish begged off more questions. She needed to go to her next event, she said.

Ben had intended to slip away quickly and head to her hotel suite as planned, but he couldn't avoid the attention of other reporters who cornered him with questions. Why Poulsbo? Why a no-name weekly? Was it to hide something that wasn't revealed last year? Is there more to the scandal you're not telling us? That the president's keeping secret?

Finally, breaking loose from the media scrum, he left the hotel, circled the block, waited ten minutes, and seeing no one from the press conference remaining in the lobby, strode quickly to the bank of elevators.

"Hey, guru, what a welcome sight you are!" said the vice president, her greeting punctuated by a long bear hug. "When you abandoned us, I was afraid I'd never see you again."

"No danger we'd lose contact," said Ben. "You're part of my political DNA."

"Great!" said Fish. "In that case, I hope you don't mind that I arranged for some food. I'm starved, and my head's on backward after flying all those hours from Tokyo. I've got some booze here. Want a drink?"

Ben was fond of Fish. She had a lively spirit and a deep well of irreverent enthusiasm. Sheila and Tenny had entered Congress in the same freshman class. They bonded quickly and both became extraordinarily successful legislators. During Tenny's third year as president an impeachment conspiracy involving some of her most powerful political enemies came close to removing her from office. When it was revealed that the vice president was among the conspirators, he was forced to resign. Tenny selected Fish to fill the vacancy. Fish then became Tenny's running mate in the campaign for re-election.

Sheila Fishburne's hometown of Utqiaġvik was 320 miles north of the Arctic Circle, the northernmost community in the US. Most people know it as Barrow, Alaska, a name abandoned in recent years as the Inupiat majority secured more political power and restored the community's original name. Fish's Inupiat mother, Alicee, could trace her ancestral lineage back infinite generations. Her late father was a math teacher from Indianapolis who came north expecting to stay a year. A young man's adventure, he thought at the time.

From her youngest days, Sheila was a star. Standout student. Compelling speaker. A sure shot when hunting for waterfowl, and one of the hardest workers when all hands were needed to pull in a shored whale. After graduating with a math degree from the University of Washington, Sheila returned to Utqiaġvik to teach in the high school. Not long after, she was recruited to represent the community in the state legislature and from there, to represent all Alaska in the US House.

Fish and Tenny were a formidable team as freshman legislators, and quickly established a personal friendship that had endured through decades of political combat. Ben hadn't favored Fish's selection as vice president. He doubted that voters were ready to accept an all-woman ticket to head the country. Fish wasn't inclined to accept the appointment either. She had built a strong power base in the House and seemed destined to serve as Speaker. But Tenny insisted, and both Fish and Ben finally acceded.

"The food should be here in ten minutes or so," said Fish. "Let's catch up. How's newspapering? Isn't it pretty tame compared to what you've always done?"

"It was until a few days ago," said Ben. He took advantage of the opening to replay the visit from Governor Bowles, his agreement to harbor Gil Adonis, Adonis's insistence on meeting with the president.

A knock on the door interrupted their conversation. Two members of the hotel staff wheeled in dinner carts. One of Fish's aides joined them, oversaw arrangements, and signed for the food delivery.

"Anything else?" the aide asked. "Just a reminder, your next appointment is at eight."

"Thanks, Karen. No interruptions 'til then, okay? I've got a lot to discuss with my friend here."

"Yes, Madam Vice President. I'll tell the rest of the staff."

Alone once again, Fish turned to Ben, her earlier lightheartedness erased by an expression that was unmistakably "let's get down to business."

"What you're saying is all news to me," said Fish. "Clearly I've been left out of the loop of some very important stuff that happened in last year's election, and now I want to know what that was. Tell me."

For the next hour, over eight-ounce sirloins, baked potatoes, and creamed spinach, Ben filled in the blanks, surprised that Fish was unaware of them. How he was recruited to go to Paris to get that evidence, how he was shot and nearly killed before he could deliver it.

"Wow, and I thought the campaign itself was filled with drama and tension. I can't believe I missed all of this."

"Not many people know. Tenny kept a tight lid on it."

"So what was behind it? Who are the bad guys here?"

"You know everything I know. I was just the messenger boy. No one ever filled me in on all the details."

"And Gil Adonis was in on it? I mean, this whole secret conspiracy?"

"I was running her campaign, and even I didn't know."

"So now you want me to tell her Adonis is here with you. That someone's out to kill him and that he wants to see her."

"You see why that's a message I couldn't hand off to just anyone to deliver."

"She may even think I'm nuts when I tell her."

"But you will tell her?"

"Oh yeah. This is too good a story to keep to myself. And I'm going to rag on her about why I had to hear it thirdhand."

"It's all yours. I want this out of my life. The sooner, the better."

"I'll see her tomorrow."

CHAPTER 7

US President Isabel Aragon Tennyson walked to a window overlooking the Rose Garden. It was a bleak February scene. Remnants of a four-inch snowfall followed by hours of thaw had designed mud-and-snow patterns where resodding had been in progress on the Ellipse. Low-hanging cloud cover squeezed ground and sky into an unusually tight landscape. The news just relayed from her vice president added to the dreariness.

Sheila Fishburne remained seated on the Oval Office sofa.

"From your reaction, I take it that this is bad news," said Fish.

Tenny turned away from the window to look at her. "I'm truly sorry, Sheila. I should have told you about this. I honestly thought it was over. I apologize for not sharing this with you."

"My goodness," said Fish, "you don't owe me anything. We've known each other half a lifetime. I trust your judgment."

Tenny returned to the opposite sofa and faced Fish over the coffee table that separated them. "Sheila, Gil Adonis knew that Zach Bowman had no business being president. The only reason he poured money and everything else into Zach's campaign was to control him. Zach was Gil's Manchurian candidate, a figurehead."

"A figurehead for who? Adonis?"

"No, Adonis's role was a lot more sinister and dangerous. He was the point man for an international conspiracy to take over this country and turn it into a dictatorship. Not for the usual reasons like power and money or even ideology. It's because they don't trust democracy. They think humanity won't survive much longer unless we get control of science. They've given up on democratic government being capable of that."

"You mean climate change? Nuclear weapons? Wars in space?"

"That's part of it. But much deeper. Also think artificial intelligence, genetic editing, out-of-control biological warfare. And who knows what else that's in the pipeline coming out of labs."

Tenny rose, walked to her desk, unlocked a drawer, and retrieved a memory stick.

"Sheila, they've recruited a lot of serious believers: scientists and business types like Adonis, high-ranking military and intelligence people, even academics. We know who many of them are. The list will astound you as it did me. Even heads of some smaller countries are on their side, people who think those like you and me will eventually make a bad judgment or mistake that will blow defenseless people like them off the map."

"How do you know all this?"

"That's what I should have told you before. About September of last year, the CIA got hold of one of the group's secret planning documents. It was all there. Identities, locations, planning for after Bowman was elected. This memory stick has all the information. View it only where there's top-secret clearance. It will blow you away."

"And it's authentic? It checked out?"

"Every bit of it. No question. It's real."

"It sure looked in September like Bowman might win," said Fish. "The polls were ugly for us then."

"They were really confident. We were blind," said Tenny. "We honestly didn't even know they existed. They successfully disguised their operations for years. Even their name, 'The Salvation Project.' Very clever. People running across them probably thought they were a missionary group or a recycling business or something. Kyle Christian over at CIA told me he was floored that we hadn't found their tracks sooner."

The admission of failure came hard for Tenny. Throughout her life she had been wrapped in a cloak of unwavering self-confidence. When she was a child living in Mexico City, her grandfather impressed upon her that she was an Aragon, part of a family that arrived in the New World not long after Columbus and that was one of the foundational families of modern Mexico and Latin America. She had rich bloodlines and was heiress to great wealth. No obstacle would be too great for her to overcome. And, with few exceptions, that *had* been the story of her life. As a young woman she achieved superstar status in her family's corporate empire. She followed that success by becoming a patron whom many called "Saint Isabel" for all the support she provided to the hungry and the homeless of Los Angeles. When she entered politics, she was rapidly elevated from the House of Representatives to the Senate and then to the White House itself. In her early years as president, she achieved a remarkable record of legislative success. But then came a devious plot to impeach and remove her from office by those she had defeated. She barely survived. Then an assassination attempt that left her physically impaired. A reelection campaign that was one long, unceasing attack on her character. And now, the knowledge that her intelligence staff had missed the signs of a dangerous plot to overthrow the government. Tenny had had little experience with failure—until lately. Acceptance of it came hard. Uncertainty over how to respond was a skill that now, late in life, she had to learn.

Tenny took a seat next to Fish on the sofa and handed her a small, sealed envelope containing the memory stick.

"So, how did Ben Sage get involved?" asked Fish. "Has he secretly been working with intelligence all along?"

"Not at all. At the time, Kyle didn't know who to trust to deliver the intelligence material to me. He knew there were moles in his own building. If he picked the wrong delivery channel, he was afraid of losing the evidence or even putting me at risk when it was delivered. He knew he could trust Ben. Did Ben tell you that they had him disguised as a Catholic priest?"

"No! Ben a priest! That must have been quite a disguise."

"Did he tell you that the disguise didn't work? Before Ben could deliver it, a couple of gunmen ambushed him at Georgetown University, and he had to run through the park at night to escape. As it was, he was shot a couple of times. Three others were killed."

"Ben told me he was chased and shot. He even offered to show me the scars from his bullet wounds. But Ben says he still doesn't know the whole story. Why would Les Bowles deliver Gil Adonis to him as a roommate?"

"After reading the intelligence reports and learning that Adonis was behind all this, I just had to know why. The same question you asked me. Why would Adonis, with his billions, get involved? So after the election, I invited him to dinner. Just the two of us. That's when he told me about the Salvation Project and what it was trying to do. After he explained it, I could see why he could be concerned enough to join a movement like this."

"You agree with them?"

"Adonis and I agree on the problem. There's no denying it. Scientific discovery is creating a world few of us understand. Not the voting public. Not most of the people they elect. No one understood Einstein, but that didn't much matter. Academics could just test his theories, write papers about them, and occasionally something would get produced that would affect our lives. Now, the world is full of Einsteins who know how to clone people, literally change us into nonbiological robots, produce designer babies, create disease we have no protection against. We still have no workable consensus about how to keep the planet from frying from global warming. Science is getting smarter, and it seems that government is getting dumber. Gil's answer is to give up on democracy and turn these decisions over to informed leaders with absolute control. That I don't agree with. I think we can protect ourselves with the government we have. But we're going to have to up our game a lot, and pretty quickly, to head off a calamity."

"So are you going to see Adonis, get him off Ben's hands?"

"Most likely. When I met with him last November, I told him I needed time to think about the problem, to process it, to talk with you and some of the others, to come up with my own ideas. I told him I'd get together with him after that. I thought I had more time. Now you tell me that his old buddies at the Salvation Project want to kill him. That means the group still exists and remains dangerous, even after we've arrested so many of their leaders. That's really shocking. The roots must go a lot deeper than we thought. It's not just a matter of solving the problem of how to manage science. It's how we stop them from overthrowing our government. The Salvation Project might have begun with legitimate aims, but it's turned into a murderous cabal and needs to be crushed. Let's get with Kyle Christian and Sam Vellman from the FBI. Let's tell them about this and see what they know. I hope to heaven they know more than we do and aren't going to be surprised again. Then let's see what we can do about getting Ben a less dangerous roommate."

CHAPTER 8

"For those who are new to this executive committee, my name is Richfield. We welcome you." The voice definitely sounded Asian. Japanese? Chinese? Korean? Identifying its source was exceedingly difficult, given the level of digital distortion applied to mask its speaker. Were the words from someone speaking in a native language, or were they the product of neural machine translation? It was hard to know.

Then, a new voice, undistorted. A woman, clearly British.

"Project Manager Thirty-Eight," the voice said.

Richfield, clearly annoyed by the late arrival and her failure to use voice alteration, replied, "Please return the code I've just sent to Project Manager Thirty-Eight."

After a five-second pause, she said, "Grayfox sixteen, three exclamation marks, two closed parens, four, extra, two *e*'s."

The woman spoke the words evenly and with deliberation, as one might when counting down a rocket launch. She did not want to appear hesitant or make an error.

"Confirmed, Manager Three-Eight," said Richfield. "You are the final manager authorized for this meeting. For you, and for all others on this call, we understand the difficulty you may occasionally encounter joining at the designated times. But everyone's security depends on our starting and ending according to schedule. Security also requires using the device you have been assigned to disguise your natural voice, with no exceptions."

"My apologies." This time the woman's voice carried the same digital echo as Richfield's.

"Let me introduce myself once again. My Project name is 'Richfield.' Remember it. I am Project control. Mine is the only name used on these calls and for all other purposes. Those new to the committee have been assigned numbers, as have all other Project managers. I know who you are. So does the Symfonia, our executive committee. Otherwise, for your own protection, you will not know one another and therefore cannot expose any other member if you are taken by government authorities. For those of you new to our committee, it is literally a matter of life and death that you conform to our protocols."

A voice interrupted, also male.

"Number Three here, Richfield. I am one of the founding Project directors, and I also welcome our new project managers. You and others involved in the Salvation Project are the vanguard of a mission whose goal is nothing less than the salvation of humanity. As has been clearly explained to you, it is a personally dangerous mission. You are replacing committee members who were exposed by last year's security breach. Because of that breach, our meetings will be fewer, shorter, and held at irregular times. And, as Richfield says, our new protocols are the best defense for all of us. They will be strictly enforced. You are the best minds, the best talent the world has produced. We cannot afford to lose any of you. Please resume, Richfield."

"Thank you, Three. For our new committee members, Three is an iconic force in this Project. He is the last remaining founder, the last survivor of a small group that launched this mission and has guided it until now. When Three and his fellow founders began, the mission seemed impossible. But, as they say, even the strongest rock can be ground into sand. Three and all who preceded you have brought us to the point where those of us on this call may reap the rewards of the Project's salvation mission. I assure you there are thousands like you, leaders in their fields, representing most countries and continents, who are with us. We have built a strong movement, which grows stronger with each passing day. The future is ours so long as we maintain our courage and discipline and are willing to sacrifice all for the cause. Any questions?"

"Richfield, this is Twelve. I would like to know more about the security breach. What can you tell us?"

"Thank you, Twelve," replied Richfield. "I cannot disclose the details of how it happened, but I can describe the consequences. American intelligence authorities got possession of documents that included the identity of many of our operatives and our plans for controlling the United States after our candidate became president. That happened at a most unfortunate time. We believe it cost our candidate the election and caused our United States project manager to reveal many of our internal secrets. Eighteen, do you have anything to add to that? Eighteen is our new project manager for the United States."

"Yes, fellow managers, this is Eighteen. Thank you, Richfield. We lost an opportunity, and it has cost us some time, but we continue to have a strong and committed network, and I see a number of opportunities for regrouping."

Twelve responded. "How do you define success?"

"One way and one way only," replied Eighteen, "control of the United States government."

"This is Fourteen." A French woman's voice. "Just to confirm, Richfield, are you replacing Marianna Lee as project control?"

"Yes."

"And to confirm further, did Marianna . . . "

The woman questioner left it at that, with the silence understood by all but the newest members of the committee.

"Marianna knew that the lost documents left her exposed, and so she acted as required to save the rest of us. She martyred herself," said Richfield.

"And what of the former United States project manager," said a younger male voice that seemed to be German. "The one who failed to deliver our candidate in the presidential election and whom you suspect of turning against us? Should we fear consequences from him?"

"Who is this?" asked Richfield.

"Oh, sorry, I'm new at this. I'm Forty-Two."

"The consequences will be his, not ours," said Richfield. "Our best protocol enforcement team has located him. They will end whatever threat he poses."

CHAPTER 9

Malik was a patient man. He waited patiently as November's rain froze into December's snow and January's sleet. Neither winter winds nor two extended blizzards discouraged him. Eventually, he was certain that Gil Adonis would reemerge, and when he did it would be here, in Columbus, Ohio, the city Adonis knew best, and that Governor Lester Bowles, his most trusted friend, would be his point of contact.

Other members of Malik's team kept Adonis's New York apartment and his Saint Bart's villa under surveillance. The Project's moles in US and foreign intelligence were alert for any sign of Adonis as well. Impatience, Malik surmised, had led to the earlier failure in the Adonis matter. The team first assigned to dispose of him was too eager to succeed, too self-confident. The timing was wrong, the risk level too high. Their failure allowed Adonis to exploit his financial resources and his contact network to disappear from the Project's screens. But a man like Adonis had too many connections with the real world to remain a phantom. Patience would be rewarded, and Malik was a patient man. That was why the Project always called on Malik for its most difficult assignments. He had never failed.

Tracking Governor Bowles was simple enough. Governors' daily schedules were generally revealed to the public. When their legislatures were in session, as Ohio's was now, governors remained close to home. So it was with Bowles, whose days were mostly spent at Ohio's Governor's Residence or the state capitol building, and whose evenings often required public appearances.

Then, with no public notice, the routine was broken by a trip to the Pacific Northwest, identity disguised. Bowles had a companion, also carefully disguised. They traveled on a private jet belonging to a wealthy contributor, not one owned by the state. The connection was with Ben Sage, well known as a confidant of the president. There could be only one explanation: the governor's companion was Adonis. With Malik's quarry located, it was now merely a matter of timing. Opportunity would make itself known.

Before a major test, Malik always studied carefully. The test at hand was to kill Gil Adonis and leave no tracks that could be followed. For five days, Malik did little but observe. He quickly spotted Adonis's security people. Adonis never left the apartment except for dinner with Sage. He considered but rejected killing Adonis when Sage was with him and making it appear to be a robbery. But both were high-profile people, easily identified. Federal authorities would immediately suspect the relationship to the Salvation Project. Killing only Adonis? Making it seem like the result of a business feud? Sage would know better and, with his Washington, DC, contacts, would quickly inform the FBI and CIA. A traffic accident? Risky. One or both could survive. But a water accident. That had possibilities. Drunk boaters often fell into the water. And if the bodies were not found immediately, identification took time.

By the sixth day of observation Malik had completed his homework.

Sage's reliable schedule was the key. Each night Sage would return from work at about the same time. After a few moments in the apartment, Sage and Adonis would leave together for dinner. Darkness came early in midwinter, and the neighborhood was not particularly well lit. Adonis's security was nested in a park overlooking the apartment. Different locations in the park, but readily found if you knew where to search. The first part of the plan, then, was uncomplicated. While Sage was in the apartment collecting Adonis for their evening meal, Malik's men would disable Adonis's security guards and quickly deposit their bodies in a waiting van. When Sage and Adonis emerged from the apartment, Malik and three members of his team would bind and gag them and throw them into another vehicle. They would drive to a secluded bayfront location, which Malik had identified, and drown them before leaving shore, making certain both were dead. Then came a more complicated plan for escape. Malik and an associate would place the bodies in a launch and motor into one of the deeper parts of Liberty Bay. A second launch would accompany them. The bodies would be dropped in the bay, and the first launch would be set adrift. Malik and his people would take the second launch to the opposite shore, where another van would be waiting to carry them to safety. The bodies and the drifting launch likely would not be discovered until morning. Both bodies would be stripped of identification. When discovered, first impressions would be that the two men were drunk and had fallen into the water. Not the first time such a thing had happened. By the time authorities identified the bodies, Malik and his team would have long dispersed. Mission completed.

On the seventh night of surveillance, Malik's team was in place. Ben, though, for the first time that week, failed to return home for dinner. Malik waited for an hour. Then two. Then he aborted the mission. Malik could not have known that Ben Sage had plans other than dying that evening. Instead, he had assigned himself to cover a Kitsap County School Board meeting.

On the next night, Ben did return. He turned into his driveway, exited his car, and took a few steps toward the front door. Then, suddenly, he was illuminated by the lights of a large, black SUV that pulled in directly behind him. Ben stood there startled, like an actor at center stage, terrified that he had forgotten his lines. Three men, all in suits, emerged from the vehicle and engaged Ben in conversation. After a few moments, Ben unlocked the apartment door, and they all entered. A half hour later, the men reappeared. Gil Adonis, carrying an overnight bag and briefcase, was with them.

Malik could only watch. His plan was perfect, but he had waited too long. Patience was one of Malik's most important assets. Tonight it was his nemesis. Adonis was gone.

MARCH

CHAPTER 10

A dozen people, each with a stack of working papers, could fit comfortably around the conference table in the White House's Situation Room. At this morning's meeting, there were just three: the president, the vice president, and the director of the FBI. Joining them on a secure video connection from headquarters in nearby Langley, Virginia, was CIA Director Kyle Christian.

Tenny insisted that the meeting be limited to this group. Neither she nor her intelligence chiefs could be certain who to fully trust, even among the highest ranks of their security teams. Last year's exposure of Salvation Project secrets had revealed a number of surprising and disturbing Project adherents in sensitive government positions. Were there others? With new concerns about the Project's infiltration, the answer was likely yes. For the moment at least, it was essential that Adonis's location remained a tightly held secret.

A week earlier, Sam Vellman's FBI agents had taken Adonis into custody and transported him in a government plane to Washington, DC. He was transferred to a safe house in northern Virginia where he underwent extensive questioning.

"I interviewed him personally for eight hours over three days," said FBI Director Vellman. "Two of my best interrogators joined me. Separately they continue to interview him each day, checking details and digging deeper. We've learned a lot and are following up on all the new leads. But it's been about four months since he was last in touch with Project people. Plenty of time for them to reinvent themselves with a different command structure and personnel. As you know, we made dozens of arrests right after we got our hands on their documents last fall. But it didn't take the remaining Project leaders very long to slam the door, take a dive, and go to sleep."

Turning to CIA Director Christian on the screen, the president said, "Kyle, the vice president had not been aware of all this until Ben Sage contacted her about Adonis. Will you please fill in the blanks for her?"

"Certainly. Madam Vice President, last September Chinese intelligence came upon a courier in possession of sensitive internal information from a group calling itself the Salvation Project. For their own reasons, the Chinese didn't want to contact us directly, and so they gave it to the French to pass along to us. At that point we didn't know who to trust to get the evidence to Washington, so we sent Sage disguised as a priest to Paris as our courier."

"I heard." Fish's smile burst into an audible laugh. "I'm sorry. Just the image of that was too much for me."

"Kyle cooked that up," said Tenny. "It damned near got Ben killed."

"Yes, it did," said the CIA director. "But it worked. And that gave us what we needed to start rounding up people."

"Why didn't any of this make news?" asked Fish. "It seems that it would have helped our campaign."

"Maybe, maybe not," said Tenny. "The political opposition would have pushed back to discredit the story as a fake political October surprise. My credibility isn't what it once was. They might have won that media battle. I just felt we had to treat it like any intelligence operation: quietly, professionally."

"And Gil Adonis was their contact? He was the money behind our political opposition," asked Fish.

"Not just the money," said Christian. "The money, and he apparently helped engineer many of the so-called scandals involving the president that turned up during the campaign. He admitted all of that during our interrogation."

"Maybe we never will hear from them again," said Tenny. "Maybe when they lost the election and failed to kill Adonis, those were their last operations. Could it be that we're just fearing ghosts of their past?"

"That's a possibility," said Vellman. "Adonis is high-profile. If they're still operating, they should have been able to track him down. We'll continue to monitor the situation. What would you like to do next with Adonis, Madam President? He's keen to talk with you."

"And I'm keen to talk with him, Sam. Before I do that, though, I want to talk with the people at Justice to determine if there are any charges that should be brought against him. I don't want to step on their turf unnecessarily. We may want to just forget about it. He's a powerful figure in the financial world. I'm not sure we want to get into an expensive, high-visibility pissing match with him, especially when it can look like political payback. Meanwhile, keep him out of sight. I'll arrange to come to your headquarters to talk with him."

With the meeting ending, Vellman scooped up his papers, placed them in his briefcase, and as he did, an image on a separate TV monitor attracted his attention.

"Turn up the volume on set number six," Vellman called out to one of the Situation Room aides.

On the screen, a young woman, microphone in hand, her face bathed in the golden light of sunrise, stood in the foreground of a scene of chaos. Behind her, uniformed police, EMT workers, and others could be seen in what appeared to be an emergency situation.

As the TV speakers gained volume, the group around the conference table heard her speak.

"Again, let me recap this breaking story. Ohio Governor Lester Bowles is dead, apparently murdered just hours ago while he was on his regular predawn bike ride on Alum Creek Trail, a popular running and biking trail here in Columbus. Police say it appears that the governor was shot in the back by an assailant and died immediately. The governor's security people were stationed nearby and said they heard no gunshots, and presume the assailant used a silencer on his weapon. The security people said it was not unusual for the governor to stop riding and talk with others he met on the trail. When this stop appeared to be prolonged, the security team responded and found him about a hundred yards from where he began the ride, facedown near the tree line. Governor Bowles was the Republican candidate for vice president in last year's election. Again, Ohio Governor Lester Bowles is dead, apparently murdered this morning."

Tenny turned to the conference screen and Kyle Christian. "Kyle, did you just hear what we just heard?"

"I did. Shocking, and pretty ominous. Adonis told us he was concerned about Bowles, but he didn't think the Project would harm someone as high-profile as the governor of Ohio. But let's not get ahead of ourselves. It could have been random. People get killed in dark parks all the time for many reasons."

"If they did kill Bowles, why him and not Adonis when Adonis was in Poulsbo?" asked Fish.

"Hard to say," said Christian. "Bowles also knew all about the Project. That's how Adonis convinced him to go on the ticket as vice president."

"And if they had staked out Bowles waiting for Adonis to make contact, they would have had even more reason to risk getting rid of Bowles," added Vellman.

"Why's that?" asked Tenny.

"Because they would have trailed them to Poulsbo and would know that we picked up Adonis. In short order we would have brought Bowles in, too, to confirm Adonis's story and add anything else he knew about the Project," said Vellman.

"But they didn't kill Adonis in Poulsbo," said Tenny.

"Could be they were just waiting for the right opportunity," said Christian. "They may not have expected Vellman's guys to snatch him first."

As they spoke, their eyes remained fixed on the seventy-two-inch drama on the screen: a growing crowd of onlookers, police holding them back to preserve the crime scene; blue-and-red flashing lights; a view from a thousand feet above provided by a TV station drone; wails of background sirens serving as a mourning chorus.

Tenny's mind raced to consider her role in all this. She called her chief of staff on the secure Situation Room phone. "Deac? You've heard?"

"Just did," Deacon said. "I was about to call you."

"Hold off any comment from me or anyone else. Call Bowles's office and offer anything they need from us. We'll be done here in a few minutes."

Then another thought occurred to her.

"If they killed Bowles," she said, "then Ben's in danger too. He spent a week with Adonis." She turned to Vellman. "Sam, please have your Seattle people get Ben out of there and bring him to Washington right away."

"What if he doesn't want to come?" asked Vellman.

"Arrest him."

"On what charge?"

"Make up something. Impersonating a journalist. Being too dense to know how much danger he's in. Find something. Handcuff him if you need to."

Vellman smiled and nodded his concurrence. "We'll bring him back bound and gagged."

Tenny turned her attention to Kyle Christian at the CIA.

"Kyle?"

"We'll alert our worldwide contacts," said Christian.

"Adonis must be devastated," said Tenny. "Lester Bowles and Adonis were like brothers. Give him some time to grieve, and when he's ready, bring him to me. It's time we talked."

CHAPTER 11

For more than a week Ben had been able to focus on his work at the newspaper without the chronic, low-level sense of terror he had felt while Adonis remained in his life. The days since the FBI van rolled out of his driveway had been blissfully routine. And yet . . .

Gil Adonis had proven to be a remarkably elevating houseguest. Art, science, economics—Adonis had used his wealth to access knowledge wherever on the planet his curiosity led him. He had been to the front lines of research and development. The laboratories. The think tanks. He had met with those who wrote the most advanced academic papers and who did the fieldwork and who financially seeded new companies. For Ben, conversations with Adonis were like exclusive TED presentations, rich not only with information but with perspective that placed everything neatly in context. Knowledge, insight, originality, all were part of the package. Having Adonis as a houseguest on the run from killers was frightening, but it was a portal for Ben into a world of infinite possibilities and dangers he until now never fully appreciated.

For decades, Ben's world had been elective politics, each election cycle requiring new insights based on past experiences. It was an exciting world, a "win or lose, no in-between" world. To the extent they affected election outcomes, most issues were in the world's rearview mirror—where we had been, not where we were headed. Adonis's world was rooted in a today few others saw, a future beyond easy comprehension, a true artist's understanding of reality and a scientist's appreciation of what could come next. Rather than paint or write words or music, Adonis converted his insights into investments. It was how he made his fortune. Even more, it was the sum of his life's purpose. He was an exceptionally curious man. He spent his waking hours pursuing answers to that curiosity.

Ben's decision to abandon the turbulent world of campaign politics was largely the result of fatigue. For decades he had greedily fed on the tension and pressure, loving the competition, inspired by the challenge, satisfied with the importance of his work, electing people he felt would be worthy servants of the public interest. But some of those he helped elect became embarrassments. And with each new election cycle, it was becoming harder to maintain discipline as changing campaign rules, new technology, and rivers of money from sources unknown competed with everything he knew about getting candidates elected. In Tenny's campaign for reelection, the opposition made Ben an issue, a weapon they used to pummel his candidate. For Ben, that was like pulling the cork and draining whatever energy and enthusiasm remained for continuing to live in a world he had once loved and mastered.

Ben's notion of retiring to a small community where he could manage a local newspaper, maybe even buy one and become both editor and publisher, had been germinating for years. Ben's college degree was in journalism. His first adult jobs were in journalism. The fickleness of chance had diverted him into politics, but one day, he thought, he would return to journalism, wiser, more worldly, more certain of journalism's true purpose, better able to sustain it as a business and as an honest broker of information for its readers. As his enthusiasm for campaigns waned, the idyll of newspaper ownership shined more brightly. Now he was here, living that fantasy in a quiet community where tourism and fishing were the highest values and making payroll was the only blood-pressure-raising event. As with most things in life, once his dream became reality, it lost some of its postcardlike luster. Nevertheless, this was his plan, and he would make it work.

That certainty, though, was now confronting the obstacle erected by his experience with Gil Adonis. Adonis had been a mind-expanding drug. In the days since Adonis's departure, Ben's newspaper life seemed smaller to him in its relationship with the wider world. His houseguest unfurled an arc of knowledge Ben never before imagined and revealed to him perils infinitely greater than whether Captain Underpants remained an option for Kitsap County's children.

But that was a discussion with himself he needed to postpone for another day. Today's reality would be writing the story of last night's Poulsbo city council meeting, lunch with the marketing director of the local Safeway to pitch the advertising value of his newspaper, and a full afternoon of editing the next edition. Small-town newspapers were important; his life experience convinced him of that. His life experience could also add value to the journalistic profession. He remained convinced of that as well. This was the path he now was on and where he would remain.

Ben woke early, showered, shaved, and dressed; no business suit required. As usual, he was the first person in the office and tuned the TV to CNN.

And there it was. Governor Lester Bowles dead. Murdered. He switched to MSNBC. The same pictures. Live from the wooded area where Bowles was shot and killed. Uniformed police combing the area for evidence. Reporters with microphones describing the scene. Images of the adjoining neighborhood, crowded with onlookers, many in tears.

Ben watched in disbelief. The same Lester Bowles who had been right here just two weeks ago, pleading with Ben to protect Gil Adonis from those who would kill him, now the victim himself. It was too real to be coincidence. This was no random murder, an unlucky encounter with a deranged guy with a gun. This had to be connected with Adonis. And if

Bowles was murdered because of that connection, then he, too, likely had a target on his back. With that realization, Ben forced himself to unlock his fixation with the TV screen and quickly check the few rooms in the office to make sure he was alone. Then he locked the office entrance.

What am I doing? Ben asked himself. *Lock or no lock, this office isn't secure. Neither is the apartment.* When Gil was staying there, knowing his security people were watching provided at least a measure of comfort. Now even that seemed naïve. If a governor, with his security detail, could be murdered, who could be safe?

Ben returned to his desk and developments unfolding on the television screen, growing more tense with each new detail. Soon, his business day would begin. His staff would arrive. Strangers would come to the office to meet with reporters, drop off press releases, buy advertising. Anyone could walk in and kill him. Later, he would be out on the streets of Poulsbo, keeping appointments, having meals, totally vulnerable to whoever had been hunting Gil Adonis. Totally vulnerable to whoever had murdered Lester Bowles. And after that, he would go home. How could he go home? Tonight, or ever again.

His ringing cell phone jarred him from his developing sense of panic. Should he even answer? He looked at the calling number and instantly recognized it as Henry Deacon, Tenny's chief of staff.

"Deacon?" Ben answered.

"Good memory," said Deacon.

"Well, I saw your phone number enough during the campaign. I'll never forget it. What the hell is going on?"

"Pack your bags," said Deacon. "Within an hour or so, a couple of guys will knock on your door, drive you to the airport, and bring you to DC. If you've been watching TV, you know why."

"Shit," said Ben. "I thought I was done with all this. Why DC?"

"I can call them off," said Deacon.

"I'll be ready," said Ben.

Was he ready for DC again? Uncertain. But he had to be anywhere but here. Of that he had no doubt.

CHAPTER 12

The SUV passed through the White House gate and stopped near the West Wing entrance. Four men, dressed in similar dark suits, white shirts, nondescript blue ties, the uniform of Secret Service agents, disembarked. For watching eyes, it was a routine occurrence. Shifts changed. Agents came and went. Sometimes they used the Seventeenth Street entrance, sometimes the garage entrance. This group entered through the West Wing and walked directly to the president's office.

To one of the group, the president's secretary Marcie Friend, said "She's expecting you. Please go in."

Gil Adonis entered the room to seen Tenny, Fish and Carmen Sanchez waiting for him.

"Good to see you again, Gil," said the president. "I imagine you appreciate the irony of coming here disguised as a member of the Secret Service. We thought this was the best way to keep your identity and your whereabouts to ourselves." She turned to the others. "Madam Vice President, Secretary Sanchez, meet Gil Adonis." She turned back to Gil. "May I get you something? Coffee, tea, water?"

"No, thank you, Madam President," said Gil. "Thank you for agreeing to see me again."

"Gil and I had a lovely dinner together last November," said Tenny. "Unfortunately, the evening ended with someone trying to kill him. Let's hope we have a less eventful parting this time."

"Luck was on my side then," said Adonis. "I survived."

"Well, we'll try to take better care of you after this meeting. I understand you're staying in one of the FBI's safe houses. Is that agreeable?

"At the moment I can't think of a better alternative. Are you aware whether I will be charged with anything?"

"Anything? You mean like last year's cyanide poisoning of Secretary Sanchez here, or working with foreign agents to stage a coup of our government? The types of things people can get executed for? Let's just say the attorney general is reviewing your file. For now, we'll forget what's passed and discuss the present. I realize how devastating the murder of Les Bowles must be for you."

"There's no one I was closer to," said Adonis. "And the fact that I was responsible for his death is a blow I'll never recover from."

"I understand he was your first contact when you came out of hiding."

"Yes. I needed a way to communicate with you. He found a way to do that, and it cost his life."

Gil Adonis, a man not prone to displays of emotion, turned his head from the others and fought vainly to control his tears. For the first time in his life, he understood the meaning of choking up. It was hard for him to breath, impossible to speak. The emotional wave crested, then subsided while the others remained silent.

"Sorry," he said. "Les bought me this meeting with his life, and I owe it to him to do what I came to do. Madam President, at our November dinner I held back many details. I had taken an oath to do that. But now, since the Project tried to kill me and obviously will try again, I wanted your intelligence people to know everything I know. More than that, I need to impress on you the urgency to act quickly on many of things we talked about last November. There's not much time. The movement keeps getting stronger. Inaction just confirms their argument that democracy can't save us. Les's murder tells us they're getting more aggressive, even reckless."

"I understand urgency," said Tenny. "What I don't understand is how a group formed with what you tell me were noble intentions could also be a bunch of murderous thugs. Even you. You're a brilliant idealist. Why are you mixed up in this?"

Adonis hesitated a moment.

"I would like that glass of water now, if it's no trouble," he said.

Sanchez poured Adonis a glass of water from the pitcher on the coffee table.

"From what I know," said Adonis, "the Salvation Project was created by a group of Asian agricultural experts furious with the United States and other developed countries that weren't taking global warming seriously. All over Asia, rice crops were being destroyed by high water. Floods were washing out coastal communities. Millions of people were being forced to migrate from ancestral homes to places where no one else wanted them. And the western countries didn't seem to care. The idea at first was to form an elite group to put political pressure on the West to take action on climate change. As the agricultural leaders reached out for recruits, they found others equally frustrated about the threat of nuclear weapons and scientists who could see the dark side of artificial intelligence and genetic editing. Before long, the movement became organized, and when persuasion failed, they gave up on persuasion and turned to action. Namely, taking over governments rather than trying to convince them."

"So how did you get involved, Gil?" asked Fish. "You're not a scientist or a health or agricultural expert."

"No," said Adonis. "But I'm a big picture guy. I could see where all the inaction was leading. We're in a place now where little mistakes can have huge consequences. A mix-up in a DNA lab. A rogue researcher creating a virulent disease or life-form. An artificial intelligence project that gets out of control. The very essence of science is that you keep making mistakes until you get it right. Now you have it happening on a scale where an innocent mistake can either wipe out life on Earth or make it unrecognizable. This is all happening without effective oversight, and even in instances like the pandemic and global warming, outright hostility to facts and reality. You don't have to be a scientist to see where all this leads."

"I can agree with the problem, Gil," said Tenny. "I've been to many of those labs and research centers myself. I've been with you on the urgency since we first spoke. What I don't understand is the violence. You tell me these are good people. What I see is a bunch of killers and usurpers. Why would they kill a decent man like Lester Bowles?"

"Frustration," Adonis replied. "Reasonable argument is getting us nowhere. Political pressure hasn't matched the money and the influence pushing the other way. Elections have changed little. What do you do if you see humanity heading for extinction and little being done to head it off? That's when the Project began turning more extreme. It sounds ruthless, I know, but the fundamental purpose of all of life on Earth is to survive. From microbes to whales, the idea is we are born, grow strong, reproduce, and die. Evolution sees to it that living things either adapt and get smarter or stronger or they die off. But we've reached a point where we humans control our own evolution. We've become our own gods, with the power to grow smarter and stronger or to kill ourselves off as a species. Seen from that perspective, a few assassinations are a small price to pay to save billions of people. I understand it. I even understand it when they're trying to kill me."

"But you say you've turned against it," said Fish.

"I have turned against it," said Adonis. "For two reasons. One, the Project leadership has lost perspective. It's an 'us against them' mentality, kill or be killed. In just the few years I've been involved, there's been a dramatic shift from thoughtful, carefully reasoned objectives to a type of bloodlust against anyone who stands in their way. The other reason I've turned against it is you, Madam President. At our dinner last November, you said the right words. Since then, you seem to have made moves in the right direction. I may not agree that you can be successful your way, but at least you're trying to combat the most urgent problems."

Tenny stood up, walked to her desk, and picked up copies of what appeared to be a bound report. She distributed them to Adonis, Fish, and Sanchez and kept one for herself.

"After our dinner," said Tenny, "I formed a number of ad hoc groups to consider the problems you and I discussed. I asked for suggestions apart from traditional government to confront them. The results aren't complete, but what I've just handed you is where we are right now. This is my agenda for the rest of my days in office. Scan the highlights, and then the four of us will take time to discuss it."

Adonis opened the report, carefully read the table of contents, and grew more animated as he thumbed quickly through the sections. He looked intently at Tenny, who had reseated herself directly across from him.

"You think you can do this?" he asked. "I'm not sure the Salvation Project could even do this if they took power, dissolved Congress, and ran a tight dictatorship. This doesn't strike me as real."

"Oh, it's real all right," said Tenny. "I heard you. I buy it. I agree we need solutions and not window dressing or half measures. We're just now finishing the program I intend to present to Congress based on that work. Carmen Sanchez here will coordinate the federal agency role in promoting that program and the outreach to the states. The vice president, who, as you know, served more than a dozen years in Congress, will oversee the campaign to get things enacted. And now I'm asking you to work with us. You have deep knowledge of the forces driving the Salvation Project. I want to make sure we're addressing those concerns. Not only that, but you've been living on the leading edge of scientific discovery and application. You can help all of us understand it and how to explain it to others."

Adonis looked up from Tenny's agenda and leaned back into the sofa.

"I'll do whatever I can to help," he said. "But explain it to hundreds of millions of people? I don't believe it can be done."

"Of course it can be done," countered Tenny. "We have an educated public, a relatively free press, a more-than-two-hundred-year investment in citizen rule. We just need to provide the right information in an understandable way. The voting public isn't a bunch of rubes or dummies. We couldn't have become the nation we are if that were true."

Adonis shook his head in disagreement.

"That was true when people could understand why you build roads and railroads, why education was essential, why you needed a balance between business and labor, why it was essential to have cops on the street and a fair judicial system and a military to defend ourselves. But we're well past that. Think of today's level of human knowledge as a school. Because of all the advanced science, in today's school most people are at a kindergarten level. How sensible is it to let the kids rule the curriculum? How much trust would they be willing to place in the unknown? Scientific knowledge has so outrun common knowledge that many fear it or are hostile to it. We haven't dealt effectively with global warming or the pandemic or stopped the disruptions caused through the internet. We still can't even feel safe from nuclear war. We've just created a whole new branch of the military to fight wars in space. Wars in space! Talk about inviting global suicide!"

Adonis shook his head in disbelief at his own words. He sipped some water from the glass beside him.

"I joined the Project as a way for people who do understand all this to make it all work with as little risk as possible, not to ask permission from a clueless Congress and a vulnerable public. In the end, I think that's what you will have to do. I realized after speaking with you last November that we were not far apart in our thinking. The big difference is that you believe we can get there, and get there in time, using democratic tools. I seriously doubt that. Maybe democracy will work again, after a period of correction, with a better understanding of what's real and what's not. Until then, I think it will require a small, elite group with extraordinary powers to save humanity."

Tenny leaned toward him, her body language a challenge. "Gil, I'm going to prove you wrong. We're going to run the most massive public education effort in history. What money I can't justify through government resources I'll spend personally. I'm not as wealthy as you, but I have billions and I have friends with even more who will support us. You say people are at the kindergarten level. We're going to provide a crash-course education. It may not make them twenty-first-century scientists, but it will be enough to maintain a responsible democracy."

"How do you intend to do that?" asked Adonis. "It's never been done, and a lot of people have tried."

"We're going to get it done because failure for democracy would have the same dire consequences as the success of your form of autocracy—dehumanization. Perhaps not the violent extinction of the human body, but the slow extinction of the mind and heart and soul and spirit that makes life worth living at all."

CHAPTER 13

Tenny asked Carmie to remain after the others had left. She poured herself a cup of fresh, black coffee from a carafe on her desk and joined Carmie on the sofa.

"Tragic. Just tragic. I didn't know Lester Bowles that well, but he was a good governor. If he had been at the top of the ticket, he probably would have beat us," said Tenny.

"I knew him from Wall Street," said Carmie. "He was one of the few governors who made the rounds for state bond issues and actually knew what they were talking about. Gil Adonis was a brave soldier to spend all that time with us this afternoon when you know his heart was breaking. It would be like me losing you."

Tenny and Carmie had been together since childhood. Schoolmates. College roommates. Carmie was a bridesmaid in Tenny's wedding. She was the pillow Tenny hugged when she needed comfort and the firm voice of practicality when she searched for direction.

"Speaking of losing you," Carmie continued, "each page we just turned in the plan looked to me like another twenty-four-hour day of work for you. You can't keep that pace. You know that."

Tenny's face messaged her discomfort at the question. She sipped her coffee to try to hide it.

"I thought we had a deal, Carmie. No more questions about my health. I got through the campaign. This won't be anywhere near as stressful. The medical team is thoroughly clued in, and the equipment in the downstairs infirmary is all there if I need it. But since you asked, I feel fine. Actually, inspired knowing what we're about to do."

Carmie threw up her hands as if to concede. "No more questions then. It's all from love, you know. I'm not normally a nag. You know I'd do anything for you."

"Of course I know that, and in fact that's why I asked you to stay after Gil and Fish left. I'm going to ask something from you. It has to do with Ben."

"Ben!" said Carmie. "Can you believe Ben got dragged into this? He ran as far as he could to get away from us. He must be both afraid he's next and furious that you've kidnapped him to come back."

"I was going to bring him back to run the agenda campaign anyway," said Tenny. "He'll kick and scream a bit, but he'll do it because it's the biggest challenge of his life and he won't be able to resist. But there's the question of security. He can't live alone and without protection while the Project killers are still out there."

"That's right," said Carmie. "What chance does Ben have if they're really determined to kill him? Where will he stay?"

Tenny moved closer to Carmie, put her arm around her shoulders and her face next to hers. "You said you love me."

Carmie suddenly realized why Tenny had asked her to remain after the meeting with the others ended.

"No, no. Don't ask, Tenny."

"It will only be a short while. Long enough to clear out the danger."

Carmie shook her head. "I don't need a roommate, Tenny. I don't want a roommate. I mean, Ben's one of my favorite people. So are you, but

I wouldn't want you for a roommate either. You and I lived together for a while in college and survived it. Barely. What are you thinking?"

"Think about it, Carmie. It's the best way to protect Ben from the killers if they come after him."

"That's a great reason for me to take him in. So I can become a target for a bunch of killers."

"Think about it," Tenny repeated. "As a member of the cabinet, you have round-the-clock Secret Service protection. By moving in with you, Ben would have it too. Moving anywhere else he'd have to hire private security, and before you know it, the media would be asking why. That would be messy. You've got three bedrooms, four baths, an open area that could host a Super Bowl party. Both of you would have your space."

"And how would we explain it to everyone else?"

"Well, last year the opposition tried to tie you, me, and Ben together as a sex triangle. The two of you as an item wouldn't surprise anyone. Are you seeing anyone else?"

"No, but what if George Clooney were to take a shine to me at some event? I wouldn't seem available."

"For what it's worth, Carmie, I think George Clooney is married now. Do you even know George Clooney—or anyone like George Clooney—or, for that matter, anyone else at all who interests you or who you seem to interest?"

"Don't embarrass me."

"I didn't think so. You're between romances. So have a pretend one with Ben."

"Don't get me wrong. I really like Ben. In fact, I love Ben. I've just never thought of him in a romantic way."

"Perfect. No sexual tension. It's a match made in heaven. And I see one more advantage to this arrangement. He's coming here to sell the public on our agenda, and you're my point person dealing with the agencies to promote the agenda. You can work together on it every hour you're awake."

"Swell. Besides the around-the-clock work life you've arranged for me, I also get a pretend sex life and the attention of a bunch of killers."

"What are friends for?"

CHAPTER 14

P ropelled by both fear and the promise of rescue, Ben Sage quickly turned over his notes from last night's city council meeting to others on his staff and assigned another staff member the job of editing the next edition of the newspaper. He cancelled his day's appointments and made management arrangements with the newspaper's owner for what he anticipated would be a short absence. All the while, he remained conscious of developments in Columbus, where cable news continued to air live coverage of the aftermath of Bowles assassination.

Deacon said the FBI would be at his door in an hour. Ben was determined to be there, and he was. Two black Suburbans were parked at his apartment, one in front, another blocking the alley connected to the back entrance. Black Suburbans. The FBI used those, didn't they? But what if the killers did too?

Ben hesitated, trying to decide whether to park or flee. He waited for a sign, something to indicate whether this was a rescue party or a hit squad. Apparently, the agents in one of the Suburbans sensed his fear. A text message lit his cell phone. Plane's waiting, said the message.

Ben pulled into the driveway, hurried inside, and within minutes had stuffed some clothes, toiletries, his laptop, and a few personal and business papers into two small overnight bags. Then, a thirty-minute drive to

Bremerton National Airport, and he was airborne on an unmarked government Gulfstream 280.

By 6:00 p.m., he was in Washington, delivered to the White House grounds by agents who met him on the private aviation tarmac. One of Tenny's aides escorted him to an empty office in the adjacent Eisenhower Executive Office Building. There, she handed Ben an ID card that certified him as a member of the White House staff. "This is your office, Mr. Sage," she said. She left Ben alone to drop his bags and survey his surroundings, a bare-bones, government-issue office. Metal desk, tired chairs, two four-drawer green metal filing cabinets, beige walls and matching carpet, and not much else.

"What in the hell is this all about?" Ben said to the otherwise empty space. Government ID? He didn't want a government job. After the election Tenny had asked him to join her staff, but he declined, more than ready to escape the lure and intrigue of Washington power.

Well, now at least he felt safe. That was no small improvement over the clutch of fear that had enveloped him this morning. Ben pulled open the drapes, inviting the early evening light to join him. It was like raising the curtain on a Broadway show featuring the brilliantly lit 555-foot Washington Monument. For decades he had lived in Washington, where its monuments were an integral part of his environment. Even after all those years, seeing them never felt routine. He stood awed now, as if seeing the Washington Monument for the first time. So large. So close.

The spell was short-lived, interrupted when the office door flew open with an enthusiastic shove and a familiar voice called out, "My man!" Ben's longtime political consulting partner, Lee Searer, threw his arms around him. "Sorry I missed you when you came in," said Lee. "I was supposed to show you to your new digs."

"My new digs?" asked Ben. "What are you doing here? I don't even know what I'm doing here."

"Aren't you happy to see me?" asked Lee, releasing his hug.

"Of course I am. But it's not like I've just been found alive after an avalanche. I only left here four months ago."

"Oh, I'm just happy that we're going to work together again."

"The hell we are," said Ben. "Who's making these plans for me?"

"Well, I guess it's Tenny herself. Deacon told me to get my ass over here to brief you."

"About what?"

"About you and me working to get Tenny's agenda passed."

"I turned down that contract and made sure she gave it to you."

"And I've been working my tail off on it. You'll love it."

"What does she think this is, the draft? I didn't enlist for this."

Ben laid his hands on Lee's shoulders.

"Sorry not to greet you properly," he said, "but this whole day's been a puzzle. I woke up three thousand miles away, intending to get my newspaper to the printer before tonight's deadline and then eat fresh crab by the water, watching the seagulls. And now I'm in DC being told I'm a government employee doing political PR work again out of the White House. I need someone to fill in the blanks."

"Well, that will be the president of the United States," said Lee. "Come on, she's waiting for you."

CHAPTER 15

Tenny looked up from her desk but didn't stand to greet Ben. "For Christ's sake," she said matter-of-factly, "can't you stay out of trouble? I've got more to do than keep swooping in to pull you out of the frying pan."

Ben smiled, appreciating the flash of a playful Tenny he seldom saw during the reelection campaign. He liked this Tenny.

"Lee," she said, "I don't know how you put up with him."

"When Ben's around, there's always drama," said Lee. "It spices up the life of a lonely researcher."

"Okay, okay," said Tenny, rising from her desk. "As long as you two are here, you might as well be useful. Take a seat."

"When I saw the news about Les Bowles this morning, I was scared out of my mind," said Ben. "Thanks for rescuing me, at least temporarily."

"The price," said Tenny, now seated opposite him, "is that you have to help me get my agenda through Congress, the one we talked about before you went off to play newspaper reporter. The plan's changed since then. More ambitious. More important. I would say even planet-saving. I need you, Ben. Don't turn me down again."

"We've done a lot since you left," said Lee. "A tremendous amount of research. Polls. Voting data. Census reports. Targeted interest group lists.

Reams of useful names. Influencers. Potential allies. Media outreach possibilities. Plenty to work with to design the strategy. And we're going international. We're aiming not only to win over the United States, but much of the rest of the world."

"Two other key points," said Tenny. "We're doing the promotion as a government information program, from right here in the White House. I've cleared it with legal. And whatever can't be legally paid for with government funds, I'm paying for personally. In other words, you and Lee tell us what's required to win this fight, and I'll see that the money is there."

Ben's day had begun with a to-do list for a small weekly newspaper. Now it was early evening, and he was being asked to create and manage one of the largest and most expensive public interest campaigns ever attempted, while fearing for his life at the hands of killers whose motives he still didn't know.

"This day's almost more than I can handle," he said. "Of course I'll help. But what is it we'd be trying to sell?"

"I'll give you the headlines," said Tenny. "The details will have to wait for another day." She outlined an agenda that would fundamentally alter much of the country's economic and social life and its national defense, and she did it with a passion he had not felt from her since her early days in the White House.

He had first met Tenny when she was a fixture in some of the most impoverished neighborhoods of Los Angeles, conceding nothing in her adopted mission to feed the hungry, arrange for their medical attention, find people jobs, establish adequate services in underserved communities, and educate children in poorly equipped schools. She was a woman with both a personal fortune to contribute and the commitment to make sure her money, and others', went where it was most needed. In fulfilling that mission, Tenny had become a local celebrity. Ben convinced her to run for Congress so she could do even more. She was elected easily in a district where she already was well known. Her work on the streets made her a formidable advocate for those she represented. Over a dozen years in the House, Tenny became a hero to minority communities everywhere while adding more issues to her portfolio: immigration reform, health care, preschool education. Her background in wealth management was a powerful lever in helping her constituents find access to the financial system. She was a compelling public speaker, too: inspirational, persuasive, unusually effective.

Throughout her political career, Ben was her counselor, her media manager, a trusted friend. It had not been an unchallenged trajectory from congresswoman to president. Tenny faced powerful enemies and endured brutal attacks on her character. During her first term as president, she had to survive a rigged conspiracy to impeach her. An attempted assassination left her with a wounded and weakened body. Her energy level had declined markedly since then. That was obvious to all those who worked with her. Ben, who knew her better than most, also could sense a decline in her spirit, her enthusiasm, the brightness of the light that she once was.

But this Tenny, the one now sitting across from him, the one who summoned him back to Washington, who sensed the danger he was in and cared enough to wrap him in a security bubble, was as excited and as exciting as any Tenny he had ever known. It was young Tenny, not old Tenny. It was "reach for the stars" Tenny, not "go through the motions" Tenny. It was "we're going to save the world" Tenny. *You and me, Ben. You and me.*

"We start in the morning, okay?" she said. It wasn't a question.

Ben, swept into her dream by the force field she had just created, said, "Let's start tonight. Lee and I can go back to the office, and he can show me everything the staff has done already."

"That's what I like to hear," said Tenny. "You're as crazy as ever. Ben, it's late. I'm sure you haven't eaten. Go home, get some sleep, and we'll start fresh in the morning."

"Home?" said Ben. "Where's home?"

"With Carmie," said Tenny. "No back talk, no questions. It's for your own good. She's there waiting for you now. She's even cooked a dinner for you."

Ben didn't protest. He turned to Lee. "Can you drive me there?"

"No, he can't," said Tenny. "I've got a car waiting for you."

"A car? And driver?"

"With two Secret Service agents. Fully armed. You're a wanted man, Ben. Get used to thinking like one."

CHAPTER 16

"I'm answering your ad for a roommate." Carmie looked Ben over as if she was inspecting him. "You'll do," she said. "Room and board. No strange friends coming and going in the middle of the night."

They laughed and hugged.

"Drop your bags, wash up, and join me in the kitchen," she said. "Dinner's just about ready. First room on the right is yours."

Carmie's apartment was in the Foggy Bottom neighborhood, a short walk from the White House. Her kitchen and living room windows faced the Potomac River and offered a widescreen view of its water traffic and activity at the nearby Kennedy Center. Ben stood marveling at the scene while Carmie heated a dish of lasagna.

"I've got a nice white wine we can have with this," said Carmie.

"Perfect," said Ben. "You made this?"

"You sound surprised that I can cook. Living alone all my life, it was either learn to cook a few things well or perish on a diet of Lean Cuisine and takeout Chinese."

Ben joined her in the kitchen. "You've never been married, have you?"

"No. Somehow I missed all that. Climbing the ladder on Wall Street doesn't leave a great deal of time for romance."

"Ever come close?"

"The closest was when I lived with a guy for two years. He worked in finance, too, so we seldom saw one another. It was kind of an audition for marriage, and neither of us got the part."

She dished the lasagna onto two plates and carried them to the dining room table, where the wine already was poured.

"Soup's on," she said.

He joined her and raised his glass in a toast. "To the chef," he said.

Carmie smiled. "Taste it first. I've got peanut butter and jelly if you don't like it."

As they dug into their food, Carmie hesitated for a moment and then said, "And you never married again? I hope you don't mind talking about this. What's it been, twenty years?"

"Twenty-three. No. It took me forever to get over it. We weren't married long enough for it to get stale or routine. There were no bad parts. It was a great marriage, and then boom, the accident and Almie was gone. Or at least gone from my physical life."

"No reason she should ever be gone from your memory," said Carmie. "You two had a rare and wonderful romance. Treasure it."

"That's where I am now. I'm over the deep sense of loss, over the anger of losing her, over any feelings of injustice or what might have been. Treasuring it is a good description."

They finished their food and carried their glasses and the wine bottle into the living room.

"What a view," said Ben. "To think I spent so many years living in Washington in an apartment without one. What was I thinking? It makes such a difference coming home to this, doesn't it?"

"What you were thinking was that you spent ninety percent of your time on the road working on campaigns, so why spend a small fortune on rent just to get a peek now and then?"

Ben smiled. "I guess that's right. God, I'm glad to get off the road. And I'd guess you're anxious to get back to New York. Did you keep your place there?"

"Yes, I still own it, and I pop back in now and then. I love living in New York. But this isn't shabby. Cabinet secretary. Best friends with the president. Beautiful apartment. Great view."

"And now a boarder taking up your space here."

Carmie laughed. "Oh, I kicked and screamed when Tenny suggested this arrangement. Nothing personal, but I've lived alone so long that the idea of a roommate just floored me. But she's so persistent. And, of course, she's right. We don't know whether you've got a target on your back, and until we find out, this is a practical arrangement. Now that you're here, I like it. I enjoy your company, Ben. I always have."

"Tomorrow I get debriefed from everyone working on agenda campaign," said Ben, will you be there?"

"I hope so. Can't promise. I've got the Commerce Department to run as my day job. If I don't show up, you can tell me all about it tomorrow night after I pull a couple of steaks from the freezer."

Ben raised his glass to her. "Carmie, I think I'm going to like it here."

CHAPTER 17

At another dinner table that night, about ten city blocks away, in the second-floor private residence of the White House, President Isabel Tennyson unfolded her napkin. Her dinner companion was Andres Navarro, her former husband.

Tenny and Andres had married while in college and divorced four years later, after her two miscarriages and his multiple infidelities. In the decades since, there had been little contact, but in the last year they had reunited. Andres was a retired surgeon and a widower. Seeing Andres again rekindled Tenny's passion for him. They had been together in the months since. Andres was temporarily living in a nearby residence hotel. He had just returned from visiting his grown and married daughters, who remained in California. Dinner tonight was the first time Andres and Tenny had been together for the past two weeks.

"Did you speak with the girls about it?" asked Tenny.

"I did," said Andres. "They really like you. Even though they've never met you, they feel like they know you. And of course I had a few good words to say about you to add to your image."

"Let's arrange for them to come here to DC in the next few weeks," said Tenny. "I'm considering a Rose Garden wedding at the White House, weather permitting. How does that sound?"

"Irresistible," said Andres. "I wouldn't think we could top our first wedding, but a White House wedding might do it."

Tenny smiled at the mention of their first wedding. The memory remained so vivid, untarnished by the lifetime of events since. "I thought I was a princess then. My grandfather went all out for it. All the best people in Mexico. Jewels and furs and roses like I'd never seen before."

"You were a princess. Now you're a queen."

"Hardly. Not a queen now or a princess then, Andres. But it was so much fun pretending to be in a fairy tale. The thing that was real then, though, was that I truly loved you. That never went away."

"And I love you, Tenny. We reconnected through the ugliest of circumstances, but this time we're going to make something beautiful out of it."

What Andres meant by the "ugliest of circumstances" was something neither the Secret Service nor US intelligence knew. Andres had been recruited by the Salvation Project to kill her. The Project had kidnapped one of his daughters, an English teacher then living in Tokyo. He was told that her safety depended on his reconnecting with Tenny. He later learned that he was embedded into her inner circle as a Plan B if it appeared she might win reelection. In the weeks before the election, with the opposition in disarray due to the Zach Bowman sex scandal, Tenny's chances of winning a new term in the White House markedly improved. That's when Andres was told to give Tenny a fatal injection as the price for saving his daughter. When the time and opportunity came, Andres was unable to go through with it. Instead, he confessed to Tenny, who, in dismay and anger, kept him under virtual house arrest for the remainder of the campaign.

A week after her election victory, Tenny had Andres brought to her. She informed him that she had arranged for the rescue of his daughter. She said she had decided not to prosecute him and that he should keep what had happened a secret they alone would share. And, to his surprise, Tenny said she wanted to remarry him.

Why would she want to marry him under the circumstances? She could hardly explain it to herself. Andres had been her first real love. She felt that love almost the moment she met him. That was so long ago. She had had many lovers since, but no loves. She and Andres had been separated for decades by distance, careers, and the lingering knowledge of their failure together. But the sight of him months ago reignited thoughts of what might have been and still could be. In their youth, Andres defined for her the meaning of love. Even now, thinking of their past lovemaking made her giddy. She knew that what they had in their twenties was not going to be recreated. His presence, though, was so comforting. He filled a need she had always had but could not satisfy with anyone else after their marriage dissolved. Would he disappoint her once again? It was a risk.

"We reconnected through the ugliest of circumstances, but this time we're going to make something beautiful out of it," Andres had said.

She desperately wanted to believe it.

CHAPTER 18

Three weeks after her reelection was assured, Tenny had commissioned Lee Searer to design a campaign that would support her agenda. "What agenda?" asked Lee. "Give me a few words that define it."

She gave him these:

An end to major wars

Income security for all

Housing security for all

Food security for all

Sustainable climate for the planet

Sustainable energy for the planet

An equitable economic system that works for all

Human rights for all

"I can work with these words to outline a campaign," Lee told Tenny at the time. "But these words also describe a utopia that philosophers have been imagining for at least twenty-five hundred years. Until you give me more, it's going to seem like the ultimate dreamy wish list. Paradise, Nirvana, Eden, not a serious political agenda."

"You come up with the campaign," Tenny responded. "I'll provide the credibility for it."

The morning after Ben returned to Washington Lee briefed Ben on what he and the creative team—an organization Ben and Lee had built over the years—had accomplished so far.

Lee envisioned delivering one hundred million individual campaigns, each one targeted to voters based on information about them gleaned from commercially available data banks: their voting histories, their issue preferences, their lifestyles, their social media contacts, newsletters or magazines they subscribed to or that were connected to their profession or hobbies or other interests. Preference would go to those who the data suggested could influence the views of others.

At the group level, separate campaigns would be directed at allies working on environmental issues, hunger, housing, racial equality, and health reform.

Campaigns would be designed to exploit and neutralize the self-interest of those most likely to mobilize opposition: weapons makers, the finance sector, agriculture, and for-profit behemoths in technology and energy.

A special team would reach out to media leaders: editorialists, columnists, TV news directors, cable news figures, magazines and their most influential writers, and every podcast with more than a thousand regular listeners.

Five books emphasizing different aspects of the agenda would be commissioned, giving their writers unlimited access to research and interviews with decision-makers.

Since the agenda's goal also involved creating a more peaceful and economically secure world for everyone, the State Department and intelligence agencies would all devise separate approaches for winning support from international audiences and their countries' leadership.

Polls would be taken in most countries on questions of war and peace, climate change, human rights, and other relevant issues in order to show overwhelming worldwide support. When the timing was right, an international telethon would be aired featuring leaders and celebrities from all fifty states and all participating countries localizing the campaigns, pledging their support, and solidifying the agenda's popularity and momentum.

Tenny herself would deliver a "speech to the world," carried in all countries and translated into multiple languages. Advance diplomacy would be required to clear this with heads of government, many of them autocrats not particularly thrilled with a US president encroaching on their turf.

All of this would occur under the single banner: "Peace and Security for All, and for All Time." It would be known as the "For All" campaign, with its own logo translated into dozens of languages.

To conduct this campaign, a full-time staff of eight hundred would be hired immediately, with more added as needed. The initial budget would be $700 million, in addition to costs absorbed by government programs.

Lee presented this plan with an artful combination of a video-laced PowerPoint, a specially designed musical anthem, and glossy handouts of program highlights.

Ben knew that Lee had been working on a White House plan, but until now he was unaware of the details and was surprised that it was so far advanced. Ben and Lee had met years earlier, during a difficult campaign for the US Senate. Lee had taken a sabbatical from a nearby university where he taught political science. He led the campaign's research group, and he did it so creatively that Ben was able to build winning media based on the information Lee provided. After the election, Ben offered Lee the job of research director for his political management firm, and Lee jumped on it. He gave up his tenured position, moved to Washington, and in short order proved himself so adept at converting research to strategy that Ben offered him a partnership. Together, they were a formidable team. Now, on the most important assignment they had ever had, Lee had once again displayed his exceptional talent.

"Suggestions?" asked Lee when he turned the last page of his presentation.

"Irresistible," said Ben.

"You mean if we do all this, we can't lose?"

"No. I mean I can't resist it. My blood pressure kept rising with every new idea. What a challenge!"

"Glad to hear that you like it," said Lee. "But come on, we've worked together long enough. I know you were mentally editing it as you were listening."

"Okay," said Ben. "Just two things. Number one, the menu's too long. If we're spreading ourselves thin over war and peace, hunger, homelessness, health, and all things that afflict us, we're not selling anything, just making a statement. We need a single point of focus, like we do in a candidate or issue campaign. We need a candidate here, something that people can say yes or no to, and a way for them to vote."

"Like, picking one issue as the poster boy for the rest?"

"Exactly. And I'd suggest war and peace. Easy to understand. Ninety percent plus would vote for peace. And if we can get world peace, with all the money saved through disarmament, we can pay for the rest of the good things we're for."

"You mean after ten thousand years of humans fighting each other, we try to sell the idea that we can stop it. With one PR campaign?"

"Why not?" asked Ben. "I think it's the easiest of the ideas to sell."

"And the military-industrial complex and all the warlords around the world will let us get away with it?"

"Can you think of a better opponent in this election campaign? We just need to develop a message strategy for beating them. You've already designed the campaign to deliver it."

"*O-k-a-y*," said Lee, his skepticism evident. "And what's your second suggestion?"

"We've got to get this done within a year, before it all gets wrapped up into next year's political campaigns. We need to build pressure to the equivalent of an election day so decisions get made, not delayed."

"Nothing gets done in Congress in a year," said Lee. "What's your idea for doing it?"

"I don't have one," said Ben.

CHAPTER 19

As Speaker of the House, Guy Rocker's support would be essential for passage of the president's second-term agenda. While the president had not yet publicly revealed that agenda, she had confided the outline to him. He was stunned by its audacity: significant cuts to the Defense Department budget and a sweeping, new arms reduction treaty; consolidation of all government research under a newly organized agency with extraordinary regulatory powers; another new agency to manage the effects of climate change, such as drought, water shortages, and agricultural and tidal land losses from rising seas—even immigration as it related to worldwide climate-caused migrations. She also intended to ask for fundamental changes in the way the government managed business and finance, to make US capitalism more socially conscious. Even though her party controlled both houses of Congress, he was doubtful about the prospects for passage.

Each of these initiatives individually would be a difficult sell. Powerful and well-funded private interests would fight back vigorously. Trying to take on all of them at once was like declaring war on every entrenched sector of the US economy and defense establishment. Rocker was not philosophically opposed to her agenda, but from what she had told him so far, he knew how politically difficult it would be for his members to go along with, and a nightmare to try to sell to the public. He shared that assessment with Tenny.

While doubting the political wisdom of the agenda, he admired her motives. In fact, if he were president he might be offering the same policy, only in bite-size portions, taking on one powerful interest at a time.

If he were president. How often he had thought of it. With the vice presidency becoming vacant last year, Rocker had felt he had an inside track for the appointment. But Tenny appointed her friend Sheila Fishburne instead. As if friendship should make a difference in choosing someone who could become president of the most powerful nation the world had ever known. It made no sense politically either. Fishburne was from Alaska, with its pitifully few votes that seldom went Democratic. He was from Michigan, an important swing state that influenced the entire Midwest.

He mulled over these thoughts more often than was healthy for him. He was aware of that. Never look back. Always prepare for the battles ahead. But still, coming so close . . .

Rocker's personal situation consumed him that night as he sat in the back seat of his government limousine. Normally he would be scanning files arranged for him by his staff. There was always too much to do and never enough time. Being alone on these drives to and from the Capitol was important time for him to review the day's events and plan for tomorrow.

Tonight, though, he stared out the car's window as they passed familiar sites in northwest Washington. His mind was on a conversation with retired General Cal Foley at an event he had just attended at the Mayflower Hotel. After his speech to one of Washington's most powerful think tanks, a group comprised largely of retired military and civilian Defense Department leaders, Rocker and Foley met for drinks at the hotel bar. Foley was a member of the National Intelligence Review Board and former head of the US Army's missile program. Foley had heard rumbles about the president's proposed cuts in the defense budget. Rocker confirmed the rumors but told him that chances for approval were grim.

"That's just the reality of it," said Foley. "The industry makes a fortune from those defense contracts. It's economic life-and-death. Can you imagine how hard they'll fight to keep Congress from passing anything like what I've heard she plans to propose?"

"You sound as if you agree we should be cutting the defense budget," said Rocker.

"Of course we should," said Foley. "Too damned much waste. Many of the programs run by idiots. And the risks. Good God, we could blow up the planet many times over."

Rocker laughed. "Hmm. That's not what I heard from General Foley when you were still in uniform testifying to Congress about your budget. Did your head spin around when you finally put on civilian clothes?"

"In uniform, you do what's expected, like it or not, agree with it or not. You put all the controls in place you can think of. But along with all the smart people running the missile program, we've got too many not-so-smart people. We've got great kids in those silos with the launch keys and not-so-smart kids. Name one technology in the world that doesn't have a bug or where materials don't develop defects or human error doesn't lead to mistakes. And not just here. People and equipment like this are on launchpads and in silos all over the world—Russia, China, Pakistan. Pakistan! It's the silos, the nuclear subs, the people dispatching nuclear-armed planes and the crews inside those planes. And, for Christ's sake, now we've got people in rooms in Florida launching killer drones everywhere in the world. Of course we should be dialing back."

"So what's the answer?" asked Rocker. "No one wants to blink. Not us, not the Russians or Chinese. Do you think the Indians and Pakistanis will ever trust one another to holster their weapons? How do we get rid of the threat? How do we get even our own Congress to act?"

Foley was quiet for a few moments. "Getting Congress aboard isn't the only way. There are alternatives," he finally said. "Would you be open to talking about it some time?"

What did Foley mean? Alternatives? The question haunted him on the long drive home.

As Speaker of the House, Guy Rocker was one of four House members regularly informed of the nation's most secret intelligence matters. That meant he also was one of the few people in the country aware that the Salvation Project was a conspiracy bent on taking control of the world's most scientifically advanced countries. He knew about the Project's role in last year's election. The agency consensus was that the threat was low-grade now that target countries were aware of the Project's existence and would be more vigilant in destroying any surviving remnants. But from what he knew, the Salvation Project's mission was control. That would make it "an alternative to Congress" and the presidency itself. What if the intelligence estimates were wrong? They often were.

Could that be what Foley meant? Foley? A man deeply embedded in US military planning and operations? A current member of the Intelligence Review Board, aware of most of the nation's deepest secrets? Could retired general Cal Foley be connected to the Salvation Project?

Unlikely. But . . . . Rocker could not leave that thought behind the entire drive home.

CHAPTER 20

Gil Adonis was in both legal and deathwatch limbo. The Justice Department was conflicted on whether to charge him with a crime based on his known activities in last year's presidential election, which would mean initiating an expensive, high-profile, politically fraught trial against against one of the world's richest and most prominent financial figures. Meanwhile, both the FBI and CIA were exploring whether Adonis was needed any longer in their efforts to smash what remained of the Salvation Project. Inside the government's law enforcement agencies there was little doubt that the murder of Lester Bowles was both an act by the Salvation Project to shut down a potentially dangerous informant and a message to Gil Adonis that they intended to kill him too. But was this just the last gasp of a few Project dead-enders or a sign that the Project was more extensive, more dangerous, more deeply entrenched than they first believed?

After his Oval Office meeting with Tenny, Adonis had been taken to an FBI safe house and not allowed to leave. Food and supplies had been provided. He was allowed to make arrangements for securing his vast investments under newly assumed names so they could not be used to locate him. Washington, DC, was a constant churn of those connected with Congress, think tanks, lobbying firms, government operations, media, and workers in the burgeoning tech and biological medicine industries. Short-term residency in the city and in many nearby Virginia and Maryland neighborhoods was the norm. A new face in the neighborhood stirred not a ripple of interest. The FBI had Adonis under current surveillance. He was safe here. He also had a lot of time to think of what could come next.

Gil Adonis was a rational man, but he had allowed his common sense to lapse, and that lapse had resulted in Les Bowles's death. Why hadn't he been killed too? He had spent a lightly protected week in Poulsbo, living with Ben Sage. Clearly, if the Project wanted to claim a victim, they would do it. They'd done it many times to others. Why not him before Les? And what about Ben Sage? Was he a target now too? Was everyone he came in contact with infected, as if he was the carrier of an incurable virus?

What next? Prosecution? Would he remain in jail for the months, possibly years, before trial? And if prosecution was avoided, what would his life be like? Tenny had mentioned a witness protection program. That would mean another name, new identity papers, most likely changes in his appearance—a new hairstyle or no hair at all, maybe even facial surgery. Would he submit to that? None of it seemed appealing or even worth doing. How could he possibly hide indefinitely? What were his alternatives?

Underlying it all was his sense of grief for June Bowles, Lester's wife, and other members of the Bowles family. He had gone on double dates with June and Les before they were married. They took trips together. She had to be distraught over his murder. Craig Bowles, Lester's oldest son and newly elected Ohio state auditor, was Gil's godson. Daughter Ann, in her final year of medical school, had been a favorite of Gil's, as interested as he was in science, traveling with him to technical conferences and advanced research laboratories. Les's father, Lester Bowles Sr., was a former US senator. Father and son were so close. Lester Sr. had to be heartbroken. Gil knew them all well. The family knew him well too. And they had to wonder why Gil had not been there with them, to comfort them, to pay respects, to offer a substantial reward for the capture of Les's killer.

Things had to be decided. He couldn't live like this, in virtual solitary confinement. He had to talk to Tenny again.

Dear Madam President:

I write with great respect for you and deep regret for events I initiated to try to defeat you in last year's political campaign. I remain convinced that if my plan had succeeded, and Lester Bowles ultimately became president under the conditions I expected, that the nation would have been more secure and humanity itself would be less vulnerable. However, I could not foresee the lengths to which my associates would go in turning what I still believe to be an essential cause into a criminal conspiracy of murderous vendettas.

In my misjudgment, I am in good company. When Alfred Nobel invented dynamite, he could not perceive that would lead to his forever being remembered as the "angel of death" for all the lives lost because of his invention. After Robert Oppenheimer led the scientific effort to create the atomic bomb, he publicly regretted the threat that it posed and still poses to life on Earth. For all the good the inventors of the internal combustion engine have created, they could not foresee that ultimately their invention would put us all at risk for how it would warm our planet.

My point is that even the wisest among us can be so close to our activities that we are blind to the consequences of those actions. I believe that's the status of humanity, particularly with its devotion to majority rule. We are too embedded in our routines to understand why we must change.

We revere the idea that "anyone can be president" (or senator or governor or member of Congress), but our history demonstrates that "anyone" can mean one who knows little about governing, one who just has enough money or charisma to grasp power. That's why I believe it is essential that the levers of governing be placed in the hands of the most knowledgeable and capable among us, apart from their so-called "popularity," and allow such a governing body to make informed, necessary decisions in a timely manner to meet the challenges of a planet with nine billion people and countless possibilities for their destruction.

We cannot assume that the people will ever vote for such a change in government control. Eventually, it will need to be imposed. Nevertheless, I applaud and support you in your effort to attempt what few of your predecessors had the courage or wisdom to attempt. And I have decided that the most effective way I can provide that support is to help remove the scourge of the Salvation Project. In that regard, I ask to be relieved of what amounts to my house arrest so that I can attend Lester Bowles's memorial service and funeral, in full public view, and thereafter to resume my past working life in New York City. I do this in hopes of luring a potential assassin who in turn would help law enforcement find and destroy the Project I once supported.

Please honor this request at the earliest moment so that I may be in touch with the Bowles family and make suitable arrangements.

Gilbert Adonis

CHAPTER 21

Saint Joseph's Cathedral seated about seven hundred parishioners, not enough capacity for all who came to pay their last respects to Governor Lester Bowles. Hundreds of latecomers stood in the side aisles and entranceways. More gathered outside the grounds of the 150-year-old Gothic stone edifice, the center of the Columbus diocese.

The mourners included fellow governors, top officials from the Bowles administration, dozens of mayors and members of the Ohio legislature, and constituents young and old who were drawn to service by Bowles and his long-established Ohio family. From a temporary unit on the grounds, FBI agents scanned faces captured by concealed cameras and analyzed immediately by artificial intelligence. Secret Service agents were deployed strategically to protect the president, who, dressed elegantly in a black wool suit, sat with the Bowles family, as did longtime family friend Gil Adonis.

Tenny had decided to come to Columbus after receiving Gil's note. Bowles's killers most likely would be there, too, and Gil was offering himself as bait. With surveillance, the FBI might be able to spot suspicious mourners inside or outside the cathedral and track them. A long-shot plan, Gil admitted, but worth the risk given the ongoing threat the Salvation Project posed to the country and to himself.

Tenny was conflicted about attending the service. She did not want to intrude on the family's grief. Neither did she want to be accused of taking political advantage of Bowles's death. If she were to appear, cable news cameras would come with her, most likely to broadcast the service live, and, indeed, those cameras were here. Despite Tenny's early hesitation, the Bowles family seemed genuinely touched by her offer to attend and to deliver a eulogy.

Gil Adonis was a prominent figure at the memorial events. He had arrived in Columbus a day earlier and met with Les's family members. He remained for hours at the public viewing the night before the service. He stayed at a local hotel, registered under his own name. After the service he greeted mourners, many of whom he knew from his early days in Columbus. He forced himself to focus on the day, not on the danger. This was the least he could do for Les and his family. Now and then he thought he saw a suspicious move or body language that seemed unnatural. Now and then he caught himself looking back over his own shoulder. Then he reentered reality. Others, trained, armed, watchful, were out there. He had a role to play as innocent prey. He needed to play the part convincingly.

Tenny also was of two minds as she greeted mourners. This was not the first sad occasion during her political career for which she was called on to provide solace. She knew what was expected, and she genuinely grieved for the Bowles family. She also could not shake her concern for Gil Adonis and his presence here. Would killers come after him today? Unlikely, but it could not be ruled out. From what she knew now of the Project, its leaders were as certain of their mission and as ruthlessly determined to achieve it as those of any Jonestown-like cult. Would a funeral stop them from killing Gil? As the victim of an attempted assassination herself, she bore the weight of many other deaths and other broken bodies. Les Bowles's murder had been made possible because she had won reelection. She felt a deep sense of responsibility.

During Bowles's service she was alert for the slightest unusual sound or click of a nearby camera or a strange voice calling her name. It was a familiar feeling, being on edge at large public events. After the assassination attempt that almost took her life, she could never again fully feel the joy and innocence of being the center of attention. Knowing there likely was a killer in this crowd stalking Gil Adonis added to her tension. She hated it.

CHAPTER 22

The trip to Columbus, the stress of speaking in a politically awkward situation before live television cameras, the mental strain she always experienced when providing comfort for grieving families, Gil's presence, and the trap set by the FBI hoping to identify Lester Bowles's killers—it all left Tenny more physically spent than usual. Within minutes of returning to the family quarters of the White House, Andres, waiting to join her for a late dinner, noticed it immediately.

"Before we eat," said Andres, "we're going to get you tested."

Normally, Tenny would have said, "Nonsense," and resisted. Tonight, she merely said, "Thanks, Andres, please arrange it."

Since the assassination attempt two years earlier, an explosion that left Tenny with broken ribs and other chest injuries resulting in acute respiratory distress syndrome, the White House medical office had been staffed with a full-time pulmonologist and state-of-the-art test equipment. Andres called the doctor on duty and told him to prepare to check the president's oxygen levels, airflow rate, lung volume, and diffusion. Also, said Andres, take blood for blood gas levels.

"Is this an emergency?" the on-duty physician asked.

"I don't think so," said Andres, "but she's unusually tired and her breathing is more labored." Decades of patient care had sharpened Andres's observations of symptoms. Tenny's concerned him. So did her willingness to submit to the tests before dinner, without the slightest hint of resistance.

The tests showed her oxygen levels about two points below what would be considered the lower end of normal. Other measurements also produced results at the low end of normal readings. Worrisome, but not alarming for a person in her condition. That buoyed her spirits, and after a bit of oxygen therapy, she even regained her appetite.

"Grace and Karen will be here next week," said Andres over their delayed meal. "I've reserved rooms for them in my hotel."

"Wonderful," said Tenny. "Let's plan a special dinner. And Grace's husband? Will he be here?"

"Can't get away from work. He has a big case on the docket. So it'll just be the girls. How would you like to schedule them in?"

"Meet the family at a scheduled time," she laughed. "But you're right, it's not as if we can spend the day together, go shopping and out to dinner. After they settle in at the hotel, bring them here, and I'll make time for them. Coordinate that with Marcie. I'll show them around the West Wing. They'd like that, wouldn't they?"

"Of course. They'll be thrilled."

"And then let's plan on dinners here in the White House, not a restaurant, so we don't attract public attention. We can begin getting used to all of us being together as a family. I want to talk with them about timing so they all can be here for the wedding. And any of their friends and yours who should be on the invitation list. By the way, I've assigned Louellen as wedding coordinator and told her to be sure you're involved in all the decisions."

"Thanks, but wedding planning isn't my specialty. I doubt I'll add anything constructive. This is your show. And, really, it will be a show. Be honest."

Tenny hesitated. "Well, I won't lie. Andres, I am looking at our wedding as a media event to help raise my popularity. I'm looking at everything I do to raise my popularity."

"I don't mind being a prop," said Andres.

She rose from the dinner table, walked to where he was seated, and put her arms around him. "Andres, if I wasn't president, there'd be no reason to get married. We could live together and who'd care? But I can't do that with the world peering into our bedroom. So if marriage it is, let's make the wedding a beautiful event."

Andres took her hands and drew her closer. "You know, at our first wedding, the vow you took to 'obey' me? I didn't expect obedience from you. But I knew that as I tried to have a medical career I would have your love and support. Now we're going to exchange vows again. And you have mine. I'm proud to be your prop."

Tenny nudged him up from his chair.

"Suddenly I have a different kind of hunger," she said. "I'm ready for the bedroom course."

CHAPTER 23

G uy Rocker's conversation with retired General Cal Foley kept competing for his attention. He wanted to talk more to Foley, to understand what Foley meant by "there are other ways to get things done." Foley's words dangled before Rocker like bait on a hook. His mind kept circling it, trying to assess whether this one held promise or danger. Rocker admired Foley for his management of the army's nuclear silo program, and he considered Foley an unusually creative military strategist. Nevertheless, Rocker had been in Congress long enough to have sensitive antennae for assessing anyone with a cause to sell. Caution lights blinked for him now as they did automatically when confronted with new proposals. This one felt particularly sensitive with its suggestion of illegality. Best not to have the next discussion by cell phone—or any phone.

As Speaker of the House, Rocker raised tens of millions of campaign dollars each year. The price of fundraising success was his availability when large contributors asked for his presence at their events and when fellow Democrats held fundraisers of their own. Some invitations could be handled with gracious "sorry I can't be with you" notes. Others could be satisfied with surrogates. Rocker had enough confidence in his staff's judgment that he seldom overrode their suggestions about which events to attend and which to politely beg off.

But tonight he had. Frank Lipscott, a fellow Democrat and chairman of the House Armed Services Committee, was scheduled for a fundraiser at the Army and Navy Club in downtown DC. Rocker's name was on the invitation as a cohost, but Lipscott assured him that his presence wasn't needed. Most of the money already was in the bank, and the event was being held just to give Lipscott's contributors an opportunity to talk to him personally. Rocker's staff had written a note of regrets to be read along with other speeches, but then it occurred to Rocker that General Foley likely would be there. Rather than call Foley or meet with him privately, an event that would show up on his very public appointments calendar, running into Foley at a typical Washington fundraiser, drink glasses in hand, would give Rocker a safe, no-commitment chance to dig deeper into those "other ways."

Earlier in the day, Rocker and four other key House members had met with Vice President Fishburne and Secretary Sanchez to review plans for enacting Tenny's Peace and Security agenda. Rocker was surprised by the depth of the plan and the money Tenny planned to invest in promoting it. He agreed with just about every part of Tenny's agenda. More than that, for the first time since being briefed by Tenny personally, he saw a flicker of possible success. With varying degrees of enthusiasm, the House leaders assured Fishburne and Sanchez that they would work to enact the program. This information would be useful to share with General Foley. He could raise the topic and test Foley's response without feeling he was entering forbidden territory.

As Rocker anticipated, there was an opportunity to isolate Foley while the fundraising crowd was at its peak and groups of conversations were taking place throughout the ballroom. He described Tenny's plan and the promotional effort behind it and cast the conversation in a positive light. Hearing this, Foley shook his head contemptuously.

"No, no, no. Waste of time. It won't work," said Foley.

"I thought the last time we spoke you felt we should be lowering the military temperature and cutting back on risk," said Rocker.

"I'm all for it," said Foley. "But it won't happen this way. Let me tell you why. It's because most people in position to make decisions about this are living in the past."

"The past? I don't understand," said Rocker.

"Few people do," said Foley. "Back when I was in college, I took a course titled 'The History of Art.' I thought the class would be a history of painting and painters, you know, like Rembrandt and Van Gogh. Instead, it was based on the definition of art as mimesis, the representation of reality. It's common to think of the artist being ahead of his time. When you think of it as mimesis, the artist is in his time, and everyone else is not. It's why military people are always getting ready to fight the last war. Since I've been in uniform we've fought in Vietnam, the Balkans, the Middle East, and all without success, even though we've spent trillions of dollars. We've just spent decades and a trillion dollars developing the F-35 Lightning II aircraft, a remarkable feat of science and engineering. Totally obsolete in the age of missile warfare. We're always looking in the rearview mirror. Technology can change. Science can make spectacular breakthroughs. We can develop extraordinary new tools, such as artificial intelligence and robots. We can land objects at precise locations on Mars. We can split atoms and rearrange molecules. That's where a few minds are. But collectively, most others are living in the past. The past is what's taught in schools. It's what passes for reality for most media. It's what most voters know best, and so when candidates run for office, they appeal for votes based on what most people believe they know. Reality is that we will never again fight a war as we have in the past. We'll never again live in a world without artificial intelligence competing with us, or robots doing so many jobs that always have been done by humans. You won't convince a majority to take a great leap into reality and make government policy to address what's real, what's ahead rather than what's behind. They don't know what reality is. Only the artists are there."

"Whoa, that's pretty heavy," said Rocker. "I'd love to talk more about it with you some time. Does this have anything to do with 'the other ways to get things done' you mentioned when we last talked?"

"It has everything to do with it," said Foley. "Tenny wants to save the world. Great. So do I. Tenny thinks people will vote to do it. I don't. The other ways? Let the artists do it."

"And you're connected with some artists?"

"I am, and you should be, too, Guy. You see things as they really are. You should be vice president instead of Fish. Hell, you should be president instead of Tenny. I think so, and a lot of my friends think so too."

"Hey, I'm flattered," said Rocker. "But the reality is that I'm not."

"But you could be," said Foley. "Would you like to know how you can get there?"

Rocker literally rocked back on his heels at this. President? Yes, he thought he should be president. Four hundred other people in the House and everyone in the Senate also thought they should be president. But here was one of the most powerful lobbyists in Washington saying it to him, and he seemed serious. Rocker hesitated before responding.

"Who are your friends?"

"Would you like to meet some of them?" Foley responded.

Rocker stood silent for a moment, considering the words and the meaning behind them. As one of the leaders of the House, and having knowledge of the Salvation Project, he instantly associated that mysterious group with Foley's "friends." US intelligence had warned that some of those plotters came from military and intelligence organizations like Foley's. But Foley was one of the most brilliant people he had ever met, particularly on matters of arms control and defense issues. And he shared Foley's views about the dangers of the nuclear-armed world. What would be the harm in learning more about how he, Rocker, could help save the world?

"Possibly," he replied.

APRIL

CHAPTER 24

Richfield noted two absences from the call. An absence often meant a project manager had been arrested or was so fearful of immediate exposure that he or she avoided the call to protect the others on the Project's executive committee.

Number Six, the Egyptian project manager and longtime committee member, had never before failed to join a meeting. Arrest in Egypt almost certainly would result in torture, and torture always led to uncertain consequences. Some previous managers withstood torture and survived without revealing anything of importance. Others had not been as resolute, leading to difficult management problems. A few less fortunate managers had died with their lips sealed. After this call, Richfield would need to investigate Egypt.

Twenty-Four also was missing. This had happened before. China monitored its communications more closely and with more technical prowess than other nations. But Twenty-Four was very skillful at avoiding authorities. Richfield had more confidence that this absence was temporary and that she would contact him later without endangering the full Management Committee.

Meanwhile, the others were waiting, and each moment of waiting risked discovery by intelligence authorities.

"Thank you all for your patience," said Richfield. "As you are aware, the timing of these meetings occasionally can be awkward for your schedules. But all have now reported, so let's begin. Our first agenda item is an important new development from Eighteen. Go ahead, Eighteen."

"Yes, I will keep this brief. A very significant asset has enlisted in our cause, someone who may allow us to accelerate our action timetable for the United States. As you know, we failed to place our team in the White House during last year's election, but there could be opportunity to do so soon. Given this situation, it is imperative that all continent and country managers be aware of the sensitivity of the American project while conducting their own operations. Any action that in any way would affect the United States must be cleared through Richfield to avoid disturbing or undermining our United States operations, which are quite promising, but also still quite fragile. Is there anything now that I should be aware of?"

"Seven here," said a male voice, speaking Spanish. "Is our translation system working? Can English and French speakers understand me?"

"We hear the translation," said Richfield. "Just speak slowly and distinctly and leave a two-second pause between statements for translation delay."

"Understood," said Seven. "Planning for the takeover of Argentina is in advanced stages. Action could take place within three months. Will this action disturb US operations?"

"Did you understand that, Eighteen?" asked Richfield.

"I did," Eighteen responded. "Will this be accomplished in Argentina by a new leadership current American policy can support?"

"I don't believe so," said Seven. "The United States government will view this as an antidemocratic coup and likely will denounce it."

"I see that as helpful," said Eighteen. "Just so that all managers understand why, let me explain the current US situation. The president is about to put forward an agenda that will attempt to unite the world's most powerful countries in an unprecedented effort to abolish poverty, feed the hungry, make common cause on disease and climate control, and to end armed conflicts among nations. The president will try to persuade all countries to disarm and divert weapons budgets into more humane and peaceful areas."

"Excuse me, this sounds like our program. Why would we oppose it? This is Thirty-One," said a man speaking through the Arabic translation system.

"We won't oppose it," said Richfield. "We will support it. Our people will enthusiastically speak out for the president's program. We hope to convince the US population and others to demand it."

"I don't understand," said Thirty-One.

"It's a perfect environment for us," replied Richfield. "US leaders and others will advance our agenda, creating demand. The entrenched money and military forces will resist. The president will lose. The public will be greatly disappointed. That improves the environment for public acceptance of our program. We will provide what the current regime failed to deliver. By trying and failing, the current president will prove to all that democracy can't succeed. We will be ready with the alternative."

"Eighteen here again. Precisely, Richfield. Thank you for that explanation. All other managers can contribute to this success by encouraging support for the president's initiative worldwide. The higher the hopes, the more disappointing will be the legislative failures, and the greater degree of acceptance we will have. Any questions?"

"This is Twenty-Eight. My compliments. A brilliant plan. I can think of no better way to succeed in the British environment."

Another British voice entered the conversation, identifying as Three.

"A word of caution here. Let's not fall into the trap of believing we will win the debate on the United States president's terms. If we could have persuaded governments to come to their senses, it would have happened years ago. We have evolved to where we are because debate has not succeeded. Force has. Our fortunes changed when we accepted the fact that we are in a war to save humanity and that, as in any war, there are casualties. Some consider us ruthless. Yes, we are, the way pilots are ruthless when they drop bombs and armies are ruthless when they attack. Victory goes not only to the wise, but to the strong. I am the most veteran member of this body at number Three because Two, who organized the Project with me years ago was killed by ruthless intelligence services. We are all in this because we are willing to give up our lives for a higher cause. We will win because we are willing to eliminate those who stand in our way."

"Well said, Three," said Richfield. "Months ago, we believed that the Project would be required to remain dormant because we unfortunately had been exposed and many of our key people had been taken. We already are back and with prospects for success more promising than ever. We are resilient. We will succeed."

CHAPTER 25

After winning her first election as US president, many referred to her as "Tenny the Tornado." She broke the decades-long impasse over immigration policy, made substantial improvements in the health care system, and won changes in economic and tax policy to achieve more equality, fairness, and genuine competition.

Then, "Tenny fatigue" set in. Members of her own party grew weary of being forced to take so many difficult votes, each one earning animosity from segments of their voting constituencies. Her third year as president produced fewer results and left her vulnerable to a powerful conspiracy that plotted her impeachment. The new immigration law spawned deadly "militias," one of which detonated an explosion designed to kill her. Tenny survived both impeachment and assassination but had paid a high price for each. Impeachment had made her politically vulnerable and nearly cost her reelection. The attempted assassination took a physical toll, one she had coped with each day since. Nevertheless, she now had a license for a fresh four-year term with renewed public support. She was determined to make the first two of those years the most consequential of her presidency.

As president, she had visited many of the world's most advanced science and technology centers. She had been given previews of a utopian future: Genetic editing and other medical developments that could raise life expectancy well beyond one hundred. New ways to generate energy and dispose of waste without endangering the planet. Agricultural developments that could eliminate world hunger. Quantum computing, data storage, next-generation communication tools—all were accelerating scientific discovery and application beyond anything ever known. Tenny could see the future. Humanity was on the cusp of a truly golden age.

But her encounter with Gil Adonis and the Salvation Project had awakened her to the dark side of a potential Eden. It would not take malign intent to create mass destruction. Innocent mistake was at least as likely. Hubris was always a risk, as was unexpected human psychological breakdown. Once she began probing for what could go wrong, she learned of many close calls that already had entered the realm of cautionary tales.

Tenny was certain that the Salvation Project was wrong in its belief that only a few well-informed authoritarians at the top could control these risks. Democratically elected leaders could manage emerging science, she believed. Perhaps not as efficiently, but in the end successfully, and without the added risk that the self-appointed leaders themselves would become more of a danger to humanity than the science itself.

Today was her first test of that theory. In the Cabinet Room sat the six key leaders of the US House and Senate, all members of the Democratic Party. Prior to this meeting, Fish and Carmie had presented the group with an outline of the Peace and Security agenda. Today was step two: previewing Tenny's planned speech to a nationally televised joint session of Congress.

House Speaker Rocker was the first to react after Tenny had completed her presentation.

"Madam President, in all my years as a member of the House, this is the most consequential program I've ever seen. My congratulations. It's the very definition of leadership. You've distilled the essence of many of the most serious problems we're facing, and speaking personally, I believe your solutions are both rational and reasonable. I can enthusiastically support it, and I'm confident I can rally our caucus behind it. What do you think, George?"

George Hernandez was House majority leader, second in command to Rocker. "My reaction entirely," he said. "Certainly there will be opposition, lots of opposition, but I think we can handle it by building in smooth off-ramps so that industries that lose will have attractive alternatives for business and profit and no one gets cut off cold turkey."

Rocker turned to Carla Redbone, his assistant majority leader. "How about you, Carla?"

"I'm in," she said. "More than in. I'm excited by it. The first thing we'll need to do is split the defense and energy lobbies so they don't form a united front against us. Before the speech, I suggest we talk privately with their top people and assure them they won't get hurt if they mute their opposition, and that we'll break their knees if they put up too hard a fight."

Tenny rose from her seat at the end of the table and walked to where the three House leaders were seated. She hugged the backs of each of them in turn. "I know I'm asking a lot," she said. "Each of these proposals is well beyond what anyone outside this room is expecting. But this is the right thing to do and the right time to do it. We have the White House. We control Congress. And we have an electorate that will welcome this agenda. The burden we have is to fight our way through the opposition and enact it."

She turned to the three Senate leaders.

"Lane," she said to Senate Majority Leader Lane Juliano, "you not only have the legislative fight, but we're going to need the Senate to approve what amounts to a worldwide disarmament treaty. That's going to blow a lot of minds."

"Oh yeah," said Juliano. "We have half a dozen people up next time who'll see many of those votes as career-ending and politically suicidal. They'll be wanting to push off votes until after the next election."

"Putting off the votes would kill the program," said Tenny. "You know what things will be like in my third and fourth years. I'll be chopped liver while the rest of you start running for president or get caught up with people who are. I understand the politics all too well. That's why I've set up my creative communications team with the biggest budget ever assembled to sell this program. We plan to move the communications in lockstep with your legislative timing. Public approval will peak just when you need it for committee and floor votes once we agree on a timetable. I'm going to see to it that public opinion will force your members to vote yes. It will be a winning vote for them, not a killer."

"Sounds expensive," said Juliano. "How will you finance it?"

"Let's just say I'm good for it," said Tenny.

Juliano smiled. She and everyone else at the table knew that Tenny could write a personal check for the kind of campaign she had just outlined.

"If you're all in like that," said Juliano, "I'm all in."

Guy Rocker flashed a thumbs-up. Each of the congressional leaders at the table seemed pleased. And when Rocker reported the details of this meeting to Cal Foley, he knew Foley would be too.

CHAPTER 26

Entering the office of the president of the United States transforms most visitors into supplicants, as if they were stepping over the threshold of a sanctuary. Power radiates from its eighteen-foot ceiling, the royal blue carpet embedded with the presidential seal, the fireplace and chairs so familiar in photos with other heads of state, the glass panels revealing the Rose Garden. Unforgettable images of John Fitzgerald Kennedy and his small children were captured here. Richard Nixon announced his resignation here. Ronald Reagan led the nation in mourning from here after the crash of the *Challenger* spacecraft.

It's an arena where the president, as the occupant of this office, carries the mantle of power, and with it the advantage of home turf in any contest of conflicting ideas.

Early in her first term as president, Tenny had discovered Oval Office magic. Today, Isabel Aragon Tennyson, the first woman to occupy the office, would attempt to cast its spell on a dozen CEOs of the business goliaths that created and manufactured weapons of warfare, recipients of billions of tax dollars each year, employers of millions, economic lifelines for communities in nearly every one of the fifty states.

Having them here the morning after Tenny's nationally televised speech unveiling her "For All" agenda to a joint session of Congress was a calculated decision. Images and stories of the event crowded out most other news for media attention. Tenny's plans for "Peace and Security for All" were a bold and electrifying departure from the customary menu of issues. Enthusiastic support from members in the congressional majority raised hope that a program as far-reaching as this could become reality. Seldom had she stood on firmer ground politically to mute the heavy guns of the defense contracting industry.

"Good morning, all," said Tenny to the nine men and three women in attendance. "I hope you enjoyed the speech and the White House party afterward."

A ripple of nervous laughter echoed across the room.

"Wonderful party," said Gillian Stockwell, Lockheed Martin's chief executive officer. "Thank you for inviting us. And I learned at the party that you are planning to marry Andres. All the best to you both."

There were nods from others in the room and murmurs of agreement.

"Planning a honeymoon?" asked Horst England, Raytheon's CEO.

"Honeymoon?" answered Tenny. "That's what I'm hoping all of you will give me."

More smiles and suppressed laughter, a bit more nervous than before.

"Let me get straight to the reason I asked you all here so I don't waste your valuable time," said Tenny. "I'm sure you're all familiar with the goals I laid out in my speech, and I'm equally sure that you all have a fair degree of heartburn for what that means to your companies. I've asked you here to assure you that I am quite serious about my initiative to set the world on a path toward disarmament, one that greatly reduces the prospect of major war anywhere and everywhere in the world. That, of course, would require phasing out many of your companies' most lucrative sales to the US government, and to every other government."

Tenny's visitors were seated on the office's sofas and chairs brought in for this meeting. She was seated, teacher-to-class style, facing them. Now she stood for effect.

"If I put to the American public, or the world public for that matter, the question of 'Are you in favor of peace or war?' how do you think most would answer? Close to one hundred percent against war, wouldn't you expect? It's safe to say that no one wants to commit mass murder or risk annihilation themselves. They don't want their sons or daughters, husbands or wives, or anyone else they know to become killers or risk being killed or injured. Yet we spend most of our national budget on weapons of war and to pay people to fight those wars and to care for those warriors after they come back in pieces or mentally warped. Why? Because we're afraid someone may attack us first or attack those who share our values or try to impose their will or ideology on us. And if none of those shoes fit, then try countries that are bent on extending their wealth and power and influence by taking what belongs to others."

Tenny walked to the window and looked out on the Rose Garden.

"In a few weeks, those brown trees will turn green, and the vegetation that now looks dead will sprout into colors thousands of people will come to these grounds to see. On one of those days, I'll be out there, exchanging vows with a man I love. I'm a romantic person."

She turned back to her visitors.

"I'm also a realist. And I know that at any moment between now and then, or during my four remaining years as president, my phone may ring or an aide my appear through that door and tell me I am urgently needed in the Situation Room. That's already happened numerous times during my years in the White House. I'll be called because something has appeared on a radar screen heading toward the United States. Are we being attacked? Is it a technical malfunction? Did a missile battery or a sub commander go rogue? Maybe the radar's telling us that the objects are heading toward

Russia and China and we didn't launch them. Or the Indians or Pakistanis lost patience with one another. Or Iran has decided to redeem its pledge to destroy Israel. And I would need to walk through that door, go into the Situation Room, and within a matter of minutes, with scant information to base it on, I would need to give orders to launch or stand down or do something else. And hundreds of millions of lives, maybe billions, maybe humanity as we know it, would be destroyed or irreparably changed by what I decide. That's a decision that should never confront anyone. Not me. Not you. Not the next person to hold this office. Not my counterparts in Russia or China or Israel or Pakistan. No one."

Tenny let the statement hang in the room's now tense air while she studiously moved her gaze from one to another of those seated before her. Then she reseated herself as a member of the group.

"Ladies and gentlemen, I am bound and determined to do everything I can in the time I have here to end the threat of nuclear annihilation. Not just the bombs themselves, but all their delivery systems, silos, subs, and planes. And I'm equally determined to end the prospect of migrating warfare to space where the consequences would be just as dire. Also, I want you to know, and this is my solemn pledge, that if I can get other nations to agree to move to a less dangerous world and we sign the appropriate treaties, that historic decision will be accompanied by a shift of financial resources to other products and services that your companies can produce that will make you, your families, and this world safer and, more stable. I've been to your companies and met with you and your people. I'm familiar with your presentations. You think and plan well into the future. I've seen your advance planning for the space program, for new forms of earthly transportation, for the work you're doing on energy replacement. You showed me all that to impress me. Well, I'm impressed. Now assume that the future is here and that what you've been planning for ten and twenty years from now will become today's new platforms for profit and jobs. And believe me, once Congress agrees, we will divert as much money as possible from war to peace to help you continue to succeed. It's as much in our interests as politicians as it is in yours as business leaders to make this transition successful—and to do it seamlessly."

Tenny poured herself a glass of water from a pitcher. No other person in the room made a sound. Not a cough. Not a suggestion of a response. All appeared riveted by this woman's intensity. This wasn't a beauty pageant winner telling the judges she hoped for world peace. This was the most powerful individual in the world expressing her determination to achieve it.

"During the next few months," Tenny continued, "I will be talking with leadership in Russia and China, India and Pakistan, Israel and Iran and with our NATO allies about developing a comprehensive nuclear and general arms de-escalation treaty. Not just reducing the number of missiles but eliminating them. Not just putting a cap on nuclear submarines and aircraft and aircraft carriers and potential space weapons, but reconfiguring them for useful purposes. While these talks are in progress, I don't want them undermined by any overt or covert activities by you or your companies or your surrogates, including those you are most connected with in the active military. Later today I will have this same meeting with the Joint Chiefs at the Pentagon. As I said earlier, I'm a realist. I know how the industry works and has worked. I served many years in both the House and the Senate, several of them on the Armed Services Committee. I know this game because for many years I played it to get jobs for my workers in California. Now I'm asking you, for the future of the planet, to shut it down and let me see what we can accomplish to lower the threat to all of us."

No member of the group interrupted with comments or questions. All were hardened veterans of commercial warfare, competing with one another for contracts, lobbying together for richer government arms budgets, at times being asked to develop weaponry and systems never before created, defending cost overruns and missed deadlines, struggling within their own companies for more power, higher positions, larger turf. But this was new: a credible threat to essentially put their entire industry out of business. How to respond? That would come later, after discussions with their staff, their lobbyists, with members of Congress they had worked with for years.

The longer the silence, the heavier the weight on all the CEOs seated before her. She purposely allowed the silence to linger, the weight to become her ally, to allow each person in the room to personalize her message and its consequences.

Finally she stood again and took her seat behind the famous Resolute desk, the desk of presidential authority used by nearly every American president since it was gifted to the United States by Queen Victoria in 1880. Tenny read the room, hearing the questions every single chief executive felt prudent not to ask.

"And speaking of threats, I'll make my own," she said. "If I find credible evidence that your company is out there working against me, I'll guarantee you that you will feel pain in the contracts you no longer get, in the ones you now have being downgraded and made less profitable. You will feel the pain of explaining the loss of sales and profits to your boards and shareholders. The people will be with me on this today. They will be with me tomorrow and every day until I achieve greater security for them. And because their voters are with me, members of Congress will be too. Fight me on it, and you will become their enemy and mine. Guaranteed. Work with me, and I'll do everything within my power to see that your companies not only survive, but thrive."

CHAPTER 27

Ben needed a timetable for congressional action so he could coordinate the public advocacy campaign with it, and Tenny had secured it from House and Senate leaders.

House committees would hold hearings in July; vote on the measures in mid-September, after the annual August recess; and schedule final floor votes in October.

The Senate would lag about a month behind and have final votes in November.

Congressionally approved legislation would be on Tenny's desk just before Christmas.

That was the schedule they would try to keep, providing, of course, they could deliver the votes along the way. No one doubted that failure would always be a huge proviso. These measures and their accelerated timetable were all adventures into uncharted legislative territory.

Meanwhile, Tenny would meet with world leaders throughout the year and secure a treaty for the Senate to ratify, ideally no later than her next State of the Union Speech.

The anticipated speed of winning approval for such a historic program defied congressional history, but a more extended schedule would give the opposition time to organize and risk delaying votes into an election year, where it would be torn apart in a grinding, scare-evoking political campaign. This had to be done quickly or not at all.

Today was the campaign's first major organizational action. The setting was the three-hundred-seat auditorium in the National Archives building, located midway between the White House and the Capitol. The audience: newly hired campaign staff; liaisons to congressional offices and government agencies; and representatives from environmental, disarmament, education and other nongovernmental support groups. Every seat was filled. Latecomers watched on closed-circuit TVs installed in the building's lower-floor offices, and on their own mobile phones and tablets.

"Your attention please," came a disembodied voice through the auditorium's speakers. "We are about to begin. Please be seated."

After a two-minute delay to allow attendees to comply, the lights slowly dimmed. The large screen on stage came alive with a series of faces— innocent baby faces, smiling, inquisitive, active and sleeping. Some of the babies were in cribs, in car seats; others, children of traditional cultures, were attached to their parents by wraparound slings and back carriers. Simple background music recalled nursery rhymes.

"Innocent, so innocent," voiced a female narrator.

With those words, the faces dissolved into those of ever-aging older children, at play individually and in groups, in schools and in schoolyards, hand in hand with parents and grandparents, showing affection for one another. As the ages of the children increased, the music became more complex, as if aging with them.

"So curious. So hopeful. So trusting," the narration continued. "They trust us.

"Us," she repeated.

Now the screen showed agricultural fields and rice paddies.

"They trust that we will provide food, not hunger."

People in schools and at work.

"They trust we will pass on to them knowledge and opportunity."

Homes of various cultures.

"Safe places to live and raise their own families."

The screen showed people at prayer in churches, synagogues, mosques, Hindu and Buddhist temples.

"Freedom to pray."

The screen erupted into a nuclear cloud.

"They trust us not to destroy it all: their futures, their lives, the planet itself.

"That's why we must. We must ensure that the world they inherit will be at peace and secure."

As the music and the narrator's voice dominated the room, the audience watched a leather-skinned grandmother hugging her beautiful, six-year-old granddaughter dressed in the colorful tradition of Guatemala. That image dissolved into a waving flag, which bore a rich, green field embellished with icons representing a dove for peace, a cornstalk for food, the scales of justice for freedom, and a book for education. On the flag were the words "FOR ALL." The flag and those words remained on the screen as the auditorium lights slowly faded on to reveal Vice President Sheila Fishburne standing alone in the center of the stage.

Her presence and the effect of the brief introductory video generated enthusiastic applause.

"Welcome, everyone," said Fish. "This is our cause. This is the flag we all will march behind to victory. What do you think?"

The room again erupted in applause.

"Thank you. There is much to report to you today. You are here as the pioneers in a historic campaign. The people of the United States and people everywhere dream of peace. If we win this campaign, they will have it. We all dream of the day we can end world hunger. If we win this campaign, we will do it. We dream of a time when we have secure economic futures, opportunities to improve our lives and the lives of our children, stable and thriving communities, a planet not threatened by the ravages of climate change or human-caused destruction. That's why we're here today. That's what our campaign is about. Isn't it all worth working for, worth fighting for?"

Again, the audience responded with enthusiastic applause.

"We have much to talk about today, but before we begin, I want to introduce some of those in Congress who will lead this fight. Let's start with our House leader, and we are so fortunate to have him as our champion, Speaker Guy Rocker. Mr. Speaker, please stand and be recognized."

Rocker stood and acknowledged the applause. Fish introduced other House members and senators who had come to the morning's session. Each received their own round of applause.

"Now," she said, "I want to introduce one of the coordinators of this campaign who will take it from here, Lee Searer."

Lee took the microphone and outlined the results of his research so far.

"Let's start with our public opinion surveys. Each of them more deeply probes into public attitudes than you will ever see. Tens of thousands of questionnaires returned from thirty-six separate countries. For the first time, we are revealing the results on the large screen in front of you. Peace is a theme that unites everyone. It's off the charts. It cannot be attacked directly, so those opposed to our agenda will use other arguments, such as the potential for lost jobs, economic harm to defense-dependent communities, and the impact on stock prices. All these arguments can be countered, and many counterarguments are in the packets you will receive at the end of the day. This is a dynamic campaign, designed to change with events, sometimes daily, sometimes even hourly. Every attack will be countered by an immediate response. Be prepared to be flexible."

Lee proceeded to show strong public support for other parts of Tenny's agenda: health, housing, human rights, food security, energy conversion.

"Polling is only one part of our overall research," he continued. "We've also compiled information that will result in individual campaigns for one hundred million registered voters."

Audible gasps and laughter came from the audience.

"Yes, that's the goal," Lee continued. "And here's how we're going to do it. Publicly available databases have been assembled from all states and cross-referenced with each person's voting history, their political activity, family size, neighborhood demographics, participation on social media, income, religious preference, education levels, marital status, age, occupation, membership affiliations, military or peace corps service, magazine subscriptions, and more. From these, we will design email and social media messages that appeal to each individual. Each written campaign will have follow-up visits and phone calls from supporters we will recruit in the target community and, in many cases, even that neighborhood. Many of you will manage those efforts, and we will provide you with all the direction and tools needed to do it."

Lee stopped, checked his notes, and from the podium picked up an electronic tablet, which he raised to show the audience.

"Before I pass the baton here," he said, "I want to explain the electronic tablets at each one of your seats. As the presentation moves along and you have questions, suggestions, or comments, please write them down on your tablet. The message will appear here, at the rostrum, and whoever is speaking will respond to it. Don't be shy. This room is exploding with creative and experienced leaders. We want all the feedback you are willing to give us."

Following Lee's presentation, members of the media team reported on their plans for contact with news and assignment editors for print and broadcast media. The social media team described how Facebook, Instagram, YouTube, Twitter, and other specialized social media would integrate with other messaging. Representatives of supporting organizations discussed their plans for communicating with their members and integrating with the main campaign. The legal team presented actions they planned to file and defenses they planned to use as many of the issues moved into the courts.

The meeting spilled over from its 10:00 a.m. start, through a box lunch, and into the early afternoon. Ben was the wrap-up speaker.

"You all know the dates we're moving toward," he said. "It's not exactly like an election, which would come on the first Tuesday of November. Congressional floor work isn't that fixed this far in advance. But we do know the committee and floor calendars. Our deadlines will be keyed to those. To peak at the right time, we are planning two major events that will involve all of you.

"The first, in early September, will be a speech to the world by President Tennyson. And I really mean to the world. It will be translated into dozens of languages and televised and broadcast on hundreds of local outlets."

Ben looked down at a monitor before him. "I see someone has asked the obvious question, 'How will we broadcast in countries that are hostile to us?'" He looked back toward the audience. "Good question. Tough problem. I didn't say it would be easy. I just said we would do it. And we will. Nothing we're asking all of you to do will be easy either, but you will do it too. We can't afford to fail."

That prompted a round of enthusiastic applause.

"Now, the second major event, also unprecedented, will be a worldwide telethon using conventional telethon techniques plus all the new ones made possible through social media and the internet. For twelve consecutive hours we will broadcast worldwide, again in dozens of languages, not asking for money, but for people to electronically sign a petition endorsing the president's Peace and Security agenda. Our goal will be to enlist a billion names, a billion people."

That prompted a gasp from the audience.

"Talk about hard. Yes, a billion names. We already have commitments from sixty-five countries to carry this telethon, and I guarantee we will need every one of you here today and many more to pull this off. When we do, the pressure will force nations around the world to demand a new era of peace and security for all. This will be our capstone, embodying everything we're trying to do. Everything that you are trying to do."

With that, the house lights dimmed again, and the screen played a montage of health clinics; classrooms; commercial wind and solar farms; fields rich with wheat, rice, and corn; glorious sunrises; countless symbols of a world of opportunity at peace with itself. Throughout, the campaign's flag waved gently in the screen's upper right corner. Now it expanded to fill the screen as a live children's chorus moved onto the stage, singing "We Are The World." Each child held a small campaign flag.

Moments earlier, the audience had felt weary after so many hours of speeches and planning. Now, recharged by the final multimedia presentation and the prosect of so many innovative milestones ahead, the audience rose with applause and spirit. Fish walked enthusiastically back onstage, surrounded by the children. She shouted into the microphone, "Thank you all. Now, let's all go out and save the world!"

As the group filed out of the room, each attendee was handed campaign flags and buttons.

Tenny's army for Peace and Security for All, and for All Time, was on the march.

CHAPTER 28

The five individuals behind all strategic decisions for the Salvation Project referred to themselves as the "Symfonia." In the Greek language, the word has multiple definitions, the most benign being "symphony." Or it could mean musical "arrangement." As with the name "Salvation Project" itself, "Symfonia" would ring harmless in the ears of anyone who inadvertently heard it. But the five individuals behind all strategic decision-making for the Salvation Project ruled their organization with a third definition of the word: "conformity." The confusion in interpretations was a small deception, but the entire history of the Salvation Project had been one of deception. Clever deceptions had kept its operations out of harm's way for most of its existence. Who, on first hearing, could be alarmed by an organization calling itself the "Salvation Project"? Or a leadership group calling itself the "Symfonia?"

Two of the original five leaders of the Symfonia no longer were alive. Number One, Singapore's former finance minister, had died in his own bed of natural causes and was mourned as a national hero for helping to create what was by most metrics the world's most stable economy. If anyone other than his fellow Salvation Project founders suspected that he had conceived and organized a sub-rosa organization dedicated to the overthrow of popularly elected governments, that never was publicly revealed. Indeed, no intelligence agencies, even years later, were aware of his connection.

Another founder, Number Two, was not as fortunate. A Chinese labor leader, Number Two was arrested in Beijing for organizing a protest over factory working conditions. He took his own life after days of severe questioning in a Chinese prison. Number Two respected the Salvation Project oath that to divulge the organization's plans, or to admit its very existence, was punishable by death—if not by government authorities, then by the Project's own enforcement team. No exceptions. He feared that he would violate that oath if tortured further.

Secrecy was the heart of The Salvation Project's survival strategy. An enforcement team always stood ready to implement execution orders issued by the Symfonia. Through the years, the Project's enforcement team had become ever more adept at its work, finding creative ways to perform without drawing attention to itself and, in many cases, without even raising suspicion that the executions the team carried out were murders. The team was headed by a man known to others as Malik. Only the Symfonia knew his background as someone who had held a similar job with British intelligence.

Today, for the first time in three months, the Symfonia met on its virtual private network. Number Three, a former British intelligence agent and longest serving Salvation Project leader, chaired the group. Richfield, a Singapore agricultural executive and protégé of Number One, now the full-time director, also served as a member of the Symfonia. The others were Forty-Eight, a nuclear scientist and high-ranking official with Rosatom, the Russian Federation's nuclear agency; Thirty-Nine, a Dutch army general assigned to NATO; and Fifty-One, the Symfonia's newest member, a Chinese expert in quantum computing.

"As you know, our procedure for maximum protection is a meeting lasting for no more than five minutes," said Three. "We will strictly adhere to this procedure starting now. Richfield?"

Richfield spoke through the network's enhanced voice modulation system. "Thank you, Three, and all of you. Did anyone not receive my last communiqué?"

No one spoke.

"I assume, then, that all did. Are there any objections to our strategy of helping the US president win support for her so-called Peace and Security agenda?"

"I object," said Forty-Eight. "Too dangerous. "Once she wins widespread support, we will lose control. We should stop it now."

"I disagree," said Three. "She's building our case. The public will be frustrated with democracy. They will be open to our alternative."

"At what point do you intend to 'frustrate' the public?" asked Forty-Eight.

"At the very end," said Richfield. "That will be the point of maximum frustration and disappointment. The final US Senate vote on her program will fail. The final vote on her disarmament treaty will fail."

"Too dangerous," Forty-Eight reiterated. "Kill it now before it gains life. I assume we can do that. The frustration level will be as great, and we won't risk losing control. Kill it in the House committee before it gains momentum."

"May I offer a compromise?" asked Fifty-One. "Let the US House approve it. They would cement the reputation of our ally, the House speaker. Then kill both the program and the treaty in a Senate committee."

"I agree," said Thirty-Nine.

"I'll accept that," said Three. "Richfield, can you arrange it?"

"Yes," said Richfield. "I can arrange it."

"Any other business?" asked Three.

"Yes, what about Adonis? Why haven't we closed that file? It is setting a poor example for others," asked Fifty-One.

"A plan is in motion," said Richfield. "I don't expect much more delay. And now we've used our five minutes. Meeting adjourned."

CHAPTER 29

Each spring in the nation's capital the White House Correspondents' Association hosts a formal charity dinner, a must-go-to event for anyone who wants to be seen as a Washington power insider. Far more people enter the scramble for tickets than the two-thousand-seat venue holds. Who sits next to whom is a self-interested calculus performed by the media and lobbying groups that buy most of those seats. First priority goes to members of Congress who serve on committees where the hosts have business or political interests. Entertainment personalities and sports stars are heavily recruited as clickbait to attract politicians of choice to donors' tables.

Retired General Cal Foley's defense-related think tank annually reserved a table, and traditionally the group had its pick of legislators to host. Defense contractors contribute generously to key legislators' campaign accounts. An invitation to their table was a signal to the industry of where to send its checks. Tonight, seated next to Group President Foley was House Speaker Guy Rocker.

Since Foley first suggested that Rocker become a link in the Salvation Project power chain, they had met multiple times in carefully arranged venues. The words "Salvation Project" were never mentioned, but Rocker was now fully aware of his situation and had become comfortable in it. While he remained concerned about the movement's methods, he shared its goals. He respected Foley for his past as one of the nation's top military leaders and found their current conversations enlightening and persuasive. *If this is my best route to become president, why not follow it and see where it leads*, thought Rocker. And if he did become president, he would know how to manage the Project's darker impulses.

The White House Correspondents' dinner was an event more to be seen at than heard. For the hour leading up to the formal program, the space between tables was crowded with those busily networking with connections they may not otherwise find as accessible: cabinet secretaries, corporate presidents, Wall Street moguls. The decibel levels were high. Two thousand guests were talking simultaneously, raising their voices to be heard over others.

For General Foley, this was the perfect venue to discuss the most important thing on his mind this evening. Standing almost lip to ear to Rocker, Foley asked, "Do you know Gil Adonis?"

"Casually," said Rocker. "Met him a few times. Handshakes and things. You know he was the money behind the campaign against Tenny. We work different sides of the political street."

Keeping his hands low, Foley handed Rocker a small, folded piece of paper.

"Put this in your pocket. Two phone numbers. The top number takes you to a scrambling device so that your next call will be garbled, undecipherable. The number below it is Adonis's cell phone. Before eleven o'clock tonight, call Adonis, identify yourself, and tell him that you have a message from the president. The message is that early tomorrow a White House courier will arrive at his office with an important piece of information. Information so sensitive that it must be delivered in person and orally. He should tell no one about this call and meet the courier alone, with no one near enough to eavesdrop or overhear."

"Why?" Rocker asked, puzzled by such an unusual request. "Have you spoken with the president? What's she have to do with Adonis?"

Foley reached out, took Rocker's arm, and pulled him even closer. "Guy," said Foley, "how many times have you voted to send our troops into harm's way? How many dollars have you approved for weapons designed to kill people and that did kill people? You did it for national defense, to protect the country, even though you knew that people would die, including our own troops. Well, consider doing this for the same reason."

Rocker realized what he was being asked to do. "You're going to kill Adonis!"

"We're going to save America and save humanity. It won't happen through talk, only action, and action means casualties."

"And you're telling this to me here, with press people everywhere?"

"It's the safest possible place, Guy. No one here gives a shit what you and I are talking about. There's so much noise, no one can possibly record this conversation."

"I can't be complicit in killing someone," Rocker protested.

"Adonis is a threat to the entire movement. If you believe in what we're doing, do this. Think of it. One death as opposed to millions or more. Once we're in control—once you, *you* are in control—wars will end. All guns will be holstered. Lives will be saved, and the money will go to saving people, not killing them. You will be the instrument for that."

Rocker shook his head, hardly believing what he was being asked to do. "But what if this doesn't work? Adonis would point the finger at me."

"Not if you use this phone," said Foley, slipping one into Rocker's hand. "I guarantee that no one will trace this back to you. And, frankly, what if they did? All you need to say is that it was someone impersonating you. You'll be clean. Who would believe the Speaker of the House would be involved?"

Animated conversations were creating a thunderous audio blanket. Women stood in ball gowns, men in black tie, some in bizarre outfits designed to draw attention and perhaps a photo or a few lines of comment in tomorrow's social page write-ups. Foley was right. No one could hear anyone else's conversation. No one cared. Guy Rocker, pressed close to Foley by the crush of those at surrounding tables, just stared at the general.

Foley lowered his voice to a level of intimacy. "Guy," he said, "I've killed people with my bare hands. In Vietnam. I've killed people using guns and knives. I've ordered people killed as a unit commander. Some innocents along with the hostiles. My country sent me to war with a mission. I fulfilled it. It was my duty. I don't ever want to be called on to do it again. Not me, not my sons or daughters. Not yours. My mission now is to prevent death, not cause it. And so is yours. You'll do it?"

Suddenly the crowd in the aisles began giving way as an army of waiters appeared with trays of arugula salad.

Rocker said nothing, but Foley detected a barely perceptible nod.

CHAPTER 30

Lester Bowles's death convinced Gil Adonis that hiding was futile. He had attended the funeral to change the game. If they wanted him, his would-be killers would know how to find him. He had hidden in Columbus. He had hidden in Poulsbo. He even had hidden courtesy of the FBI. Now, he was done hiding. Adonis's success had been built on confronting situations no matter how difficult, not running from them.

After the funeral, Adonis informed federal authorities that he was returning to New York. If they planned to charge him with a crime based on his activities in last year's election, they would find him there. On his return he quickly reconfigured his Upper West Side office to add sleeping quarters. The office building, he decided, would be more secure than his apartment. Not as plush, but safer because of the building's location and design. In addition to the building's regular crew of guards, he bulked up his own security team, placing them on a twenty-four-hour schedule. He limited his own activities to infrequent outside meetings and social events, and only then with extensive protection. How long would this last? Until the Project's hired guns again tried to kill him, as he was certain they would. One more attempt, one more failure, and then perhaps they would be caught and the Salvation Project would be shattered, shuttered, or at least would give up trying to kill him. He was betting his life, but he felt he had no alternative. He was marked for death whether he was hiding or in plain sight.

The call from House Speaker Rocker had dropped into his voice mail box the night before, after he had turned off his cell phone and retired for the evening. He found it the next morning. The fact that the president wanted to get a private message to him was not particularly surprising, given their past conversations. But sending someone to deliver it in person? That seemed odd. And why was Rocker serving as an intermediary if this was so confidential?

He called the White House and asked to be put through to the president to confirm Rocker's message but was told the president was not yet in her office. Nine a.m. and not at her desk? That was odd too. Maybe it had to do with the courier. Maybe it was something she did not want to discuss by phone.

At 9:10 a.m., Adonis's secretary, Lois Adkins, entered his private office to report that building security was with a man in the lobby who claimed he had to see Adonis personally. The man had an envelope with the presidential seal and "Eyes Only" stamped on its face. Adonis told her to meet the courier in the lobby and ask whether he would hand it to her.

From the lobby, Adkins called and said the courier planned to leave without delivering the envelope unless he could deliver it in person. "Come up with him," said Adonis.

Adonis's office was on the eleventh floor of an eighteen-story building. A private elevator opened directly into his office where, this morning, four others were at work: two assistants and two members of his security team. James Lazarre, one of Adonis's security guards, met the courier at the elevator and asked to see his credentials. After inspecting the courier's White House photo ID, Lazarre waved him in. Adkins led the courier to Adonis's office where he rose to meet him. The courier turned to Adkins and said, "I'm sorry, ma'am, but I must deliver this message privately."

Adonis nodded. "It's okay, Lois," he said. "Please leave us alone and close the door."

CHAPTER 31

F BI Director Sam Vellman sat quietly across the desk from President Tennyson, waiting for her to digest his written report without comment. Tenny looked up from the paper and shook her head in wonderment. "This had to be someone he knew. How could someone just come in off the street and kill him? Knowing Gil, he had to have had it organized as an armed fortress."

"His security people didn't recognize the person," said Vellman. "They knew most of Adonis's contacts, but not this one."

"And he had White House credentials?"

"He had a White House badge that apparently looked authentic. And Gil told them in advance he expected a White House courier, so they were primed to accept it."

"Did Gil's security write down the name of the courier? Take a photo of the badge?"

"Apparently not," said Vellman. "But security cameras in Gil's office and the building lobby all have the killer's photo. We're checking our image files for an ID. The assassin must have known there were cameras, but he did nothing to hide his identity. It was incredibly brazen."

"And so," said Tenny, "walked right into Gil's office, closed the door, stabbed him with a hypodermic needle, walked out, told Gil's people Adonis needed time alone with the document and disappeared?"

"That's the story. It appears that first the assailant shoved a rag in Gil's mouth to keep him from shouting, used an ether-like substance to render him unconscious, injected him, and left. Gil's secretary told New York police that the assailant was with him no more than three to five minutes."

"And Gil died on the way to the hospital?"

"Yes. It was a powerful poison, apparently ricin. It destroys the muscles around the injection site immediately. In this case, the injection went right into his heart. His organs failed very quickly."

"Tragic, Sam, just tragic. It sounds too audacious to be true. Why wouldn't Gil have called here to confirm that the courier was really from the White House?"

"It looks like he tried, Madam President. A call from him was recorded at the White House switchboard about a half hour before the attack. You were getting your daily intelligence briefing at the time, and your staff didn't interrupt. He was asked if he wanted to talk with anyone else, but he declined. And he left no message."

"Good God," exclaimed Tenny. "I could have saved him!"

"You had no way of knowing. Gil was too secretive to trust anyone else, even people on your staff."

"Horrible, just horrible. Is there any doubt this is the work of the Salvation Project?"

"Either the Project or the work of a foreign intelligence agency," said Vellman. "The killer obviously was a professional, and a strong one to overpower Gil before he could call for help. And there had to be a skilled organization behind him to produce believable White House credentials and fool Gil into thinking the contact was authentic. The New York authorities, of course, don't know about the Project. They'll check all of Gil's personal and professional contacts, including Gil's own security people, to see whether they set him up for this. They also are unaware that we've monitored Gil's phone calls since he returned to New York. Last night he got one through a device that used ZRTP, a cryptographic protocol that encrypts voices end-to-end using connections over the internet. Our people are working on that to see if we can locate the origin of the call and identify the caller. The system often is used to deliver confidential financial information. In this case, it could have a connection to Gil's murder."

"Is it a difficult code to crack?"

"Not really, but once we do, depending on how expert the sender was, we might reach a dead end at the call source. We'll see. It's helpful that the caller left the message on voice mail and that Gil didn't pick it up until this morning. That gives us more to work with. Other than that, we found nothing unusual to run down. Madam President, if it turns out that the Salvation Project gets by with the Adonis murder, it might encourage them to go after others, even you."

Tenny stared hard at Vellman. Of course he was right. They already had tried to kill her, through Andres, a fact she had shared with no one. Andres. They might also see him as a threat. Andres's family. They held his daughter hostage once. Ben? Certainly Ben. That was why he was living with Carmie, for the Secret Service protection. And now Carmie? If Gil's protection couldn't save him, what chance did Carmie and Ben have?

"Good point, Sam," she finally said. "Let's make sure we have sufficient Secret Service protection for Andres and his family. And double Secretary Sanchez's regular protection and at her residence. Also, I want Ben Sage protected wherever he goes."

"I'll set up a meeting with Simon at the Secret Service and Chief Valdez at the DC police department," said Vellman. "We'll coordinate on all of this. I'll also let Kyle Christian at CIA know, since the Project is international. You're aware, I'm sure, that the Adonis case jurisdiction is with the New York City police department. Do you want us to intervene on the basis of a suspected hate crime or civil rights violation?"

"No, Sam. There's been nothing in the media about the Salvation Project. Only a few congressional leaders are aware of it outside of the intelligence services and your office. Let's keep it that way. And I want to know everything happening in the investigation. This is getting too close to home."

Vellman left the office. Tenny sat at the desk of the most powerful office in the world, feeling momentarily powerless to compete with the murderous scourge that threatened her family and closest friends.

"Close to home," she said aloud. And then her mind returned to that night in a New York hotel room when she and Andres were about to make love and he came within inches of injecting her with a potentially lethal dose of poison. His explanation was that his daughter was being held by a mysterious group who had threatened to kill her if he failed to do as he was ordered. But could that kidnapping and that story have been staged to put Tenny off her guard? Could Andres actually be one of them? They seemed to be everywhere. She and Andres were about to remarry. Then they would live together, share many meals together, sleep together. She had misplaced her trust in him when they first married decades ago. She had misplaced her trust again during the campaign when he might have killed her. How could she be certain she could trust him now, when the Salvation Project seemed more devious and murderous than ever?

CHAPTER 32

Each Friday at four-thirty, Ben had a standing appointment to brief Tenny on campaign progress. Together they reviewed the latest polls, made adjustments to media and organizational plans, and assessed costs and financial arrangements for underwriting the extensive and expensive work that was gradually growing into an international behemoth.

Ben came prepared for all of that today, but those details were secondary to what he had waited days to discuss with her—his safety.

Often there were others at these agenda update meetings. For this meeting, Ben had warded off company. He needed Tenny alone. While she wrapped up a phone conversation, Ben spread his briefing documents on the coffee table between the room's two facing sofas. She finished her call but was not yet ready to talk with Ben. Tenny walked to the office door and called out to her secretary.

"Marcie, arrange a meeting for me this weekend with General Castle here in my office." After a pause, she said, "Yes, Marcie, this weekend unless he's out of the country. You know my schedule, just fit it in." Another pause. "I think half an hour should be enough. The topic? Nothing he needs to prepare for. Tell him just the two of us. I think he'll understand the topic."

She finally turned to Ben. "Sorry, Ben. My generals don't seem to understand how serious I am about arms reduction. I need to bring them in after school to tell them they've been bad boys trying to undermine me. They love their toys and have no interest in giving them up." She sat down next to Ben. "So, where are we? What do you have for me today?"

"I have a lot of anxiety," said Ben. "Or let me put it another way: I'm scared shitless."

As president, Tenny was accorded the deference of the office by just about everyone in the world. But after decades of working together in high-intensity political battles, no veil of power separated Tenny and Ben. They were just people. Best friends.

"Let me guess," she said. "You're having Gil Adonis anxiety syndrome."

"And Lester Bowles syndrome. And flashbacks to the killers who chased me through the woods last year when I was trying to deliver a package to you. What in the hell is going on? I appreciate the protection from the Secret Service, but who are they protecting me from? And why has the guard at Carmie's apartment been beefed up since Gil's murder? And right here in the West Wing, I get the impression I can't take a piss without an armed guard watching to see whether I zipped up right. I haven't pressed you for this before. I figured it was national security. Top secret. Eyes only. That sort of thing. But come on, Tenny, I deserve to know."

"Yes, you do, Ben. And it is eyes only, top secret. Hardly anyone knows except for the highest-ranking intelligence people. Ben, we're looking at a very serious international conspiracy that's trying to take over not just this country, but others. Last year Gil Adonis was their key operative in the United States. He recruited Zach Bowman to run against me. He also recruited Les Bowles to run for vice president. If they had won the election, after a while, not too long, Gil and his friends would have seen to it that Zach had a fatal accident or heart attack or something. Les would have become president, and the conspiracy would have had the keys to the White House."

Ben shook his head in disbelief.

"I can't buy that, Tenny. It makes no sense at all. Especially the part about Les Bowles being on their team. Nothing in his background would ever suggest that."

"Nothing," said Tenny, "except the fact that Les and Gil were as close as you and me. And Gil was an extremely persuasive person."

"How can you be so certain?" asked Ben. "This sounds like one of the maybe-it-could-happen scenarios the intelligence people are always dreaming up."

"I'm certain," said Tenny, "because Gil told me himself. Right here. Right where you're sitting now. He explained everything. That's why they killed him."

"And Bowles?"

"He also knew all about it. That's why they killed him too."

"And you think I'm next?"

"I don't know, Ben. I do know that these people are ruthless. They're killing people in other countries too. Gil spent a week with you in Washington. He obviously didn't tell you what I just did, but the people he was working with don't know that."

Ben sank deep into the sofa, trying to process all this. His mind had constructed many scenarios to explain his situation, and now Tenny had confirmed one that was even more deadly than he had imagined.

"If I could wrap you up and put you in storage until we destroy this conspiracy, I'd do it, Ben," said Tenny. "I'd never forgive myself if anything happened to you because of this. Last year when I heard about the close call you had, I nearly fainted. Few people in life mean more to me than you. You know that. That package you carried for me was hard evidence of the conspiracy. It allowed our people to round up many of their top leaders, here and elsewhere. We thought it was over, that the group was either out of business or too weak for us to be concerned about. I thought we were all out of danger. But when you told Fish that Bowles had delivered Gil to your doorstep, and that Gil was in hiding, that showed us they not only remained in business but had the resources to still be dangerous. That's why I insisted you come here where we could protect you. When I learned they'd murdered Gil, I told the FBI and Secret Service to add to that protection."

"So you're sure this is why Gil was murdered."

"No hard evidence, but it's the only explanation that makes sense. The motive and the cunning it took to get access to him? Not the work of amateurs."

"And where are we in trying to break up this crowd, really break them up so I can get out of your bubble?"

"I wish I could tell you we're close, but honestly, I don't think we're anywhere close."

"Does this have anything to do with why you've got this extraordinary agenda and you're investing so much of your own money in it?"

"Of course it does. What I have told you I just used my prerogative as president to declassify. Needless to say, it can't leave your lips."

"It won't," said Ben. "It also won't leave my brain. It's going to be hard to think of anything else until either you get them or they get me."

CHAPTER 33

The Adonis murder was big news in New York. For more than a decade, Gil Adonis had been one of Wall Street's heaviest of heavy-hitting financial power brokers. His hedge fund and other investments could move markets. His rare public comments about companies or industries quickly entered the calculus of research analysts.

Unlike so many others in his position, Adonis avoided the spotlight. He never appeared on CNBC or Fox Business or gave media interviews. He just did his thing. Adonis had largely disappeared from public view after the election, reemerging only weeks ago at Lester Bowles's funeral service. Then he once again became inaccessible. Most phone calls went unanswered. Most invitations were declined. His business activity was conducted through a small group of longtime aides. Adonis was in New York. That was well known. But he may as well have been in Outer Mongolia for others in his financial world.

His murder, then, was shocking. The absence of a quick arrest was unfathomable. The media reported that Adonis was in his private fortress, protected as if his body was in Fort Knox. Yes, he had business enemies, lots of them. Adonis could be ruthless where money was involved. People in the financial world had been known to kill themselves over deals gone bad, but they didn't kill one another. Could there have been a woman? A jealous husband? In past years Adonis had been seen with female partners, but not lately. Adonis had no wife, current or divorced. He had no known children. No siblings. No family tensions that might have erupted in violence.

In the absence of clues or leads that made sense, the media opted for conspiracies. He was about to be arrested for financial fraud, and others had silenced him before he could testify against them. It was clearly the work of professionals. Who's more professional than the Mafia? He was laundering their money and got too greedy. He was about to dump a boatload of stock in a company and tank its price. Major shareholders had to stop him or else they would be ruined. He had inoperable brain cancer and arranged the murder himself so he wouldn't die a slow death, and besides, the cancer already had scrambled his brain to a point he didn't know what he was doing. That would explain his support for Zach Bowman and his peculiar behavior afterward.

For days, the story had what the media calls "legs." New York police officials had few clues to follow. The lack of information was interpreted as facts they were hiding. The FBI was involved, but no one would say why they were investigating a murder that was not in their usual jurisdiction. A few "persons of interest" were interviewed, but then released. Police checked every security camera within ten blocks of Gil's office building but would not say what they found, if anything. Despite the lack of hard news, speculation about the Adonis murder sold newspapers and raised cable news ratings.

Then there was an announcement with real news. In his will, Gil had left some of his fortune to Lester Bowles's family and the bulk of it to various foundations for laboratory research and scientific scholarships and education. This prompted a new wave of revelations.

The connection between Gil Adonis's murder and Lester Bowles's was too obvious to be simply a coincidence. What was that connection? Political, certainly. Was there a financial tie with criminal elements?

The scientific bequests were also a surprise. For many years Gil Adonis has been a quiet but frequent presence at advanced scientific centers around the world, attending their conferences and meeting with those working at the frontier of many scientific disciplines. Eulogies were published by well-known researchers about Adonis's devotion to their causes and how hard he studied to understand their work. The word on the street had been that Adonis did this to gain an investment edge for new technologies and businesses. It now was becoming clear he was fully immersed in that world beyond the profits that would result from it.

Since there was no family, there was no elaborate funeral. After police investigators released his body, it was cremated and, according to his will's instructions, placed in a vault in a Columbus, Ohio, cemetery, near Lester Bowles.

Sam Vellman personally reported to Tenny every day about developments in the investigation. Most days the report was the same—leads that led nowhere. On the day of Adonis's interment, Vellman did have something to report. The FBI technical lab had succeeded in tracing the mysterious murder-eve call to its scrambled source. But that was just a black box, with nothing to identify the source of the call itself.

"Is it technically possible to crack that code, or whatever they need to do to find the caller?" asked Tenny.

"Our people have never done it. It's a technology they've never encountered," said Vellman. "The National Security Agency has more advanced coders and equipment. Do you have any objections if we ask them to give it a try? It's a domestic case, but it could have national security implications."

"Do it, Sam," said Tenny. "Do it."

In a hallway of the Rayburn House Office Building that day, House Speaker Guy Rocker accidently encountered retired army general Cal Foley.

Foley stopped to shake Rocker's hand and convey a whispered, "Thank you." No one walking with either Foley or Rocker could hear the exchange.

But Guy Rocker did, and he knew, as he had known from the moment he heard that Gil Adonis had been murdered, that for him there would be no turning back.

CHAPTER 34

Bauman Kabiri was certain he recognized her voice, and the recognition stunned him. Could Renetta Chance also be a Salvation Project manager? Renetta Chance was a towering figure in the narrow world of biostatistics, a relatively new field of biological science. Her textbooks were required reading in graduate schools. She held a prized seat in the statistical department of the London School of Economics.

Today, Chance chaired a hastily called gathering of experts to examine post pandemic management of virus behavior and continuing threats. Two dozen English-speaking virology experts had been invited to participate, a group large enough to provide a range of opinions, but manageable enough to be conducted in the Mayfair Suite of London's Saint James Hotel, where out-of-town participants were housed.

During the COVID-19 pandemic, Bauman Kabiri had made his mark in biostatistics with a well-received paper, "Microanalysis of the Gamma Mutation." He was thrilled when he had received an invitation to present his findings at this meeting. He knew of the other attendees, but never before had he been considered a peer at this level of research.

Kabiri had no trouble gaining approval from his department chairman at the University of Virginia to attend the London meeting. He quickly packed his bags and worked out a schedule that would allow him to spend a few extra days in the city to meet personally with colleagues and visit museums. What he did not expect was to discover that Renetta Chance also was a project manager. He was certain of it from her opening remarks at the two-day session.

For Kabiri's purposes the day's events went well enough. As a newcomer to this distinguished group, he was at first hesitant to join the conversation and express his views. But the presentation of his paper seemed to go well and respectfully. By the afternoon session, Kabiri felt comfortable with the subject matter and his own participation. Now he was anticipating an enjoyable group dinner. He knew that Salvation Project managers were forbidden to recognize or communicate with one another, but the temptation grew as the day wore on. What would be the harm of a few brief moments alone with Renetta Chance, an influential star in his profession? And if he had misjudged the situation, it was an opportunity to enter her orbit in any case.

That opportunity came moments after the day's final session as Chance walked next to him, heading to the hotel's bar.

"Very stimulating day. Thank you for inviting me," said Kabiri.

"Your contribution was quite valuable," said Chance. "Joining us for drinks?"

"Yes, Forty-Six," he replied.

Chance froze in place, stared at him for a moment, and quickly recovered.

No question about it, thought Kabiri.

"Thirty-Five," he said simply. "Talk?"

In control of herself now, Chance continued walking toward the bar with him.

"Room number?" she asked, looking straight ahead.

"Three twelve," Kabiri responded, then changed direction and headed toward the elevators. Once there, he placed his copies of the day's working papers on the desk. And waited.

Not long. He had left the door slightly ajar, and she quickly slipped through it.

"This is very dangerous," Chance said. "How did you know?"

"Linguistics is a hobby of mine. Languages, accents, regional variations."

"But I've said so little on the calls, and our voices were electronically distorted."

"It was enough," said Kabiri. "I'm very good at it."

"Why did you expose yourself to me? You know how dangerous this is."

"I guess to confirm my linguistic hunch and, frankly, to get to know you better. I've admired your work for such a long time."

"Thank you." She hesitated. "Is it Bauman? Is that how you prefer to be called? I've just known you more formally as 'Kabiri.'"

"Yes, Bauman is fine. I hope I haven't distressed you with this . . . recognition."

"Actually, no," she said. "In some ways it's a relief to be able to discuss it. Frankly, I'm worried. I'm curious to see if I'm the only one. It's all the killing. Is it necessary? I've been in this movement for many years, and at first I thought like a scientist and a statistician. I knew vaguely that some unsavory things were happening. I didn't know what, and that was fine with me. Our cause is to save humanity from itself. That's bound to be a bit messy. As long as I wasn't directly involved, it seemed acceptable. But there have been so many killings lately, almost routine. Now that I'm a project manager, I'm deeply concerned that I may be asked to order some killings myself. I'm wondering if we've created something that's out of control."

Chance sat down in one of the room's straight-backed chairs. Kabiri took a seat on the bed facing her.

"You aren't alone thinking that," he said. "But this structure we have—each of us isolated, no communication among us, no common understanding—it's really hard to know what's happening and why. And why are they keeping us isolated? If we're the governing board, how can we govern this way? How did you get involved?"

"Global warming," said Chance. "Early on I looked at the data, and it was obvious we had a humanity-survival scale problem. I did what I could to try to sound the alarm outside the scientific community. I joined the committees, signed the petitions, gave media interviews, spoke at parliamentary inquiries. It was just remarkable how little effective action resulted from our efforts. Then, I was exposed to the Project by a friend. And I thought, 'If she's involved, why not me? This may be the only possible way to get real results.' And you? How did you get involved?"

"Oh, I'm not political at all. I'm a statistician who works mainly with microbes. Nothing political about them. I just know what works and what doesn't and keep trying to discover useful things. I don't know much about politics and frankly don't care. But a lot of what needs to happen just isn't, so it makes sense to me to pull together people who know what they're doing and try something else. That's why the Project appealed to me. And like you, I got recruited by someone I trust. I guess they were having trouble finding American scientists to join up with them. I was surprised when they asked me to be a project manager."

"And do you share my concern about too much killing?"

"Very much so," he said. "I'm in the life business, not the death business. I was really surprised when they killed Adonis. I presume it was Project people who did it. Maybe they had reasons they didn't share with us."

They allowed silence to make the next statement.

"I need to get back downstairs," said Chance. "You do too. Let's try to stay in touch. No phone calls. No contact of any kind. Except in person, like this. Agreed?"

CHAPTER 35

When Tenny first told Andres she wanted to remarry him, her vision had been a simple, private ceremony. Carmie and a few other close friends. Andres's two daughters and their families. Privacy also was Andres's preference. He had spent his life as a prominent California surgeon, with little experience in the spotlight outside the medical world. Ben's return to DC changed that. He quickly recognized the wedding's possibilities as a major media event to boost Tenny's popularity for the difficult agenda campaign ahead.

"Don't you see?" Ben argued. "You're living a romantic dream. Reunited after decades apart. A flame that never died. A Rose Garden presidential wedding, one of only two in American history. A chance to highlight Andres's lifesaving work as a surgeon. It shows you as the hopeless romantic you really are, softening your hard edges after so many highly visible brass knuckle fights. We can relive your Mexico City wedding, with all its color and grandeur. You want to sell Mexico and Latin America on your Peace and Security plan? Your wedding would be a showstopper on Spanish-speaking TV and websites. I couldn't buy enough advertising to melt hearts the way this wedding will."

"For Christ's sake," said Tenny, "this isn't the coronation of the queen of England or Diana's wedding at Westminster Abbey."

"No, it's the typically American version of that," said Ben.

"Typically American? Get serious, Ben. You're talking about two Mexican Americans here, kind of sticking it in the eye of the anti-immigration people. You're talking about a made-for-TV spectacle between two people who many believe aren't typically American people."

Ben would not be diverted. He continued to weave mental images.

"I see it in late April. The trees will be young, full, and at peak green. The azaleas and dogwoods will be gorgeous. The grounds crew can also see to it that some late-blooming cherry blossoms and tulips are prominent. I see about two hundred guests seated in the Rose Garden. A custom-made white altar, live TV broadcasting the spectacle to the world . . . "

"Stop, stop," Tenny said. "Enough. Yes, I'll do it. I'll be your media spectacle. Will this get my agenda passed?"

"With this, if I can't get your agenda passed, I'll quit and go back to my newspaper in Poulsbo."

"You're planning to do that anyway, you faker. I'll talk it over with Andres."

While Tenny feigned resistance, she knew Ben was right. This could be spectacularly positive media at a time she needed maximum political power.

Once Tenny agreed, wedding preparation became its own feverish promotional industry. Who was this man who had won Tenny's heart? The White House helpfully fed the media details about the lives Andres had saved as a surgeon, awards he had won, public service he had performed during his decades as one of San Diego's most prominent medical experts. The White House press office also provided details of the couple's glamorous first wedding, including contact information for many who had attended so they could tell their own stories. The only other office-holding president to marry at the White House was Grover Cleveland, and that was in 1886. Details of that event were minutely researched and became the topic of countless feature articles. Everything about Tenny and Andres's wedding preparations became news: what they would wear, how grounds crews were grooming the Rose Garden, how the normal Mass would be compressed, music that would be played, and who would attend. Those invitations became the hottest tickets in Washington.

The Sunday afternoon ceremony took place under a rich, blue, late April sky. An altar was erected a few steps from the entrance to the Rose Garden. As Ben had envisioned, two hundred white folding chairs were placed on the lawn, separated by an aisle where latticed arches were covered by medleys of red and white roses. TV cameras controlled from nearby broadcast vans captured the event from a dozen perspectives: the presidents of Mexico and Brazil and the prime ministers of Canada, Great Britain, France, and Spain and their spouses sitting in the front row; the recognizable political and entertainment celebrities; lilac-colored azaleas in bloom; the Marine Corps band, in dress uniform, augmented by a string section, serenading the guests while waiting for the ceremony to begin; a twenty-person chorus from the Cathedral of Saint Matthew the Apostle in full regalia.

Tens of millions watched an hour of pre-ceremony commentary on broadcast and cable networks. Each network deployed its A-team of news anchors, positioned at elevations on the White House grounds, providing viewers the perspective of being guests at the spectacular event.

At precisely noon, foregoing the traditional walk down the aisle, members of the wedding party emerged from the White House and took their places at the altar. When Tenny and Andres first married, the ceremony was conducted by the archbishop of Mexico. Presiding over this marriage was Father Bennett Morgan, Tenny's social work ally from her pre-political years in Los Angeles, who remained her friend. In Mexico City, Tenny, then known to friends and family by her given name, Isabel, wore a floor-length satin gown, a floral tiara, and jewelry so valuable it was stored in a vault. For this wedding, her dress was far more modest, but reflected her lively, break-the-rules spirit. Instead of the traditional white gown, she wore a cerulean blue, finely tailored Ralph Lauren long-sleeve, knee-length dress with padded shoulders, a modest V-shaped neckline, and gathered folds at the waist. Around her neck she wore a necklace of graduated diamonds with matching earrings, family heirlooms given to her by her grandmother.

Following the ceremony, wedding guests assembled in the East Room of the White House for a seated lunch. Champagne donated by California vineyards flowed freely. The foreign heads of state offered toasts. An obviously nervous Andres recounted humorous and ribald stories about their first wedding, interrupted by hoots and asides from those who had been there. Finally, Tenny rose to thank all who attended. She spoke briefly but movingly about her love for Andres, her excitement for being part of this new family of his daughters, their husbands, and her inherited grandchildren. She described the peaceful world she hoped she could help ensure for their young lives, a bountiful world where humanity would be at peace and secure. When Tenny appeared in public, invariably it was connected with politics and controversial issues. Few had ever seen this Tenny—a radiant woman in love.

All of it—the spectacle of the White House wedding ceremony; the gala event that followed; the bride-president opening her heart to the world; the exuberant dancing by their president with her new husband, world leaders, and celebrities, today without the usual masks of office and fame—all of it was televised live to the largest viewing audience ever measured on a Sunday afternoon.

It was a feast for romantics. For Ben Sage, it was everything he hoped it would be, a major media event to launch Tenny's Peace and Security campaign. He was ecstatic.

CHAPTER 36

How long had it been since Ben danced at a wedding? Or felt this giddy? Why not? A ten-strike of a media event. Tenny radiating so much love there was a surplus of it spilling from the East Room of the White House and flooding the nation's cable channels. A memorable party. Endless flutes of fine champagne. He and Carmie laughed for the entire short ride home to her apartment. Their Secret Service driver fought every impulse not to join in.

It was late afternoon, the sun was still well above the horizon. Yachts and tour boats plied the Potomac River in force.

"More champagne?" asked Carmie. "Let's watch the scene."

"Champagne?" Ben replied. "Why not. I've invested too much into my buzz to let it go easily."

Carmie uncorked a bottle of Gloria Ferrer and poured them each a generous flute. They stepped out on the balcony into the mild, late-day breeze.

"I can't tell you how much I love this view," said Carmie. "Look at the blossoms over near Roosevelt Island. Ever walk over there?"

"Many times," said Ben. "For many years my office was in Georgetown. The office had a shower, and nearly every day I would try to make time for an hour run from there. Sometimes around the Mall.

Sometimes into Rock Creek Park. Sometimes across the bridge to the island."

"More ambitious than me," said Carmie. "I just stand here when I can and admire it all."

"Hey," said Ben, suddenly turning toward her. "Let's do it now. I'm hyped."

"Do what?"

"Get on your running stuff and we'll run over to the island. There's still daylight."

"I don't run very fast."

"Doesn't matter. In my condition, I won't either."

Ben alerted their Secret Service guardians, who scrambled to find running clothes of their own.

Twenty minutes later, all of them, Ben, Carmie, and two guardian agents, were jogging on a path to Theodore Roosevelt Island, eighty-eight acres in the Potomac River across from Washington's Kennedy Center and reachable from a footbridge on the Virginia side of the river.

"There's a memorial not too far into the park," said Ben. "We'll just go there, rest for a few minutes, and run back."

"I hope it's not too far," huffed Carmie. "You might have to carry me."

Within minutes they were immersed in the lengthening shadows of the park.

"Not so bad, was it?" said Ben.

"Actually, no. You're not as crazy as I thought when you suggested this. It's actually fun."

"One day if we get time, we'll start earlier and make the whole circuit. It's amazing that all this is so close to downtown."

People were using it today. The parking lot was three-fourths full even as the sun waned. After a brief respite, Carmie and Ben jogged their way back to her apartment.

"Thanks, Ben. I thought the day couldn't have been any better. This was a wonderful new experience. Let's shower and change, and I'll make us some dinner."

Ben went to his room, undressed, and stepped into the stall shower. The glass door quickly steamed in the heat. He worked shampoo into his hair and closed his eyes. Before he could rinse out the suds, his eyes still closed, he heard his shower door open.

"I just thought of a way to make the day even better," whispered Carmie, as her soft, warm, naked body pressed tightly against his.

CHAPTER 37

Ben opened his eyes to semidarkness, struggling to focus. Head still firmly attached to his pillow, he could see the luminous dials on his bedside clock: 5:30 a.m. The next attack on his senses was the aroma of frying bacon. That prompted a pang of hunger. And, finally, a vivid memory of the night before.

He extended an arm to the other side of the bed. Empty. Ben swung his legs over the side into a sitting position and realized he was naked. He never went to bed naked. Throwing on pajamas and a bathrobe, he shuffled into the kitchen. Carmie was at the stove top, wearing a pink cotton nightgown and nursing bacon strips to perfect crispness.

"Good morning," she said. "I thought frying bacon would be a good way to wake you."

He walked up behind her, put his arms around her waist, and nuzzled her neck.

"Does this mean you aren't angry with me for last night?" she asked. "Honestly, I didn't intend to seduce you, but when I took off my clothes, all I could think of was a wonderful man I was incredibly drawn to, and he was just a few steps away. What a waste to miss that moment."

Ben turned Carmie around and kissed her with passion.

"So you aren't mad," she whispered. "Not if you want to kiss me before I've even brushed my teeth."

Ben pulled her tightly to him. "I hope there are more last nights," he said. "I hope it wasn't just the champagne and seeing Tenny in love and the glow of a great party."

She put her hands around his neck and kissed him.

"I'm really fond of you, Ben. I have been for a long time but never really admitted it to myself. There was something about yesterday that made me want you physically. I still do. Right now."

"Then turn off the bacon and let's go back to bed." Carmie playfully pushed him away.

"Sorry, my friend. I've got the United States Department of Commerce to run. Trade treaties to negotiate and all that sort of thing. And you and the president of the United States are taking advantage of the high she's riding this morning to explain to bankers why you're taking away some of their favorite toys, remember?"

"I thought you just said you were hungry for me."

"You and food. I started a chain reaction last night that didn't involve dinner. How do you like your eggs?"

MAY

CHAPTER 38

The men who wrote the American Constitution knew they were creating a governing obstacle course. They feared democracy could be supplanted by monarchy or anarchy when passions ran high. Better to slow things down, do little, even nothing, than to race headlong into an ill-considered, dangerous unknown. For more than two centuries, the governmental system based upon distrust had mostly succeeded in avoiding self-destructive public passions.

Tenny was openly defying this governing model. She was proposing major structural changes—now. Overturning entrenched economic models—now. Proposing the most radical change in the nation's defense policy—now. Legislative sprints seldom succeeded except in times of great national peril. Congressional leaders who shared her goals had no illusions about achieving her agenda on what they called "Tenny time," but confronted with relentless pressure from the White House and increasing levels of support from their constituents back home, they had little choice other than to try. The positive wave stirred by Ben's campaign and Tenny's wedding made her initiatives politically hard to resist. At least for the time being.

In mid-May, two months into the effort, Guy Rocker assembled his congressional leadership team to evaluate progress.

"I gave her my word we would bring her program to a floor vote by October," said Rocker, "so let's get the timing right. Frank, you've got the defense budget in your committee. I see that as the toughest of all. Where are we?"

Frank Lipscott, a veteran House member from California, represented a Los Angeles area district whose largest employer was Northrop Grumman, one of the nation's largest defense contractors.

"The money guys are going nuts," said Lipscott. "To get this through, I'm going to need extended hearings and build an airtight case for it. And I need to take care of my own political situation. I need time to make this saleable to my district's voters."

"Can you move the bill before the August recess?" asked Rocker.

"Depends on the support I'll get from the White House," said Lipscott. "She needs to keep selling hard."

Rocker turned to Lucille Nobel, chair of the energy committee. "Can you keep up with our schedule, Lucille?"

"Don't think so," she said. "The oil guys are matching Tenny's PR campaign dollar for dollar. My goodness, I never expected to have an issue where the game is no limit, table stakes. They've built their own effective grassroots campaign. Like Frank, I'll need Tenny in the field to counter it. Public appearances, not just media. She needs more creative ways to make the climate change case. As long as we keep the poll numbers strong, I can count on the committee to stay together. But they'll run pretty fast if it looks like we're losing public support."

After the final committee chair reported, Rocker said, "I'm staying close to our Senate guys and their Christmas targets. Right now, they're optimistic. But of course, nothing's happened yet. No committee votes. Not even hearings. They're trying to get a lot of the must-have other work out of the way first."

"What do you hear from them on a new arms treaty?" said Ingrid Stolski, chair of the House foreign affairs committee. "I can't do much until they take the lead."

"And they can't do much until Tenny and the State Department do more advance work," said Rocker. "Tenny tells me she's been having private conversations with top people in Russia and China. We'll see. It's out of our hands."

"Seriously," asked Stolski, "what are we dealing with here? A show, or a real effort to do in a year what Congress hasn't been able to do in decades? It makes a difference in how I handle this and how many bridges I need to burn."

"Tenny's dead serious," said Rocker. "I've never seen her more intent on anything, not even that immigration bill she got us to pass a couple of years ago. She sees this as her legacy. And let's face it, everyone in this room would feel damn proud if we can get it done, or even part of it done, so let's try as hard as she is."

It was an inspiring message of leadership from Rocker, but the system wasn't built for wholesale change, and the barriers for success had defied countless other well-intentioned legislators before them.

That was just fine with Rocker. Tenny's PR effort would raise public expectations. He was confident that he had a tight enough rein on committee chairs and key members to ultimately win House approval. He also was confident that he had close enough ties with key members of the Senate to ensure that it lost in their chamber.

CHAPTER 39

Secretary of State Stanley Decker's entire adult life had been spent in the US Foreign Service. A graduate of the Johns Hopkins School of International Studies, Decker's first assignment was as a low-level attaché to the US embassy in Bolivia. In between that post and the coveted cabinet position he now held, Decker had served in Asia, Europe, and Africa, distinguishing himself throughout as a hard-driving, effective diplomatic representative of US interests. He was one of Tenny's first appointments after being elected president, a rare instance of a career foreign service officer making it to the top.

Now, Tenny had presented him with a challenge he doubted that he, or anyone, could meet. Total disarmament. Not just a fig leaf, not just comforting words on paper for a high-profile photo op, but actual destruction of most existing weapons, enforcement mechanisms to ensure compliance, and agreements from leaders of most of the world's nations that military combat among them would no longer be an option. Even if the Russians, Chinese, North Koreans, Iranians, Indians, Pakistanis, and our NATO allies agreed to sign up for this, would the US military establishment, the US arms industry, and the powerful, hawkish political civilian defense lobby accept this radical reordering of the world?

Tenny had rejected Decker's counsel that she not spend all her political capital on such a bold effort. Progress could be made, he assured her, but the process would require time and diplomatic delicacy.

Months after receiving this far more difficult assignment, Decker now was on Air Force One, returning to Washington with the president after two weeks of negotiations in Geneva, in awe of what had been accomplished.

"Whatever you said to President Voronin appears to have been effective, Madam President," said Decker. "I just received word that his foreign office has responded with workable first drafts. May I ask what you and he privately discussed?"

Tenny smiled at the validation of her strategy. "I told him the truth, Stan. Just the truth. It helped that our intelligence people had collected so much truth. He tried not to be surprised that I knew at least as much about his military capability and economic problems as he did."

"You shared our intelligence with him?"

"Yes, I did. Why else do we spend so much time and money and take so many risks? If it's usable intelligence, why not use it?"

"And how did you use it?"

"I said, Anatoly, here's the number of your real unemployed. Here's the extent of your food shortages. Here are the places street protests are growing. Here's why your economy is tanking and won't much improve: because as the world migrates away from fossil fuels, very soon all your oil will be virtually worthless. Now, here's how much you spend on weapons and military stuff, most of which is nonsense. Are you really going to order a nuclear attack on the US? Of course not. You're as likely to do that as I am to use our vastly superior arsenal on you, which is never. Let's get real here. All of this is a charade, a waste of money. But it's a huge risk that those decisions could be taken out of our hands by idiots or psychopaths—or technical glitches or system failures. Let's just stand down, all the way down.

Divert your military spending to civilian spending, infrastructure, education, resource development. We're phasing out our oil industry. During the transition, take over many of those markets while we withdraw from them and use the time to stash money for Russia's own transition. This is a no-lose package for you. Improve lives of Russians, lower risks of catastrophe, improve your economy, be a hero."

"You said that?" asked Secretary Decker.

"I did. And using the same language I just described to you. I used numbers and other data to show he had no secrets from us."

"And how did he react?"

"He asked about the Chinese and the others: Do we get naked while they stay dressed? And I said, 'Let me take care of the Chinese. Premier Wong Ho wants to spread Chinese influence everywhere. He wants to build roads in South America, harbors in Africa, send spaceships to Mars. Let him. He can't afford it if he's in an arms race with us. His infrastructure building is no threat to us if he doesn't have nuclear weapons and a million-man army. If the three of us are together on this, we can get the others to fall in line.'

"'You've spoken to him this way?' "Voronin asked me. I did. I couldn't do this in public, obviously, and I even felt that doing it with our diplomatic staffs present wouldn't be wise. I had to do it in person, not in a phone call where he might think our generals were at my elbow prompting me to read from a script, trying to lay a trap for him. I did this one-on-one with him, without notes, sitting just a few feet apart and looking him straight in the eye, trying not to blink."

"Well," said Decker, "I always knew you were good at political sales, but this is extraordinary. It obviously had the desired result."

"My first job after college was recruiting rich clients for wealth management accounts. It taught me a lot about selling to powerful people."

And how did you handle Premier Wong Ho on the North Korean issue?"

"Since Wong Ho is from Guangdong province, where so much Chinese business is transacted, I decided to treat my offer as a transaction rather than a political proposal. My argument to Premier Wong was that he had crazy North Koreans on one border and unstable Pakistanis on the other, right next to an India that's been taken over by Hindu fundamentalists who believe this life doesn't matter as much as the next one. Wouldn't he sleep better if all those nuclear missiles on his border went away? Sign on to my program, I said, and we can work together to make China much safer. I said the US has no interest in having a sphere of interest in Asia. The deal is this: We would mothball our fleet and aircraft, withdraw our troops from South Korea, and pose no threat to China's regional economic interests if China would guarantee it would not invade Taiwan or militarily threaten Japan or other countries in the region by lowering its military temperature. We would work together to neutralize North Korea. No nuclearized North, no million-man standing army on the border with the South."

"That's a pretty breathtaking set of proposals, Madam President. Risky too."

"That's the offer," said Tenny. "The threat if it's not accepted is to pull all of our factories and other business out of China, set up stiff barriers for importation of Chinese products to the US or Europe, and encourage Japan to develop its own nuclear weapons. It's either Peace and Security or face us as the bigger and more dangerous bullies you've always claimed we are."

"And how did he react?"

"Well, you see they agreed to return to Geneva next month for a second round of talks. I'll get them there, Stan. You reel them in."

CHAPTER 40

Tenny was struck by how the day mirrored her mood: joyful, peaceful, beautiful. She felt she was on the cusp of a series of events that would bring the nation and the world closer to peace and personal security than any in her lifetime. She was confident that before year's end Congress would enact her proposals for massive shifts in budget priorities from military spending to a range of long-deferred domestic programs. It also seemed possible that she could reach agreements with Russia, China, and other key nations to begin phased reductions in all weapons systems and standing armies. Would the Senate agree to ratify such a plan? She had enlisted a dozen senators to join the ongoing Geneva negotiations, and so far the results looked promising. She already had made three trips to Geneva to personally negotiate the underlying treaties. Hardly a day passed without her involvement by video conference.

All major countries were now being influenced by her Peace and Security for All campaign. She had spent nearly a billion dollars of her own fortune and billions more in government funds to whet the appetite of people everywhere. That campaign tapped into universal desires. It was blooming as quickly as orchids in the rainforest. Her speech to the world and the worldwide telethon would turn those desires into popular action. Leaders of all nations would feel maximum pressure later in the year.

As she looked out at the Rose Garden, Tenny felt a surge of pride and personal fulfillment. This would be her mark in history. Yes, it would take years to implement. Her programs would be tested in the courts. Disarmament would occur in stages over many years. But she would still have three White House years remaining to manage the transition. After that, hopefully Fish would succeed her as president and in the next four or eight years finish the work. Once the machinery of peace and security was turned on, it would be increasingly difficult for anyone to stop it.

On impulse she walked to the line of visitors standing near the east entrance of the White House. Seeing her, the crowd cheered and applauded. Many pushed forward as she stood and smiled for hugs, handshakes, photos, and bits of conversation. Then, with one final wave, she returned to her office, where she knew Fish and two members of her legislative staff would be waiting.

She met them buoyantly, high from the prospect of passage of her Peace and Security package, turbocharged by her moments with hundreds of happy citizens in the White House garden. It took a moment for her to recognize that neither Fish nor her legislative aides were smiling. In fact, they wore expressions better described as grim.

"Bad news," said Fish. "We're getting sandbagged. You may need a quick trip to the Capitol."

Tenny was too high to fall to their level quickly.

"Who did we lose?" she asked.

"No one yet," said Fish, "but the word is that there's going to be a kill switch in the Senate with the filibuster or by packaging anti votes with senators who have safe seats and can take backlash. Luckily, Pete Quist from Seattle leveled with me. The Boeing people apparently are giving some House members a pass to vote for it, feeling sure they won't have to worry about the Senate."

Tenny was now at their level of concern. "How could this happen? I have promises from the Senate leadership," she said.

"The defense guys are working hand in glove with big pharma and energy," said Angel Suarez, one of the White House legislative assistants. "They figure there's safety in numbers. You can't punish everyone if this fails."

"But what about Rocker?" asked Tenny. "He should be able to head this off, or at least give us plenty of early warning."

"From what I understand, he's getting wobbly," said Fish. "That's your first call."

Fish had served in the House for fifteen years. When Tenny selected her to be vice president, she was assistant House majority leader. Tenny trusted her judgment. If Fish said the package was in trouble, it was.

"I can't believe it," said Tenny. "Guy Rocker has been in on all our planning. He's been our strongest advocate. He knows that I'll guarantee that any member who gets into election trouble because of this vote will have all the money needed for a reelection campaign, and plenty of pork to bring back to the district. There's little risk."

"Here's the list we have of people who could desert you at the last minute," said Suarez. "We'll let you know if we ID others."

"Rocker!" she said again. "I can't believe it."

The sky was still a brilliant blue. The White House grounds were still bathed in late spring colors. The crowds were still there, happy and excited. But Tenny's sunny day was over.

CHAPTER 41

S he had been too sure of victory, too convinced she had won. The stakes were higher than any bet she had ever made, the consequences for failure too devastating to consider. Rationality was having a hard time fighting through her churning, angry thoughts.

She asked Fish and the legislative staff to leave her for a few minutes, feigning a headache. Then she realized she actually was having a headache, a pounding ache at the back of her head. Her difficulty breathing, which had begun in the garden, as she hugged small children and posed for photos, lasted longer than the usual spike to which she had become accustomed. Few knew that she kept a portable oxygen tank secreted in her desk. At times in recent months, she felt the need to use it. Now was one of those times. Her desk also contained a oximeter, a simple clip she could attach to her finger to check oxygen levels. She found it in a drawer and placed it on the middle finger of her right hand. Within seconds it registered below normal.

While she was loathe to admit it, the fact that Andres was a medical doctor was one of the reasons behind her decision to remarry him. He was someone she could grow old with after her White House days ended. Because of her fragile condition, she would always need a doctor close by. She needed him now.

Andres was upstairs in the private residence when she called. He moved quickly to her office.

"Symptoms?" he asked, now the doctor, not the husband.

"Short of breath, excruciating headache."

"Where?"

"Back of the head."

"Have you taken anything? Aspirin? Motrin?"

"No."

He took the small oxygen tank from her desk and attached the tube to her nostrils.

"Any better?" he asked, after she drew a few deep breaths.

"Some," she said. "Order us a couple of sandwiches and drinks so people will think we're having a quick bite together."

After ten minutes on the oxygen, Tenny gave the portable tank back to Andres.

"Okay, I think that will do it," she said. "I've got to make some urgent phone calls now."

Andres looked at her closely. Her facial color concerned him. She still was reaching a bit for air. He checked her pulse and blood pressure.

"No, he said, "you need to go down to the infirmary for a full check." On his cell phone, Andres called to learn that White House physician Dr. Lucille Walker was away on a personal errand. She would return in ten minutes.

"Let's go down," said Andres.

"No," said Tenny, "I've got some calls to make that can't wait. Ask Fish and the others to come back in."

"Ten minutes, until Walker returns, no more," said Andres. He opened the door and motioned for the others.

Tenny rose to join them in the seating area. Immediately on standing, she felt light-headed. *Too fast, I got up too fast,* she thought. Gripping the side of the desk for support, she said, "Be with you in a minute."

She feigned looking at a piece of paper on the desktop to provide an excuse for not moving, but was alarmed that even that simple act produced only a blur. She felt her legs lose their support and had just enough time to say, "I need help," before she lost consciousness and fell to the floor.

CHAPTER 42

Within minutes, the medical team always on standby on the White House grounds transported Tenny to the emergency room at George Washington University Hospital, just seven city blocks away. There was no hiding the fact that the president was the patient. It was midday, and the White House press rooms were fully staffed. Network programming was interrupted. Instant messaging and tweets flooded cell phones and the internet. Crowds quickly formed in Washington Circle immediately outside the hospital. Two years earlier, the vigil had been for Tenny, victim of a massive explosion designed to kill her. Now she was back in the same emergency room, victim of something yet to be disclosed, prognosis uncertain.

Andres was in the ambulance that carried Tenny to the hospital. With his briefing of her condition to the hospital's emergency medical team, and the hospital's records of her post-assassination treatment, the doctors on duty could move quickly from diagnosis to treatment. She was sedated, intubated to increase oxygen flow to her vital organs and minimize fluid in her lungs, and given blood thinners to prevent clotting and to stabilize her blood pressure.

Once these procedures were completed in the intensive care unit, Andres and Mark Rosenthal, the hospital's chief medical officer, conferred privately and then met with Fish, Carmie, Ben, Tenny's chief of staff Henry

Deacon, and White House press secretary Claire Liston in a nearby conference room.

"I'm not sure whether all of you know this," said Andres, "but the assassination explosion left Tenny with long-term lung damage. We've been managing it discreetly with Nintedanib, an anti-scarring medicine, and periodic uses of portable oxygen, but today it got away from her and turned critical. I was concerned originally that she had a stroke, but that's not the case. Dr. Rosenthal here will give you the medical details."

"Yes," said Dr. Rosenthal. "The medical term for her condition is idiopathic pulmonary fibrosis, or IPF, and it's fairly common after recovery from ARDS in those who suffer the internal trauma the president incurred. It can be a dangerous, life-threatening condition, one that could rapidly transform into full blown respiratory failure. Basically, the lungs scar and lose some of their function, which is to supply oxygen to vital parts of the body. The president has been aware of her condition and, as Dr. Navarro just said, she's been managing it carefully by limiting her exertion and augmenting her oxygen when needed. But there is no cure. The medical response to the setback she suffered today is standard in most cases: stabilizing her oxygen, preventing oxygen loss from causing further damage, and once that's accomplished, getting her up and about as quickly as possible so she doesn't lose muscle or motor abilities. Her chances of recovery are good. But she's suffered a shock and related modalities are still possible. Some patients on ventilators also incur mental loss, and so we try to remove them as quickly as possible."

"Other modalities?" asked Fish.

"Yes, Madam vice president," said Dr. Rosenthal. "Lungs don't have an ability to regenerate. Once they've been damaged and they become incapacitated to this degree they permanently lose function. We need to be alert for pneumonia, and the possibility of sepsis, which is massive leakage of white blood cells through the damaged lung cell walls to the circulatory system and damage to other organs. And if there's additional loss of lung function, there's always the possibility of the need for a double lung transplant. These are the modalities we watch for."

The room fell silent. Lung transplant? Even Carmie and Deacon, both of whom knew about Tenny's ARDS condition, were startled to hear that possibility.

Sensing the distress Dr. Rosenthal's medical report created, Andres quickly tried to put a more optimistic face on it.

"Dr. Rosenthal has mentioned a realistic number of worst-case outcomes," said Andres. "We need to be aware of them, but Tenny is not close to that stage. He said her chances of recovery are good, and in his opinion and mine, that's the most likely outcome. She's getting the best medical care available, and she received it quickly, always a plus in these situations."

Dr. Rosenthal nodded in agreement. "I agree," said Rosenthal. "I believe her chances of recovery and resumption of her normal duties are quite good."

"How much of this can we tell the media? The TV trucks and reporters are all over Washington Circle," asked press secretary Claire Liston.

"As far as the hospital is concerned, you can tell them what I've just told you," said Dr. Rosenthal. "She's being treated for idiopathic pulmonary fibrosis. We are optimistic about her recovery. We need to wait for her response to our treatment."

"How would you characterize it?" Liston asked.

"I'd say serious, not critical," said Rosenthal.

"Is it necessary to say 'serious'" asked Deacon.

"The media will make it sound worse if we don't give them an official word," said Liston.

"Let's put it in writing so that there's no misunderstanding," said Deacon. "Claire, get together with the hospital press office right away and prepare a statement that has everyone on the same page. And have someone from hospital administration read it to the press, not anyone from the White House. Right now, this is a medical situation, not political."

"And when it's ready," said Fish, "let me know. Before it goes out, I want to personally call the secretaries of defense and state and the intelligence agencies, so they know what we're dealing with."

Fish and Deacon returned to the White House. Carmie and Ben moved to another meeting room to wait, helpless to do anything. Ben noticed that Carmie's face was wet with tears. He was surprised to realize that his was too.

"Oh, Ben, my heart is breaking," said Carmie. "Ever since the explosion I've expected this. I asked her not to run. For a time, I even secretly hoped she'd lose. The work was killing her. I could see that."

"No, you couldn't," said Ben. "The work kept her alive. She's had a purpose, a mission, and knowing her life expectancy may have been compromised has caused her to fight harder than ever."

CHAPTER 43

The main campus of George Washington University occupies forty-three acres of some of the most valuable property in Washington, DC. Locals are largely inured to the sight and sound of ambulances arriving at the hospital's emergency center, sirens wailing. It's a scene repeated often, day and night, seven days a week. But not since Tenny had been rushed to the hospital in critical condition two years earlier had the hospital, or the campus itself, been the center of a scene such as this.

The vigil began within moments of her arrival. It intensified three hours later, when LaVenna Seraphin, the hospital's assistant administrator, appeared at the hospital entrance to read the official medical statement:

"At approximately 3:10 p.m., President Tennyson was admitted to the emergency room. She was met by George Washington University's emergency medical team and diagnosed with idiopathic pulmonary fibrosis, a condition that reduced her oxygen levels. She was conscious when she arrived and now is sedated and receiving supplemental oxygen through a ventilator, a routine procedure for patients in this condition. She is in the intensive care unit and will continue to be monitored until her oxygen levels return to normal. That's all we have now. We will provide more information about her condition when it is available. Thank you."

Immediately, reporters began shouting questions.

"Will she need surgery?"

"Is this related to her assassination injuries?"

"Has she suffered brain damage for lack of oxygen?"

Spokesperson Seraphin ignored all questions and quickly disappeared into the refuge of the hospital's administrative area, leaving much room for speculation.

In CNN's studio, anchor Josef Lorenz turned to the network's medical expert, internist Darren Fitzgerald. "Not a lot to go on there, Darren. Can you add to what we just heard?"

"Well, Josef, I don't want to jump the gun, but it sounds like this is very much connected to the injuries from the bomb blast two years ago. It's not uncommon for people who've been through a trauma like that to have ongoing lung problems."

"Is it life-threatening?"

"It certainly can be. It depends on the severity. Normal lungs have a foamy substance called 'surfactant' that keep the lungs fully open so a person can breathe. In damaged lungs, with the condition the hospital just described, tiny openings develop in the lungs' air sacs, preventing the lungs from filling with air properly and moving oxygen through the body. Over time, the lung tissue may scar and become stiff."

"Just a second, Darren, we have Charlotte Gambel outside the hospital now. Charlotte, what more have you learned?"

The camera switched to a chaotic scene outside the hospital: an endless sea of faces in the crowd, blocking access to Pennsylvania Avenue; flashing lights from an ambulance trying to make its way to the emergency room; other reporters talking to their studio anchors.

"Josef, I've spoken with an off-duty nurse who was here when the president was treated after the assassination attempt. She said it was well known among the hospital's medical staff then that the president was suffering from acute respiratory distress syndrome, but the White House did not want that information publicized. So it appears she's been living with this secret for nearly two years now."

The camera switched back to the studio.

"Acute respiratory distress syndrome? Can you explain that?" he asked Dr. Fitzgerald.

"It means simply that her lungs are damaged. Idiopathic fibrosis refers to the scarring that resulted from the trauma of the explosion. It's treatable but in this case something happened. Possibly deterioration of the lungs. Even exceptional levels of stress can trigger an acute response. Clearly she's been living with this condition since the attempted assassination."

"Amazing," said Lorenz. "Imagine being able to keep the news quiet for so long. Obviously she didn't want it to become a campaign issue. How much danger is she in now?"

"Quite a bit," said Dr. Fitzgerald. "The standard treatment is supplemental oxygen until the body stabilizes, blood thinners to help prevent blood clots, and really little else. There's no surgical procedure involved, unless the lungs become so incapacitated that she requires a lung transplant."

"Sounds like this situation can be described as 'critical,'" said Lorenz.

"Well, officially the hospital says it's serious, so the medical team must not feel surgery is required, at least not yet. Double lung transplants, by the way, are more common than most people realize. Many Covid patients with long term problems have had to undergo them. Not only lung transplants, but many Covid patients on ventilators afterwards have reported cognitive issues."

"And the president is on a ventilator. There may be much more to this than the hospital's statement indicates. We may be in for a long night," said Lorenz.

"Possibly many of them," said Dr. Fitzgerald.

CHAPTER 44

Prayers and messages of hope for Tenny's recovery came from world leaders and ordinary people everywhere. Tenny was the face of America, and a popular one. The country's first female president. A wealthy heiress who used her fortune and her political power for a broad range of social causes. Her disarmament campaign had only recently been ignited and was extremely popular. Her wedding, which had taken place little more than a month earlier, was still a heartwarming memory. Her health now was a worldwide concern.

At the White House, Fish moved quickly to ensure that there would be no gap in US leadership. Within hours she convened a meeting of the presidential Cabinet and invited the media to cover it. She personally called heads of many foreign governments, state governors and business leaders. Privately, she met with key members of Congress to discuss a contingency plan in the event Tenny died or could not continue to function as president. The 25th amendment of the US Constitution provides that the vice president assumes the power of the presidency immediately if the president dies or becomes incapacitated. Fish seamlessly took that authority, but she refused to move to the Oval Office to exercise it. Tenny would return, she said with an assurance that remained in medical doubt.

For the first twelve hours after Tenny was stricken, Carmie and Ben held vigil at the hospital. Then the Secret Service intervened. Both were still considered major targets of a Salvation Project death squad, and the service insisted they move to a more secure location. Carmie argued that because of her close association with Tenny she needed to be there to provide comfort when Tenny woke from sedation. Ben was helping Deacon and the White House press office field questions from the media camped outside the hospital. Only after the Secret Service secured rooms at the Washington Circle Hotel, directly across Pennsylvania Avenue from the hospital, did Carmie and Ben agree to leave the hospital's office area.

The wait seemed endless, interminable, but it was little more than twenty-four hours from the time Tenny was admitted that Andres called.

"She's awake, breathing normally; I think it's going to be okay," he said.

Carmie and Ben had braced themselves for Tenny's death. The news that she would recover was like experiencing a resurrection. They had spent the last twenty-four hours in shock, in fear, in hope, in tears, in each other's arms, lost in their own thoughts. Now that ended as abruptly as it began. It seemed so much longer ago than yesterday.

CHAPTER 45

Richfield's predecessor as the Salvation Project's executive director had failed, and in failing, she had become an unacceptable organizational risk. Too many of her operatives had been compromised. Too many paths were open for government authorities to follow and ultimately destroy the Project itself. And so she had to die. It was the price established when she became the Project's working executive director. She had accepted it.

Richfield also accepted the potential consequences for failure, but he had no intention of failing. He had unquestioned belief in the Project's mission and unshakable confidence in his ability to succeed.

Richfield's first stop after his appointment as executive director was Buenos Aires, where a Project-inspired Argentinian coup had taken place without significant opposition. The UN held a special session to condemn it. The United States had issued a ban on the country's beef imports. The Pan-American Union refused to recognize the new government as legitimate. None of that affected actions on the ground, where a junta secretly organized by the Salvation Project's Argentinian cell was now in firm control. Except for a few active human rights groups, Argentinians were either accepting of the new regime or willing to give it an opportunity to end the governmental chaos that had made the coup possible. Argentina was a bright spot Richfield could point to when visiting his other outposts.

Richfield also visited the Middle East, where the Salvation Project's operatives were working with supportive imams to integrate the Project's civil authoritarianism with the region's Islamic culture.

Europe presented a more difficult situation. Inroads were deepest in Great Britain, whose centuries of monarchy promised a platform for control if a member of the royal family sympathetic to the Project ascended to the throne. A very active UK cell was at work trying to achieve that outcome. Separately, another active group was working to take control of the new antiroyalist party.

All were sideshows to the main event—control of the United States government. Yes, last year's plan had failed and failed calamitously for the Project's cause, but it demonstrated the vulnerability of a government resting on a fragile foundation of ambition, greed, malleable information, and a system for attaining power open to anyone determined enough to grasp for it.

Now, this new opportunity. A US president whose medical condition no longer could be kept secret or denied. A condition open to exploitation. An untimely death that would come as no surprise. And the formulation of a new plan with great short-term promise for success.

Richfield had just such a plan in mind. It was time to perfect the details, to present it to the other members of the Symfonia, and to set it in motion. After so many years of survival and progress, Richfield now had the endgame in sight.

JUNE

CHAPTER 46

For seven days Tenny remained in the hospital. Her body was healing but her anxiety level was not. She feared the consequences of detachment from the Peace and Security agenda campaign. Any suggestion that her physical ability or resolve had weakened would provide potent ammunition for the powerful forces lined up against her. She had to return to the White House.

Tenny's medical team was ever more anxious as well. Tenny's condition was improving, but she remained a candidate for pneumonia, sepsis or other physical setbacks. Mortality rates are high for those suffering the type of lung damage Tenny endured. Andres and the hospital medical team explained these risks to Tenny and insisted she remain in their care longer. You may not know you have an infection until it's too late, they warned. In the hospital, at the first sign of infection, antibiotics could be administered, blood pressure could be maintained. She would have the benefit of every treatment option medical science has available.

"Test me at the White House," Tenny responded. "I'm ten minutes away. That ten minutes can't be the difference between life and death."

Tenny had an agenda to enact, a treaty to negotiate, a public to convince. She could not do that from a hospital bed. She could not convince wavering members of congress that she would have their backs from the hospital. She was going to check herself out. As president, she could do that, and no one could stop her.

And so, a week from the day she arrived in an ambulance, Tenny walked through the hospital's front door holding tightly to Andres's arm, and waving and blowing kisses to the crowds who lined the streets to cheer her. She played to the cameras, offering evidence that she was back in action. The presidential caravan motored the seven blocks between the 23rd street hospital and the 1600 Pennsylvania Avenue White House. Tenny emerged, stopping for a few moments to feed more positive images to the microphones and cameras waiting to greet her there.

Then, she went to her bedroom and with help from Andres, went directly to bed.

Another week passed, a week of frequent tests, physical therapy, few appointments but an active phone blitz to promote a charade of normalcy before she felt strong enough to return to the Oval Office for a semblance of her previous schedule.

Fish continued to field visitors and handle executive branch business but remained out of most camera range as she seamlessly transferred the spotlight back to Tenny. Each day, by arrangement, Tenny presided over a high visibility public event. As far as the public and Congress knew, Tenny's physical emergency was old news. Her mental capacity appeared unaffected,

For months before Tenny's hospitalization, Fish had planned to attend the annual late June whaling festival in her hometown of Utqiaġvik, Alaska. For Utqiaġvik, the whaling festival was a highlight of each year, a celebration of ancient culture, skill and courage, and an important source for food, clothing and other valuable assets required for Arctic life. Last year, for the first time ever, because she was a candidate for vice president and the campaign needed her, Fish was unable to participate in the festival. She was determined that nothing would interfere with her trip home this year.

Her staff protected the dates, warding off all other demands for Fish's time. When Tenny fell ill Fish had no choice but to cancel.

Now, Tenny was back at the White House, each day spending more time in the Oval Office, each day feeling a bit stronger, her improving health confirmed by multiple daily tests and physical therapy.

"For God's sake, go," she told Fish. It's not too late. "Go. You travelling to Alaska just confirms that I'm back to normal. The media will stop magnifying my every cough or sneeze."

Fish at first resisted with a bullet list of "what-ifs." But the pull of home and culture was too strong. Resistance quickly melted. The festival would begin in a few days. There still was time.

CHAPTER 47

North of the Canadian border, and even farther north, above the Yukon River, the Arctic Circle, the caribou migration routes, the oil derricks at Deadhorse, and the north slope of the Brooks Range, is the town of Utqiaġvik, population about 4,500, elevation ten feet above the Arctic Ocean, the northernmost community in the United States, formerly known as Barrow, Alaska.

People have inhabited the Utqiaġvik area for thousands of years, from when a land bridge existed between Russia's Siberian coast and Alaska's western edge. Most ancient migrants continued south, where the climate was more tolerable and food and other resources more plentiful. Those who settled on the Arctic coast lived in near total isolation and lack of awareness of other human history—the dynasties of China, the pyramids of the Nile, Greek and Roman culture, the rise of Christianity and Islam, the European Renaissance, voyages of Columbus, lives and fortunes of other Indigenous people on the American continent, and later, the migrants who created the United States of America or even the tsars who ruled the nearby Russian mainland. What the village people of Alaska's Arctic coast did know was how to survive in one of the least hospitable regions on Earth. They knew how to convert the Arctic's unique animal and plant life into food, clothing, hunting implements, and housing and how to sustain those resources for each new generation.

That isolation ended when Vitus Bering, a Danish explorer employed by the Russians, made contact with the village communities along the Gulf Coast of Alaska. Bering opened the sea-lanes for Russian fur traders. Decades later came the whalers from New England, as well as guns and alcohol and diseases the people of the north had never before been exposed to. Later came the contacts made possible by air travel and an entity known as the State of Alaska and, just a clock tick in time later, the discovery of oil. Enormous pools of oil.

Vice President Sheila Fishburne was a daughter of that culture, raised by a grandmother and mother and others whose lives began before sled dogs were replaced by snow machines and before there was oil money to build Iḷisaġvik College, the only tribal college in Alaska, where Fish once taught a course in basic science.

In addition to her formal classroom studies, Fish's education included how to sew skins together for clothing and use rounded ulu knives to cut meat from bearded seals. Her mother taught her how to whip caribou fat to a froth with her hands and mix in berries until it became a local delicacy. In her late teens, Fish joined her uncle Tulak's whale boat crew, camping on the ice pack near open water during the spring hunt; waiting, often for many frigid and windblown days, to see the spout of a bowhead whale; learning to row silently with others until the prey was within harpoon-striking distance of their small skin boat.

She loved it all. The traditions and ways and legends of her people.

Her late father was Reed Fishburne, a math teacher who arrived in Utqiaġvik from his home in Indianapolis, Indiana, as a recent college graduate expecting to have a year's adventure teaching at Barrow High School. At that school he met a beautiful girl by the name of Alicee, married her, and remained in Utqiaġvik for the rest of his life. Fish's mother traveled widely with her husband and became comfortable in his world as well as her own.

Fish inherited her mother's dual citizenship in modern and ancient societies. As Alaska's lone member of the US House of Representatives, she was proficient in her Washington work while remaining firmly rooted in Inupiat culture. She returned home as often as time permitted and particularly on important occasions, such as Utqiaġvik's spring whaling festival.

In the past she would fly from Washington, DC, to Utqiaġvik on commercial airlines, changing planes in Seattle and again in Fairbanks to get there. Now and then she would be accompanied by an assistant. Making the trip as vice president of the United States was another matter. She had her own plane, a military version of a Boeing 757-200, otherwise known as Air Force Two. And she had a lot of company—members of the White House press corps, network TV crews expecting colorful footage of Fish at the festivities, and six Secret Service agents for security. An advance team of agents already was in Utqiaġvik to plan for her arrival.

"You're going to love it there," she good-naturedly told the security team before it left Washington. "Every home has high-powered rifles for shooting caribou; twelve-gauge shotguns for shooting geese and ducks; razor-sharp knives for slicing up whale, seal, and walrus; and dynamite-tipped harpoons. I leave it to you to decide how to protect me from bodily harm."

As so often happens in Alaska, weather conditions took control of planning for Fish's arrival in Utqiaġvik. Air Force Two flew into a turbulent northern storm, one that closed Utqiaġvik's airfield and forced Fish's plane to make an unscheduled landing at Eielson Air Force Base near Fairbanks. Finally on the ground, the plane's mostly pale and storm-shaken passengers headed for either the bar or the toilet, assuming their flight was over and thankful that they had survived. But Fish was no stranger to Alaskan aviation. She had flown on countless single- and twin-engine aircraft through rain and snowstorms and was not inclined to be deterred. She appealed to Eielson's base commander to somehow get her home that day.

After a flurry of phone calls to cut red tape, Fish was told that although conditions in Utqiaġvik likely would not clear until late tomorrow for a 757 landing, a plane with a shorter runway requirement possibly could land if it arrived during a lull in the storm.

That was all Fish needed to hear. She commandeered an Alaska Airlines Embraer 170 temporarily based at Eielson on a military contract. Dozens of unhappy and wary media people, staff members, and Secret Service agents followed her grudgingly up the ramp to seats on the twin jet.

Her influence landed her an aircraft, but nothing she could say or do could change the weather. Fish knew better than to tempt the elements when traveling by air in Alaska, but this was the whaling festival. Now that she was vice president, her people would be sorely disappointed if she failed to be there. A century earlier, the nation's most famous aviator at the time, Wiley Post, made the same calculation with the nation's most famous entertainer, Will Rogers, as his passenger. Their plane crashed fifteen miles from Barrow, and they both were killed. The local airfield ever since had been named the Wiley Post–Will Rogers Memorial Airport.

But Fish won her bet with fate. As the plane approached Utqiaġvik, the storm temporarily subsided. The last ten minutes of the flight were moments the passengers would not soon forget, but the pilots assured Fish that they could land safely. They had done so under comparable conditions many times before.

Fish was met by hundreds of townspeople, most of whom she knew by name. They came out in the storm to cheer and wave welcome signs and to take photos of her and with her. Whatever doubts she may have had about risking this flight melted in the warmth of the welcome. She was Utqiaġvik's rock star.

Also waiting at the airport was Fish's mother. "Foolish, foolish, foolish," said Alicee Fishburne to her daughter once they were alone in the car that was taking them home. "Weather rules, you obey if you want to live. You know that."

"Yes, Mama, I know. I pushed a little. Maybe a bit too hard," said Fish. "I just so much wanted to be here today."

"You know that being an important person doesn't protect you," said Alicee. "It didn't help Nick Begich or Ted Stevens." A plane carrying Begich, who was the state's lone member of Congress at the time, along with House Speaker Hale Boggs, was never found after it disappeared on a stormy night on its way from Anchorage to Juneau. Stevens, Alaska's US senator, died with others when their plane crashed on a fishing trip near Bristol Bay.

Utqiaġvik was home. For Fish, it always would be. Now that she was here, she was looking forward to socializing, enjoying local delicacies, and participating in the games. Could she still fly high in the sealskin blanket toss? Not as high as she once did, and not without feeling her age afterward. But it would be fun, and the video footage and still photos and the stories that the traveling media sent back would be good politics.

And then she thought of her nervous Secret Service detail watching her being propelled twenty feet in the air from a taut blanket and wondered how they would explain that in their reports to Washington, DC.

CHAPTER 48

Fish rode an emotional wave, returning to Washington after three days immersed in her Inupiat heritage and convinced that she had a concept that could help win support for the Peace and Security agenda. Her first call was to Ben Sage.

"Welcome back, O great whale hunter," said Ben. "Catch any good belugas while you were up north?'

"Don't mock it," replied Fish. "Those whale crews are my heroes."

"Sorry," said Ben. "No offense, but you were a whale hunter yourself, weren't you?"

"My uncle Tulak's crew."

"I've always been curious: How do people like you manage to pull in something like a fifty-foot whale?"

"You should try it sometime," said Fish. "Maybe I'll ask Uncle Tulak to send you an invitation. Then you can spend a year in training, learning how to sharpen the harpoons, properly load the whaling guns, tie all the rope knots, and get the floats ready. You'll need to learn how to shoot a rifle and not miss if a polar bear decides to join your crew. Then, when it's spring whaling season, be prepared to go out on the pack ice, ice with ridges jammed together so's there's hardly any flat path. You'll need to chop a road through the ice so you can haul the boat and tents and stoves because you might need to stay awhile. Whales don't show up by appointment, you know. So you may need to go miles out there, right to the water's edge where you can launch your skin boat. And wait. Days. Maybe a week or more until a whale's sighted. While winds are blowing forty or so miles an hour and you're trying to keep from freezing in your tent, where you can't stay indefinitely because you need to pee and shit somewhere and take your turn on lookout and keeping things tied down.

"Okay, then someone sees a whale. Eight of you launch the boat into choppy water, water so cold it will kill you in a minute if you fall in. You oar out to the whale. Really close to the whale. The crew captain will decide how close. He's likely been doing it all his life. It's not for amateurs. And then the guy with the harpoon takes his shot. And it better be a good one. You don't want to spend a lot of time next to a wounded, angry whale. So let's say his shot is true. Now, you need to tow the forty-ton catch back to the ice, and with your snow machines back to the edge of town. Are you interested in what comes next? What it takes to prepare the food that feeds the community and the clothes that make it possible to live in that climate?"

"No," said Ben, awed at Fish's description of the whale catching experience. "I've heard enough. Cancel that request to your uncle. I don't think I'll be up for it."

"Good, and don't knock it. This is really hard, dangerous, skillful work. That's why the communities celebrate it. That's why I celebrate it."

Anxious to change the subject, Ben noticed an embroidered caribou skin hanging on the wall behind Fish's desk, a piece of art he had never seen. It depicted a high summer sun above a vast, unbroken stretch of the Arctic Ocean, on which was a multicolored inscription in what appeared to be the Inupiat language.

"It's new," she said. "It was given to me during the whaling festival."

"And the words, what do they say?"

"You don't speak Inupiat?"

"I didn't think anyone did any more."

"We're graduating dozens of kids every year with college degrees in it. Picking it up from the dead, so to speak. Rosetta Stone even sells a course in a boxed set."

She walked to it and began pointing to each line of the inscription.

"*Paaqjaktautaieeiq* means think positive, act positive, speak positive, and live positive.

"*Nagliktuutiqabniq* means compassion. Live with warmth, kindness, caring.

"*Paammaabigeiq* translates as cooperation. Together we have an awesome power to accomplish anything.

"*Ixagiigeiq* is family and kinship. As Inupiat people, we believe in knowing who we are and how we are related to one another. Our families bind us together.

"*Qieuieeiq*. Humility. Our hearts command that we act on goodness. We expect no reward in return. This is part of our cultural fiber.

"*Quvianbuniq*. Humor. In a tough environment like the Arctic, hardship around every temperature change and west wind, we laugh and keep our sense of humor.

"*Afuniallaniq*. Hunting. Traditions. Reverence for the land, sea, and animals. It's the foundation of who we are.

"*Leupiuraallaniq*. Knowledge of our language. Yes, we're getting back our language, and so are many other Indigenous people. Language means identity, expressed in ways no other languages can.

"*Piqpakkutiqabniq suli Qiksiksrautiqabniq Utuqqanaanun Allanullu*. Love and respect for our elders and one another. Our elders model our traditions and ways of being. They bind our generations.

"*Qiksiksrautiqabniq Ieuuniabvigmun.* Respect for nature. Our creator gave us the gift of our surroundings. We respect this magnificent gift so we can pass it on to those who come after us.

"*Aviktuaqatigiigeiq.* Sharing. We share with one another and acts of giving are returned.

"And the last one is *Ukpiqqutiqabniq.* Spirituality. We are a spiritual people. There's power in prayer."

Fish walked over to where Ben was observing this.

"One more thing, Ben," she said. "These are not just random words. These are Inupiat values. Children are taught them at home and in school. Most homes have them posted in one form or another. All of this was suppressed for decades when the government's goal was to make our language and culture extinct. But now we're in a period of cultural rejuvenation."

"Impressive," said Ben. "A beautiful piece of art you have there, and beautiful sentiments. Now, what's on your mind? Why'd you call for me?"

He sat down in a straight chair in front of her desk.

She followed him to the chair, clutched his shoulders with both hands and shook him. "Wake up in there," she said, raising her voice. "This is why I wanted to see you the moment I returned from home. This is a powerful piece of our Peace and Security campaign."

"It is?" said Ben, clearly surprised at her agitation.

"I didn't think I'd need to dope slap you about this," said Fish, still clutching Ben's shoulders. "We're talking about the North Pole, the home of Santa Claus and polar bears and whales. All instantly recognized as positive symbols. Throughout the world. And the people. We're on ice cream bars as Eskimos. The tails of every Alaska Airlines plane. And not just Alaska. The Arctic is commercial magic. Lapland reindeer. Saint Nicholas.

Sled dog races. Huskies. How many companies do you think call themselves Husky this or Husky that? Hans Christian Andersen stories. *Frozen!*"

Fish released her grip on Ben and walked to her desk. "My God, Ben," she said. "The Arctic, our people, our wildlife, generations of stories, can you think of more positive or more universal symbolism?"

Ben shook his head in awe of Fish's enthusiasm. "I don't know how to answer that, Fish," he replied. "I'm not creating ice cream bars or Christmas sleigh images or storybooks. Where are you going with this?"

Fish looked across the desk at Ben with an assertiveness he seldom recalled. "Ben, you may never have heard of such a thing as the Arctic Council, but it's a big deal. All the Arctic countries belong: Canada, Denmark, Finland, Iceland, Norway, Sweden, Russia, the US. And just about every country in western Europe and along the Asian side of the Pacific Rim. Why? Because the Arctic Ocean is melting. New sea-lanes are opening. Lots of gas and oil and minerals will be accessible. Meanwhile, the place is no longer pristine. Environmental problems. Habitat loss. Military people jockeying for advantage. Like I say, it's a big deal. And it's a microcosm of what we're trying to do with our agenda—bring people together peacefully, drop the weapons, save the environment, the sustainable resources. And with the Arctic Council it's actually being managed without the baggage of animosity that goes along with UN involvement or any other international institution. The history and symbolism and future of the Arctic is a great hook for a lot of the things we want to say and do with our campaign."

Ben waited for more, but she just sat and focused on him silently with eyes and an expression that said more than words. He knew he had to respond, even though he had no idea what to say.

"Do you have anything specific in mind?" he finally said.

"Nope," she answered. "I've laid out all the ingredients. You put it together."

"I'll give it a look," he said.

"Yes, you will," she replied.

JULY

CHAPTER 49

O n the third day of the International Conference on Experimental Biology and Biomedicine, Renetta Chance signaled Bauman Kabiri that she wanted to talk. They had not communicated since discovering in London that they were both Salvation Project managers. Now they were in Toronto, each having delivered scientific papers to their assembled colleagues. Neither had acknowledged the presence of the other at the conference. Until now.

At the coffee break before the final plenary session, Chance approached Kabiri with two business cards.

"Excellent presentation, Kabiri," she said, trying to talk over the din. "I have two recommendations for you to follow up on for your study on how machine learning can quantify long-term health effects in COVID-19 survivors."

She handed him the cards back side up. On one she had written, "Let's talk here. Safer."

Kabiri looked at the card and nodded. Even though he was not sure meeting in the open like this was a good idea, he could hardly avoid it now. "Thank you," he replied. "I'll contact them."

In a lowered voice, she said, "This will just take a few moments."

Kabiri nodded, uncertain of what else to do.

"Just before I left London there was another murder. Actually a friend of mine, Janice Gainsboro. Although I never spoke with her about it, I believe she was one of us, a believer in the Project, but recently I learned she backed away from it."

"Sorry to hear that," said Kabiri. "Could it have been an accident, a robbery, something else? How sure are you that it's"—he hesitated to even say the word "project" in public—"it was really murder?"

"Certain enough that I plan to bring it up at our next Project meeting," said Chance. "It's time we had this out. If we're a real executive committee, we need to act like it and question the direction. All this killing. I hope you will support me."

As her intensity rose, so did Kabiri's alarm level. It peaked with the suggestion that they both engage in what Project leadership surely would consider a mutiny. He fought to keep his composure and not draw attention from others in the crowded hotel reception hall.

"Renetta, my God, please don't even think of that," said Kabiri. "I've been on this board longer than you, and I know how intolerant they are. You don't want their death squad coming after you."

"Why would they do that?" she said. "I joined because I believe in the cause. I went on the committee because I thought my experience and contacts would be helpful. I've never been a puppet or a yes-person. All my life I've believed in action. It's served me well through my career and allowed me to reach the top of this profession. I joined the Project in the first place because I saw no hope for resolving the great problems any other way. But I didn't sign up for indiscriminate, senseless killing. I've been on too many committees where people failed to speak up. That's not me."

Kabiri scanned his surroundings. Did it appear anyone was listening? Anyone paying unusual attention to them? It didn't seem so. There was much chatter. The clatter of coffee cups being jostled. Music from the hotel speaker system consuming a share of audio space. Some attendees moving through the crowd with suitcases and backpacks ready to leave the conference early. No. He didn't believe this conversation in itself would put them in danger. But Renetta Chance's naivete would. Kabiri was far more attuned than she to their operations. He knew how effective the Project had been in learning state secrets, in identifying sympathizers and enemies, how ruthless the leaders had been in enforcing discipline. Clearly Renetta would be in danger. And because of his association with her, he could be as well. He agreed with her concerns, but there were ways to achieve change without being as direct as she planned to be.

"Renetta," he said, "promise me you won't challenge them on this at the next meeting. Things are happening in the United States, they tell us. We may be on the verge of success. If that happens, we win. There's no need for killing anyone. We can all focus on doing what we signed up for: to help administer a science-based government that actually can get things done. We're almost there. Don't put yourself in danger."

Renetta Chance looked at Kabiri, balancing what she felt she had to do against what Kabiri advised.

"Bauman," she finally said, "I'll trade promises with you. I promise not to make waves at the next meeting. But if we fail to take control of America and there are more killings, I want you to promise to back me up later."

Bauman Kabiri was alarmed by her proposal, but at least it resolved the immediate threat. And what choice did he have? His relationship with her already made him suspect. If she was targeted, he very well could be collateral damage.

"Deal," said Kabiri reluctantly. "Deal."

AUGUST

CHAPTER 50

P roduction arrangements for Tenny's speech to the world were nearly complete. Difficult arrangements, with Russia, China, and many other countries that much preferred that she not speak directly to their constituents. What would she say? How would she say it? Other leaders respected her oratorical powers and feared the result.

But Tenny had persisted. In private conversations, she had made her top-line arguments: The financial benefits of total arms control. The dangers posed by nonstate forces with growing arsenals of advanced deadly weapons. The scientific developments that few political leaders understood, but whose risks to their countries, their reigns, even their own lives, was increasingly apparent. The existential need to invest trillions to keep the planet habitable and using money diverted from their war chests to pay for it. Her logic was inescapable, and the proposals she made to accomplish disarmament were generous. A more peaceful and predictable world was an attractive prospect to all countries, large and small, friendly and hostile, democratic and autocratic. *So why not,* other country leaders decided. *Let her try.*

As long as she had breath in her body, Tenny was determined to deliver that speech. That breath had returned to what for Tenny now was normal. Her bout with mortality signaled to her that she might not have much more time to speak, to plan, to persuade, to serve. She was not going to postpone the speech or alter the plan's deadlines. The drama of her collapse and the uncertainty of whether she would recover would drive world interest in this speech to a larger audience than she earlier had hoped. Curiosity alone would boost ratings. She could not allow that opportunity to pass.

Months earlier, Ben and Lee assembled a speech writing team to build Tenny's presentation. Public and private archives were searched for information that would provide solid pillars for her arguments. State Department consultants were enlisted to vet words and images for their universal appeal. Experienced editors combed drafts for conciseness and accuracy. Artistic consultants were hired to transform the Oval Office as a powerful one-day TV stage, with visual props and symbols to reinforce her words. Tenny was a dynamic speaker, but the format would require an intimacy, a worldwide appeal felt personally by everyone who watched.

Congress was in its annual August recess. Members were home, her allies working to explain Tenny's agenda. She travelled to states and districts where more local support was needed to help promote the cause. On each return to Washington she would rehearse the latest version of the speech. Each line was vetted for accuracy, political impact, whether it would open her to political attack. The final draft would be placed on a Teleprompter. But she already had rehearsed so many times that the words were etched in her memory. Every move she was to make during her delivery was as familiar to her now as it would be if she was a cast member of a long-running Broadway play.

For Tenny, just two months beyond a serious bout of lung failure, the schedule was far more demanding than her doctors warned was advisable. Medically, they were correct. Emotionally, they were not. The month of August was one of the most exhilarating of Tenny's life. She was drawing strength from crowds who came to see and hear her. As she rehearsed she recalled those who pressed against the rope lines at her public rallies. She heard their voices, many called out to her, some whispered as they hugged her and encouraged her. And she could see the faces of the children, many in their parents' arms, others just barely tall enough to see over the ropes. She could see those faces with every line on the teleprompter. And the signs, so many signs. Yes, her advance team had done well to have many signs produced and distributed in advance. But so many were not. They clearly were the spontaneous products of people in garages and basements and school yards. As she rehearsed, she saw those signs, and the people holding them, so excited. People longed for this, the security of this, the future that could be so much more hopeful if Tenny succeeded.

Mission. This was her mission. Not a casual use of that word, but a reason for being. She was a messenger for peace on Earth. She would give her long-planned speech to the world, but if there was no Teleprompter, in fact if there was no written speech at all, she could speak to the world about her plan for permanent, enduring peace in a way everyone would understand. Because the people had spoken to her and the words she would deliver would be theirs'.

On the second day of September, the entire team conducted its final rehearsal. Tenny walked through her part and delivered her lines. Camera positions were fixed at optimum angles. The director's cue sheet was prepared. A few words were changed, a sentence here and there deleted. Technicians checked all the worldwide local delivery preparations.

"We're ready, Madam President," said Ben. "Are you?"

SEPTEMBER

CHAPTER 51

"Hello. My name is Isabel Aragon Tennyson. The people of the United States of America have elected me as their president. I speak to you for them and for our nation."

The camera pulled back from a head-and-shoulders shot of Tenny to a medium view that revealed her standing in the Oval Office. She wore a dark blue blazer over a white blouse adorned with a pearl necklace and matching pearl earrings.

"It is traditional for United States presidents to speak to the American people on television. It is most unusual for a United States president to use this office, where I work, to speak to all the peoples of the world. I know of no other occasion where it has been done."

Tenny walked to the window facing the Ellipse. The perspective shifted to outside, revealing the Rose Garden and red roses in full bloom against a blue sky and wispy clouds.

"Outside these windows is what we call our Mall, acres of space that are home to monuments recalling America's past: a monument to George Washington, our first president. Beyond it is a memorial to Thomas Jefferson, who wrote our Declaration of Independence. At one end of the Mall is our monument to Abraham Lincoln, who strove to keep America united during a terrible civil war; and to Franklin Roosevelt, who saved our country during the great economic depression of the last century; and to

Martin Luther King Jr., who did so much to advance the cause of racial justice. These are a few of America's most revered heroes. At the other end of the Mall is the United States Capitol. We Americans call our Capitol the People's House. It's where our elected Congress makes decisions for all Americans. Because of our country's economic and military strength, those decisions often affect the world and affect you personally. Just across the Potomac River is the Pentagon, the headquarters of America's worldwide military operations, and Arlington National Cemetery, where four hundred thousand veterans of America's military are buried."

As she described each monument, film footage, artfully shot and edited just for this occasion, slowly panned and dissolved from one monument to another. Then the scene dissolved back to Tenny, who had turned away from the window to face the camera.

"It's those four hundred thousand military veterans I want to talk with you about today. Those four hundred thousand, and hundreds of thousands more in veterans' cemeteries in the United States and graves in seventeen countries beyond our own borders where we asked them to serve. And I want to talk about millions more. Your people. Your countrymen who died in your service."

Tenny walked slowly to the office's sofa, sat down, and lifted a tabletop book. The camera zoomed in on the title, *The Book of War*. She looked up from the book directly into the camera.

"No matter on which side of battle your flag flies, war comes with a terrible cost of lives lost, communities destroyed, countless survivors who live the remainder of their lives with wounds, disabilities, and memories of war's horrors."

The camera moved in more tightly on her.

"As terrible as wars have been in the past, they pale against what any future war might bring. It is not an exaggeration to say that we would be facing the possible end of civilization as we know it."

Tenny reached to the floor in front of her and showed a leather valise to the camera.

"This valise is what we call the 'nuclear football.' It's anything but a game. As president of the United States, I can open this at any time. It contains codes that on my order would launch any number of nuclear weapons. Our secretary of defense must verify that the order came from me. Otherwise, he has no authority to reverse my decision. Nor do any American military commanders. Those nuclear armed missiles are in silos buried in American soil, on American submarines now active in most of the world's oceans, and aboard long-range military aircraft positioned strategically in Europe, Asia, and the Middle East. The weapons they carry, if ever used, would create the greatest holocaust humanity has ever known. Possibly one from which humanity as we know it would never recover.

"Nuclear missiles launched from the submarines alone could end life on Earth. Each submarine carries twenty-four missiles. Each missile is armed with eight hydrogen bombs with thirty times the power of the bomb dropped on Hiroshima, Japan, during World War II. The United States has eighteen of these submarines."

Tenny placed the valise back on the floor and picked up another book.

"The reality of today's world is that I am authorized to destroy civilization. And I am not alone with that power. Russia's nuclear arsenal is as large as ours. China, Great Britain, France, India, Pakistan, Israel, North Korea all have nuclear arsenals. All have leaders with authority to use them. Like the United States, all have systems for maintaining them, upgrading them, protecting them. All those functions require people who follow orders, never disobey them, systems that must never critically break down, accidents that must never occur. And all these weapons must be protected from falling into the hands of those with malign intentions."

The displays on millions of TVs shifted to historic footage of the Cuban missile crisis, with Tenny narrating over it.

"In a well-known 1962 incident, a Russian submarine commander who had lost contact with Moscow mistakenly believed war had begun between the United States and the Soviet Union and ordered the use of nuclear torpedo against the American fleet. Fortunately, the fleet commander refused permission to launch. We came that close to a worldwide nuclear war."

File footage of Khrushchev at the UN in 1962 was shown.

"US nuclear forces once went on high alert when our radar equipment in Greenland mistook a moonrise over Norway as a large-scale Soviet Union missile launch. Premier Khrushchev was in New York at the time, which raised doubts as to whether an attack was under way. Otherwise, those who controlled US nuclear weapons very well might have mistakenly launched them."

Khrushchev's image dissolved into a B-52 in flight.

"In another incident, one of our nuclear-bomb-carrying aircraft broke up during a flight over the US East Coast, and one of the bombs came very close to detonating. A calamity was averted only because of a single faulty switch."

The camera returned to Tenny, at her seat on the sofa.

"We've had false alarms because of temporary lost communications, solar flares, untimely power outages, computer errors, faulty sensor readings, and misinterpretation of military exercises. It is nothing less than a miracle that during the nuclear era, with its tens of thousands of nuclear-carrying weapons, a holocaust has been avoided."

Tenny rose from the sofa and walked the few steps to her desk. Still standing, she picked up a folder, opened it, and looked at the camera.

"Each morning I receive briefings like this one from my government's intelligence agencies. They inform me about military matters, weapons developments, political and natural events that could pose dangers to our country and the world. Through these briefings I am aware of plans to build and deploy what are called self-launching weapons. Yes, you heard that right. Weapons that decide, without me or my approval, when and what to destroy. Software is trained to distinguish, for instance, military tanks from school buses. The United States has already developed armed ships that can go to sea almost indefinitely, military aircraft and ground equipment that need no crews. Once these weapons are activated, they can select and engage targets without intervention by any human being. And the United States is not the only country in the world developing this type of arsenal."

The screen shifted to images of high-speed computers, Wall Street, and other scenes evocative of stock trading.

"For many years, stock traders on our Wall Street have used computers that are programmed to buy and sell stock in milliseconds, on their own, without any human intervention. Some of the finest minds and most skilled operators in the digital world created these systems and manage them daily. They run almost to perfection. Almost, but not one hundred percent."

The screen presented headlines of huge, unexpected stock price drops and other major events triggered by computer error.

"Mistakes happen. Programming mistakes. Market changes that were not anticipated. Odd events the programs had not been designed to respond to. And when they happen, some people may lose a lot of money or make a lot of money. The errors are caught and fixed. If they were to happen, and they surely would happen with self-launching weapons, how do we correct the destruction? How do we prevent escalation, one error leading to a more devastating one?

"This is not science fiction. It is reality. These weapons exist today. The United States has them. So do Russia and China."

The screen showed computer simulation of satellites being attacked and destroyed.

"We all also have weapons that can destroy satellites and have had that capability for many years. So far, there's been no arms race in space. But think of the situation today. Thousands of satellites are circling the planet in low and high Earth orbits. Imagine what would happen if nations of the world began purposely knocking each other's satellites from the sky. Communications would be lost; navigation services for cars, airplanes, and ships would disappear; a deadly rain of debris, much of it radioactive, would fall on us from the sky."

Tenny put down her folder and returned to the sofa.

"There was a time, centuries ago, when leaders of nations would be expected to ride onto the field of battle to share the risk of death and defeat with their armies. There was a time when wars were fought on battlefields only among those armed for combat. Now, all Earth is a battlefield, and every living man, woman and child and all God's creatures are at risk. Not just of invading armies, but of death and destruction from the skies, from weapons I and others could launch at the push of a button. Worse, that a robot could launch under some circumstances or someone with deadly intent could commandeer digitally and launch or a technical mistake could launch or an unintentional accident could launch. And millions of us, tens of millions of us, hundreds of millions of us, could die. War is no longer war. It's suicidal madness. And that's how we must think of it."

Tenny sat on the sofa. There were ten seconds of silence, dead air, while the camera tightened on her and showed the emotion of the last statement run across her face.

"And it's not the only madness. We are destroying the harmony of our planet. The ability to live above ground because of extreme heat, fires, storms, rising seas. Or to have sufficient drinking water. Or to maintain the soil or the food of the sea. All of this is predictably leading to deadly competition among us for the very essentials of life. We have inherited the only place in the entire universe we know about where we can live and sustain ourselves, and through changing climate and our failure to treasure the Eden that is ours, we are creating conditions where that may no longer be possible for our children."

She lifted an official-looking document from the coffee table to show it to viewers.

"For many months, I have been discussing these facts and truths with leaders of other nations. And offering this proposal."

The camera cut to graphics with the heading of the proposal being discussed.

"Nuclear disarmament. First, we must all agree to disarm our nations of nuclear weapons. All nuclear weapons. That we stop research, production, and deployment, whether the weapons are designed for use from land, sea, air, or space, and that we all destroy the arsenals currently in existence and shut down the facilities for making more. And that we create a system for verifiable inspection for assurance that we have all complied. And, further, we create a system for detecting attempts to build or deploy nuclear weapons by any non-nation-state, and then if we do detect such violations, we agree to jointly act to engage and disarm that offender.

"Total disarmament. Next, we all agree to stand down all military operations except those necessary to maintain order in our own countries and assist in disasters. No standing armies trained for combat. No militarized ships at sea. No aircraft equipped for war. No weapons in space. No uniformed military or military bases outside our own borders except by request of host countries for protection or humanitarian reasons. And a total moratorium on manufacture of military weapons. Again, supported by inspection and enforcement agreements. This would limit opportunities for terrorists to arm themselves and engage in violent acts. It also would limit opportunities for so-called minor wars or terrorist attacks because there would be fewer weapons in circulation.

"Human security initiative. The nations of the world now spend ten trillion dollars each year to maintain their military forces and to buy and deploy weapon systems. The priority for diverting that money would be to address other threats to human security: hunger, health, housing, education, economic opportunity. The nations of the world would contribute to a common pool of money, manpower, technical and academic resources to ensure that everyone on the planet would have access to food, health care, a livable home, and educational opportunity. The tens of millions of people worldwide now engaged in the arms industry and who serve their countries in military services would be offered opportunities to migrate to jobs that build the newly peaceful and prosperous world, not threaten it.

"Planetary health initiative. Ending worldwide militarization also would provide the resources needed to restore our planet to maximum habitability. As quickly as possible, we will end all use of fossil fuels, ban toxic substances from the oceans, and make a massive worldwide effort to restore rainforests and despoiled soil.

"Other potential megathreats. Scientific advances offer unlimited possibilities for health care and benefits for all human activity. They also pose potential threats that must be recognized and controlled. No one nation can do this alone. For example, the internet has changed life for most of us, and mostly for the better. But it also has been the instrument of social disruption that has directly resulted in countless deaths, religious conflicts, and divisions among us based on lies, deceit, and evil intent. The internet is a creation of my country, but your country likely has borne adverse consequences from it. With advances in artificial intelligence and quantum computing, these threats will only grow. We can no longer look on these developments as private commercial matters. Similarly, in recent years we have learned the basic code of life itself. Scientists now can edit our genetic makeup to heal, yes, and to do much more. We must learn to cope with and control the developments of science and technology that most of us don't even understand. This is not a problem for a single nation, and it will take international cooperation to define it, explain it, and regulate it for service to humanity, not a threat to us all."

The camera returned to Tenny.

"This is my proposal to the leaders of the world: Nuclear disarmament to end the threat of unspeakable, planet-destroying conflict; total military disarmament to put an end to increasingly deadly and inhumane warfare; a human security initiative to use money saved from war and weapons to provide health, housing, education, and job security for everyone on Earth; a planetary health initiative to preserve the livability of our Earth; and a joint initiative to control scientific advances that pose great threats as well as promise."

She stood and walked to her desk. Still standing, she addressed the viewer again.

"As I said earlier, in recent months I have spoken with leaders in Russia, China, India, Japan, the European nations, Canada, Mexico, and dozens of others. Like me, they find appalling the possibility of armed conflict among us where millions, tens of millions, perhaps hundreds of millions of us die. Like me, they would rather use our resources for life, not death. And so they have listened to what I have to say. And each has honored my request to create working groups in their own countries to consider the program I've just outlined for you. Could it happen? Well, it gets much less attention, but most of our countries already work together within treaties and agreements on many things that are controversial.

"The United States, Russia, the Scandinavian nations, and others work together on common issues regarding the Arctic. We have similar agreements among nations governing the Antarctic. We have nation groups and treaties that manage the law of the sea, the control of poison gas in war, satellite cooperation, the international trade of goods and services, crime, and extradition of criminals. Much good, cooperative work goes on daily to extend health and education opportunities. Why not agreements on the most essential issue of all, preventing a holocaust that could destroy human civilization?

"This would not happen tomorrow or next week. I believe it would take ten years to transition to the world outlined in my proposal. Each stage, if faithfully carried out, would set the stage for the next. And so, yes, it could happen. It is practical. In fact, it is necessary and urgent."

The camera moved in more tightly on her.

"This is my Peace and Security for All, and for All Time proposal. The next step is up to you. Beginning now, a worldwide petition will be available to you. You can sign it online or with an email or mobile device or by verified telephone call or by post. It will be available in two hundred languages, so everyone in the world, no matter who you are or where you are, can read it."

The screen cut to instructions on how to sign.

"Let the leaders of your nation know that this is what you want. Not nuclear devastation. Not war of any kind. Vote for peace. Vote for security. Vote for a better life for yourself, your family, and for generations to come."

The camera returned to Tenny, seated behind her desk, pen in hand.

For the next sixty seconds the screen showed how to sign, interspersed with images from earlier in the production and ten-second cameos of artful, moving slides that say "End Wars," "Peace and Security," and "For All" while a male narrator described how to sign up.

With the broadcast ended, the cameras' red lights blinked off.

CHAPTER 52

Anticipating Tenny's speech, the powerful industry that since World War II had built the airplanes, ships, missiles, heavy and small arms, electronics, satellites, and components of warfare's infrastructure was ready with its response.

Retired generals and admirals immediately appeared on newscasts, podcasts, and talk shows to characterize the president's speech as aspirational, but impractical and dangerous: "It's what we all want, of course, but not possible in a world as conflicted as it is today." Editorialists and newspaper columnists, nearly in lockstep, criticized Tenny for failure to do her necessary homework on issues beyond her understanding. Letters to the editor, phone calls, social media posts, and all other forms of communication questioned whether her recent illness had affected her judgment or whether peacenik doctors had administered drugs that now controlled her mind. There was more than a whiff of sexism undergirding the opposition. You would never hear a male president making such proposals. In major media markets, crowds formed, carrying signs that read, "Save Our Jobs," "No Disarmament," "Impeach the Traitor," "She's Wrong, Stay Strong!" Tenny's Mexican heritage also provided fodder for the organized anti-immigrant movement. A flood of phone calls and emails swamped Congress, many of them from governors, mayors, and state officials urging their representatives and senators to speak up immediately against the president's agenda and save the economies of their defense-work-dependent communities.

It was an impressive show of popular opposition organized by an industry experienced in leveraging its economic importance to win ever more billions for defense budgets.

Ben and Lee anticipated this deluge of opposition and had a morning-after plan in place as well. Peace being far more popular than war, it was easier to generate street demonstrations that supported Tenny's initiatives than opposed them. The numbers and depth and emotion of the supportive crowds dwarfed the opposition's, and the comparison was itself a major win in the battle for public approval. The ready-to-go letters and phone calls and emails generated by the pro-agenda campaign easily matched the industry's, with a crushing additional advantage. Ben approached this day as he would an election day. In elections, Ben's clients always had an army of volunteers organized to call presumed supporters, urging them to vote. He adapted that strategy for this day. A bank of tens of thousands of volunteers, organized over the past six months, made calls to friends, acquaintances, relatives, and coworkers, asking them to support Tenny's plan. Triggered by Tenny's speech, they built a contact tree of millions and activated those contacts to demonstrate their approval. Backing up the "ground game," and unmatched by the opposition, was a massive advertising campaign made possible by Tenny's unlimited campaign budget.

Ben and Lee were determined to "win the day," in this case meaning the narrative that would drive media coverage. Their story: an amazing universal demand erupting for disarmament. The opposition's: a physically wounded president proposed an unrealistic, dangerous, job-killing plan.

What neither side fully appreciated was how deep a vein Tenny's argument touched. Her speech was a magnet, surfacing desires universally held but mostly suppressed until now. In the days that followed, pro-disarmament street demonstrations continued, many in cities and towns where Ben's teams didn't need to generate them. And they kept growing. And the emails and phone calls and expressions of support kept coming. And editorialists and columnists and other opinion influencers who initially were skeptical or expressed outright hostility had to take notice. This campaign now had unmistakable momentum. It had to be taken seriously.

CHAPTER 53

What began as dismissive commentary now focused on implementation. How long would it take? Was ten years enough? How would it be enforced? How could two million defense-related jobs really be converted to peaceful industries? Difficult questions. From the intensity of public support, however, there could be no doubt that people the world over wanted their leaders to find the answers and act on them.

Since one country does not make a treaty, the level of support by the Americans needed to be matched by the populations of dozens of other countries. Achieving that, persuading one billion people worldwide to add their names to a petition demanding that their governments support the Peace and Security for All agenda was the goal of the telethon. What could be more dramatic than a billion names collected in twelve hours of airtime?

High-pressure situations and Ben Sage were not strangers to one another. A line in Rudyard Kipling's classic poem, "If," begins, "If you can keep your head when all about you / are losing theirs and blaming it on you." Ben lived that line multiple times in each campaign he managed, but no previous experience could prepare him for today.

On a Hollywood studio's sound stage the size and shape of an aircraft hangar, Ben sat before a bank of video screens displaying televised images fed from thirty-four separate sites located on every continent, including

Antarctica, and from NASA's orbiting space station. Another feed, by some form of technical magic, was a live image from a submersible a mile deep in the Pacific's Mariana Trench.

On a separate panel were dozens of screens with streaming internet images cued to private homes, workplaces, and urban and rural sites. A third bank of monitors was poised to insert prerecorded video at specific times during the live program. A fourth board of images was dedicated to those managing live video from drones, aircraft, and satellites.

Four banks of control stations, four sets of directors, editors, camera operators, and switchboard stations, all under one central command center. That was the plan for "Speaking for the Earth," the worldwide telethon. It would happen live with no opportunity for retakes. If things went haywire, the whole world would be there to witness it.

Ben had no operational assignments now that the program was about to go live. Instead, those jobs were assigned to some of the world's most experienced media directors, who would call camera shots according to the script and make judgments to go off script when visual and emotional opportunities presented themselves. Ben's role was to sit near them and sweat.

Ben and Lee had conceptualized the event, but it was a far more massive undertaking than they could produce on their own. State Department officials had been called on to negotiate participation agreements by Russia, China, and other key countries. Artists, cinematographers, and producers had been identified, hired, and deployed. An advance team had recruited on-air personalities and celebrities from the worlds of entertainment, sports, politics, and the military. Anthropologists and linguists had been hired to modify program designs for dozens of distinct language and cultural groupings. An intricate programming schedule had been developed, with some segments being broadcast worldwide, some in just their own geographic regions and countries, and others in what the creative team termed local broadcasting and video streaming "pods." All of this required coordination with those handling broadcasts in each of the world's time zones.

A telethon is generally organized as a marathon fundraising event, but Tenny and many of her wealthy friends had underwritten all the costs of Speaking for the Earth. Rather than raising money, the single-minded focus would be the recording of one billion individual names on a petition supporting Tenny's agenda.

For months, Ben and Lee had done little more than oversee creation of this media juggernaut, fielding problems as they cropped up, adjusting and making personnel changes as needed. Their staff topped out at twelve hundred. Lee had moved to London to handle European operations.

Now it was out of their hands. All they could do, through bloodshot eyes and fatigued bodies, was observe, knowing that the success or failure of Tenny's plan likely depended on the next twelve hours of worldwide communications.

Media control rooms are kept cool in deference to the needs of sensitive broadcast equipment. Despite that, as the go-clock counted down from ten, Ben was surprised to notice that the back of his shirt and his armpits were as wet as if they had just come through the rinse cycle.

CHAPTER 54

The screen came alive with a full-length image of a young Asian man working in a rice paddy. The man looked up, directly into the camera lens, as if pleasantly surprised to see a friend.

As the camera pulled back to reveal the full scene, the man gestured to the paddy with open arms. The image squeezed down to a small, oval portrait frame that came to rest in the lower right-hand corner of the picture. Delicately overlapping it, another image, a Caucasian woman playing a violin, a few bars of Mozart's Violin Concerto no. 3, slowly zoomed to full screen. She stopped playing and looked directly at the camera and smiled.

She resumed playing as her image slowly zoomed down into an oval portrait next to the live image of the first man still working his rice paddy.

A third image appeared, a young African girl, about eight years old. She was at a school, in class. She looked up from her desk to the camera and smiled.

The pattern continued. An American in a hospital room with his wife and newborn child. A merchant sailor at sea, a laborer welding a bridge beam, people making things, working fields, others at computer keyboards, driving trucks, managing retail counters. The pace grew faster, accompanied by an original musical score that evoked happiness, promise. The screen filled with individual images, each shrinking in size as more were added. The volume of background music increased gradually with the pace of the onscreen scenes. Upbeat music. Festive music.

The screen's images began to sway in synchronization with the music; then the images transformed into a circle. The circle became the iconic photo of the blue Earth familiar since astronauts began to capture it from the earliest space capsules. Suddenly the audience realized that it was not a photo of Earth they were seeing, but a live image from the International Space Station.

"It's our home," said a narrator. "The only home we know. The only home there is. Earth. Beautiful Earth. Bountiful Earth. Provider of food and shelter. Beauty to enrich our lives and souls. All good things we know. Life itself. Earth."

The narrator's voice was familiar. Most viewers would recognize the voice as belonging to Kellen Monroe, one of the world's best-known actors, international star of dozens of movies and the most popular current streaming series, "Unto This Earth."

The image of the planet dissolved to reveal a man wearing the suit of an astronaut, helmet off. He was inside the space station; later, audiences would admit they were surprised to see that it was Kellen Monroe—not just narrating but actually aboard the ISS.

"For the next twelve hours," said Monroe, facing the camera, "the time it will take this space station to orbit the Earth nearly eight times, we will pay tribute to Earth. More. We will be on a mission to preserve it as the home we know. The home that must survive if we, you and I, and all we love and cherish are to survive. It's a mission for all of us. The greatest mission mankind has ever been asked to undertake. And you and I are on it together."

The camera switched to a preproduced graphic presentation, filled with moving images and creative art that evolved into words as Kellen Monroe narrated them. It was all reinforced by a musical score written to synchronize with the pictures and narration: "An end to major wars," "Income security for all," "Housing security for all," "Food security for all," "Economic opportunity for all," "A sustainable climate for the Earth," "Sustainable energy for life on Earth."

As the musical score and visual graphics built to a crescendo, Kellen Monroe's image integrated into the picture.

"Is this just a fantasy? A dream? Until the last few years of human history, the idea of me speaking to you from space, this very broadcast, would have been considered fantasy. Dreams can come true if we make them come true. If a billion of us, from all the world's nations, the world's religions, the amazing cultures that inhabit the Earth, sign the Peace and Security for All, and for All Time petition, the dream of ending wars and building a secure peace can come true. That's our goal. A billion of us strong, voting with our names, making our wishes known. So please, for yourself, your families, for all of us, during the next twelve hours, sign the petition. One person at a time until we become a billion-person march for Peace and Security. For All! Here's how."

The programming then switched to each of the thirty-four separate broadcast sites and the multitude of internet streaming locations worldwide that were connected to the telethon, where local personalities described instructions for signing the petition.

Over the next twelve hours, these channels would feature entertainment by some of the world's best-known celebrities, musicians, actors, athletes, popular figures from politics and the arts, localized for each audience. The programs would conduct e-sport video competitions, drawings with valuable prizes, opportunities for those who were watching to become part of the programming itself.

Every fifteen minutes a name would be drawn in each broadcast and streaming region for locally targeted prizes: dinners and lunches with celebrities, time and activities with their favorite athletes, acting roles written for them in upcoming movies and streaming drama series. Two grand prize winners in each region would win trips into low-orbit space on the new, privately operated space liners.

For every moment of those twelve hours, except for bathroom breaks, Ben sat with the core directing team at telethon central command in Hollywood, occasionally commenting or making suggestions. There was no time for idle conversation. Directors' calls were moving quickly: "Zoom camera one! Pull back camera twelve! Wider! Wider! Cue the talent in Sri Lanka. Five, four, three, two, one, take it! Roll graphic forty-five! Hold on that shot of the kids at the pyramids. Hold. Hold. I know, but it's a great shot. We'll make up the time later!"

The production moved so quickly and intricately that three directing crews were needed, working alternating one-hour shifts. Any longer was much too stressful, even for experienced sports action directors.

While Ben watched the program unfold largely as planned, he knew that what was on his screen was only one version being fed to six world regions. Lee was monitoring others out of London. Members of their staff were assigned to control centers in Tokyo, Cairo, Prague, and Mumbai. All of them were connected by a separate communications system and describing events to one another through their own private audio network.

The only constant for Ben was a small square in the bottom left corner of the monitor in front of him. It was the only constant being shown worldwide: a running tally of how many had signed the petition. Those numbers were being collected and updated through ten interconnected data centers.

The totals moved slowly at first. In the hundreds of thousands. Then the millions. Tens of millions. When one hundred million appeared on the screen, everyone in the directing room and in Ben and Lee's communications loop cheered. But the program was three hours old by then, and the pace was far too slow to reach a billion.

When programing reached the halfway mark and only three hundred million names had been recorded, the directing team advised all on-air live personalities to dig in harder, push for names harder, scrub some entertainment segments, and focus on name generation. If the numbers fell short, would it be impressive enough to win converts in world capitals where it mattered? Ben mentally was preparing contingency arguments. How to spin it? Should the program be extended an hour? Two?

553,240,961

705,432,006

825,116,112

At eleven hours and forty-five minutes, the petition project was still short of its target by 150 million names.

Fifteen minutes to go. And now the final scene. Fish had lobbied hard for this. Ben finally saw the value of her argument and made it the last segment, the segment they needed to generate one last rush of names.

On cue, all screens lit up with a brilliant bouquet of flags from the US, Russia, Canada, and the Nordic countries.

"Welcome to Fairbanks, Alaska," said an offscreen woman's voice. "Welcome to the Arctic. We are nations of the polar north: Canada, the Kingdom of Denmark, Finland, Iceland, Norway, the Russian Federation, Sweden, and the United States. We are the Arctic Council." As each nation was mentioned, its flag unfurled prominently on the screen before giving way to another montage of flags. "And all these nations also participate: France, Germany, Italy, Japan, the Netherlands, the People's Republic of China, Poland, India, the Republic of Korea, Singapore, Spain, Switzerland, and the United Kingdom."

Out of the graphic swirl of national flags, Fish walked onto a stage followed by dozens of others. It was her voice the audience had been hearing. She gestured to all those around her.

"These are not just names and flags; they're people. People who have been working in harmony for decades on ways to make life better, safer, protecting the land and its resources. We're not all alike. We have our differences. But our common interests are so much greater. Take a look."

For the next five minutes, the screen filled with a fast-moving montage of Indigenous peoples from the polar regions giving testimonials about how the Arctic waters were being protected, health was being improved, resources were being developed sustainably, rights were being guarded. Then Fish reappeared, live and speaking directly to the camera.

"For those who question whether the nations and peoples of the world can work together in peace and security for the good of all, this is our answer. We've done it. We continue to do it. Except for dealing with military issues, there is no part of life we in the Arctic are not addressing together. There's no reason we cannot include those military issues too. With me are those who represent most of the world's largest nations, smallest nations, and Indigenous peoples who have made the Arctic home for thousands of years. We're all here with the approval of our governments. We are working to build a more secure, more peaceful world. Let's make what's happening in Arctic happen everywhere. We are the world."

And then the entire group on stage began to sing "We Are The World" while cameras zoomed into their faces. Hordes of children joined them, and the screen all swirled into a closing montage encouraging viewers to sign the petition.

The tally increase moved into overdrive:

902,476,209

924,380,124

962,100,014

1,138,327,007

Ben watched the numbers climb, felt the passion and drama of what had unfolded in Fairbanks, and fell back, exhausted against his seat. All he could think of, and say over and over, softly to himself, was "Well, I'll be damned."

CHAPTER 55

Two hundred million more people signed the petition after the telethon concluded. They came from every region, every country in the world, even those with limited broadcast or internet connections, places where no effort had been made to reach them with the telethon. It was a stunning result. Newscasts worldwide would continue to rebroadcast highlights and engage in commentary for days after the telethon ended. Internet streaming services added segments of the telethon to their free offerings.

Immediately after the last segment, Ben raced for Los Angeles International Airport and a waiting government aircraft for an overnight flight to Washington. Lee did likewise from London. These were precious hours. The team had to meet quickly to develop plans for maintaining momentum, particularly directed toward congressional action.

Before the next day ended, they gathered at the White House, their euphoria barely contained. Staff members who had remained in Washington strung banners and balloons reminiscent of an election night victory. Cases of champagne lined the floor of Ben's office.

Within minutes of Ben and Lee's arrival, Tenny came to the office to join the party. She had watched most of the US version of the telethon from the private residence, her level of excitement for it growing as the onscreen petition numbers moved relentlessly toward the billion-name goal.

Tenny had had no visible role in the telethon. Her presence would have Americanized the program and made it more difficult for leaders of other countries to offer the agenda as their own. Her speech a week earlier had done its job. Another appearance this soon would have risked overexposure. The starring role, if there was to be one, would go to Fish.

Tenny welcomed Fish's new stardom. If the Peace and Security agenda was to survive elective politics, Fish had to succeed her as president long enough to implement all the provisions and prevent backsliding. The program needed time to get past inevitable organizational problems and embed itself so deeply in popular support that it could survive no matter who followed as the nation's leaders.

It was a happy and gracious Tenny who spoke briefly to those at the victory party.

"I've never been as proud of anything we've done," she said. "We set impossible goals, but honestly, after the success of the speech and the telethon, all those names signing up, unbelievable feedback I've been getting from all over the world, we might just pull this off."

She hugged Ben and Lee and others in the room. Then she picked up a file folder and waved it.

"My notes," she said. "My ideas from watching the show and reactions that have been coming here since. Now, let's all get to work on the final push. Next stop, Congress approves it!"

Ben and his team took their bows, downed a few glasses of champagne, and turned to leveraging their petition success. The phone banks were reactivated to flood members of Congress with calls, emails, and texts from constituents. The media team pitched and placed waves of locally targeted stories about those citizens who won telethon prizes. They provided photos and biographies on those who had appeared live on the telethon. During the twelve hours of the telethon, some members of the team had been assigned to find nuggets for feature stories: heartwarming coincidences, glitches that occurred but turned out well, tables that showed percentages and numbers of petition signers from various nations, comments from world leaders and other notables. The team was now covering its own story as a major newspaper or TV network might, all of it adding to the growing belief that passage of the Peace and Security agenda was inevitable.

Two hours into the post-telethon campaign, Deacon appeared at the door of the media room and motioned for Ben to step into the hall. In all the years they had worked together, Deacon had been the steady hand, unfazed by any development, positive or negative. This Deacon was clearly shaken and upset.

"What's wrong?" asked Ben. "Is Tenny sick?"

"Not Tenny," said Deacon. "Fish. This morning, she and some members of the Arctic Council left Fairbanks on a flight to inspect the Arctic Wildlife Refuge. Their plane's fallen off the radar. It's missing."

CHAPTER 56

The plane, a de Havilland DHC-6 Twin Otter, took off from Fairbanks International Airport at 11:14 p.m. Alaska Daylight Time. The takeoff was routine and tracked by the FAA's Air Route Traffic Control Center on a northerly heading. The pilots filed a flight plan that had the plane turning west after a visual inspection of the Arctic Wildlife Refuge, then an overfly of the Gates of the Arctic National Park before returning to Fairbanks. The estimated time of the flight would be three hours.

Midway into the flight the pilot radioed that he was returning to Fairbanks. No explanation for the change of plans was given. The pilot did not signal a problem or emergency of any kind before the FAA lost contact.

The Twin Otter was a charter from New Alaska, a Fairbanks private air taxi company with an otherwise spotless safety record. The plane's pilot was the company's owner, Hank Leidimeier, a former commercial airline pilot and a veteran of nearly ten thousand hours of Alaska bush flight. His copilot was Carol Vincent, also an experienced Alaska pilot who had never been involved in an air accident despite many difficult trips through the state's often harsh weather and wide range of problematically small landing strips.

Since Twin Otters have a low cruising speed and up to a six-hour range, the plane was perfect for the type of trip the vice president had organized. There was a faint hope that the problem was in radio communications and the plane would still appear in Fairbanks or elsewhere. So far there had been no reports that it had landed or crashed. There had been no reported sightings by other aircraft in the area.

Fish's prominence in capping the telethon the day before made the search personal for hundreds of millions of people around the world. The members of the Arctic Council and local Indigenous figures who shared the stage with her had become minor stars. It now seemed certain that some of those people were also aboard the missing plane. Which ones? That was uncertain.

Secret Service agents assigned to Fish's traveling party had compiled a trip manifest before takeoff and checked security clearances for each traveler. The manifest included the council's representatives from Russia, Sweden, Denmark, and Norway and meeting observers from China, Korea, France, and the United Kingdom. Two Secret Service agents also were aboard, along with two council staff members, a charter company employee serving as flight attendant, and the two pilots. Sixteen passengers total. The plane had capacity for nineteen. It was not overloaded.

Upon hearing the news, Tenny called Secretary of Defense Garrett Baumgartner who in turn patched her into a three-way call with General Carter Edsell, commander of the Eielson Air Force Base near Fairbanks. Edsell said he had mobilized a team of helicopters, spotter planes, and a search and rescue ground crew including medics, experienced mountain climbers, and weapon carriers to guard against the grizzlies and other dangerous wildlife prevalent in the mountains. Alaska's Air National Guard had an experienced search and rescue team, which was mobilizing as well.

Baumgartner also arranged to retarget available military satellites to scan the Brooks Range using advanced infrared imaging that could spot objects on the ground as small as five inches wide.

"What else do we have that can help find them?" Tenny asked.

"This is really difficult terrain, Madam President," said Edsell. "I've been up there myself hiking and hunting. We're contacting all the local guides and air services in the region. Depending on where they're found, it may take local knowledge to get there. And we'd need it do it quickly. It's wild country: grizzly bears, wolf packs, wolverines."

"That's discouraging," said Tenny.

"We've got a lot of resources, Madam President," said Secretary Baumgartner. "We're using all of them."

Tenny ended the call and turned to Carmie and Ben, who had joined her in the Oval Office and listened to the conversation on speakerphone.

"What else is there to do but wait?" said Ben.

"Just one thing I can think of," said Tenny. She buzzed Deacon on the intercom. "Deac," she said, "go to Fairbanks right away and set up our own communications center. I want the most reliable information we can get. Only reliable information."

CHAPTER 57

At 11:00 p.m. Eastern Daylight Time, Tenny, Ben, Carmie, and Andres watched television and cable news channels in the private residence. There was an open phone line to the Situation Room, where staff members were monitoring developments. Other staff members fielded calls from members of Congress, governors, and friends. Tenny had spoken with members of Fish's Alaska family who reported that local pilots were moving their planes to Deadhorse, the airstrip servicing the Prudhoe Bay oil facilities about one hundred miles from the presumed crash site. Ground parties from nearby villages were also prepared to move quickly when a location was identified.

"No one will sleep here tonight," said Alicee Fishburne.

Shortly after the news broke, House Speaker Guy Rocker arrived at the White House. The U.S. Constitution designates the speaker of the House of Representatives next in the line of succession after the vice president. If Tenny died or became incapacitated and Fish was gone, Rocker would become president. At the first report that Fish's plane was missing, the Secret Service added security to Rocker's regular detail, protocol for such a situation.

"Whatever Congress can do," said Rocker. "Equipment. People. Money for support. Anything."

"You're very kind," said Tenny. She described the military and civilian resources already deployed.

"If it won't interfere," said Rocker, "I've already contacted a number of people representing the big airframe and communications manufacturers to see what they can mobilize."

"Whatever it takes," said Tenny. "Whatever it takes to find them. I've sent Deacon to Fairbanks to coordinate and to keep a direct line open to me. Work through him."

"Of course," said Rocker. "You know that Fish was my deputy leader for many years. I feel as close to her as I would any member of my family. I won't give up hope. And neither should you."

"God bless you, Guy."

Shortly after Rocker's visit, Defense Secretary Baumgartner called back.

"Not great news, Madam President. Dense fog rolled in across a wide area of the search terrain. There's no possibility of a visual sighting until it clears and no possibility to get light aircraft to land if we spot them from satellite observation."

"But the satellite search can continue?" asked Tenny.

"Yes, and it will," said Baumgartner. "If the plane's down, it's a small footprint in a huge area. It could take a while to spot it. We're working through the night here."

"I appreciate it," said Tenny. "I'm here too. I want a call any time there's news, no matter what time that is."

When the call ended, Andres, normally careful not to interject himself into anything involving Tenny's presidential business, spoke up.

"Tenny. There's nothing more you can do tonight. Even if they get a satellite reading, nothing will happen until the fog lifts. And when it does, that's when you'll be needed. Get a few hours' sleep. You need it."

"I can't leave here," Tenny insisted.

"It's your duty as president to stay strong now," Carmie insisted. "The country and world can't afford to see a sleep-deprived president at a time like this."

Tenny shook her head more in despair than in resistance. "I won't be able to sleep."

"I'll get you a mild sedative," said Andres.

"We'll wake you if there's any news," said Ben.

"News? That's such an inadequate word for Fish. Brilliant, wonderful, loving—that wonderful spirit. Oh, Fish!"

During her years working the sad streets of the poor in Los Angeles, serving California constituents in Congress, years in the White House as the nation's consoler-in-chief in times of tragedy, Tenny had learned to live with, and deal with, human loss. Now, for the first time, tragedy overwhelmed her. Her eyes welled with tears. She placed her forehead on Andres's shoulder and sobbed loudly, uncontrollably.

CHAPTER 58

Russia, China and the European Union offered coordination of their satellites to scan the area. The Nordic and Alpine nations dispatched climbers experienced in mountainous terrain. From Washington, Guy Rocker sent members of his staff to Fairbanks and mobilized Boeing, Lockheed, and other aviation giants to devote their resources to the effort. Tenny's chief of staff, Henry Deacon, commandeered a military flight, arrived in Fairbanks the next morning, and established communications with the National Security Council at the White House.

Not since 1972, when a twin-engine Cessna 310 carrying House Majority Leader Hale Boggs and Alaska Congressman Nick Begich disappeared in marginal flying weather, had such a massive search effort been assembled. Despite thirty-nine days of intense search in the mountains and waters of southcentral Alaska, no trace of the plane carrying Boggs, Begich, and two other passengers was ever found.

That history was very much on the minds of those leading the search for the plane carrying the vice president of the United States and other prominent international passengers.

Literally inch by inch, satellite observation was scanning the likely route taken by the missing de Havilland Twin Otter. Normally there would have been a definite flight plan to track, but this was an observational flight.

The flight could have ended up anywhere within the twenty-million-acre Arctic Wildlife Refuge or even the nearby eight-million-acre Gates of the Arctic National Park. The fact that the pilot radioed he was returning from the flight earlier than planned only added to the mystery.

With its slow cruising speed and short runway capability, the plane may have landed in a riverbed or flat plain. Both the pilot and copilot were skilled Alaska bush veterans. If there was a possibility of an emergency landing that spared lives, this crew would have known how to maximize their chances. But if they survived, why had there been no radio communications?

Neither the plane nor its passengers had carried cold weather gear, food, or weapons. Finding them quickly would be essential, particularly if there were serious injuries. Searchers simply needed to know where to look. Day two ended with no clues. Even if there had been, low-lying Brooks Range fog hung on stubbornly. Small planes, even helicopters, would not be able to carry searchers near the site when it was found, or if it was found.

CHAPTER 59

In the White House, the wait and the uncertainty cast a pall over every thought, word, and action. But the rest of the world did not go on pause waiting for an answer. Foreign and domestic issues, so important before the plane disappeared, still required a president's attention. Tenny did her best to function, even though she felt she was in a state of mental and physical paralysis. Fish was the one who would carry the torch for the Peace and Security agenda when Tenny herself was gone. If Fish was dead, what next? Who to turn to? The weight of personal loss made every waking moment a trial. The prospect of losing her entire Peace and Security agenda was crushing. Andres increased the dosage of her blood pressure medicine. She found herself reaching for the portable oxygen container more often, even if she didn't feel she needed it.

Congress remained in session and committees were still at work on the Peace and Security program, but deadlines and schedules were on hold. Ben's robust plan to build on the momentum of Tenny's speech and the telethon, the dispatch of surrogates, the advertising blitz, all now was in limbo. The momentum provided by the telethon was gone. The scene from Fairbanks with the Arctic Council, which days earlier had seemed like a brilliant public relations triumph, now took on the pall of a fatal mistake.

Ben and Carmie spent much of each day with Tenny. She obviously needed the company of those she considered family. Andres remained in the Oval Office, watching closely over her health. They were all there when the call came on the early afternoon of day three of the search.

"It looks like one of our satellites has spotted them," Defense Secretary Baumgartner told Tenny. "Can't be positive; we're trying to verify now. They picked up what looks like a plane on the ground in the Mount Chamberlin area of the Brooks Range."

"Can you tell the condition of the plane?" asked Tenny.

"Not yet," said Baumgartner. "But the fog's lifting and I think we can get a ground party in there soon."

Moments later CNN's screen lit up with a bulletin: "MISSING PLANE FOUND!"

Carla Bounty, hosting that hour of CNN's programming, followed quickly with the sketchy report.

"After nearly three days of search, the location of the missing plane carrying Vice President Fishburne and fifteen others has been spotted. We have special correspondent Farley Caragin standing by in Fairbanks. Farley, what do you have?"

"Yes, Carla. Searchers believe that satellite observation has located the missing Twin Otter aircraft in the Mount Chamberlain area of the Brooks Range. Crews are scrambling here in Fairbanks, and from the airfield at Deadhorse, where the oil companies have their Prudhoe Bay facilities. I understand that military search parties from the Alaska Air National Guard's search and rescue squad are on the way."

"What do we know about the terrain there? Where is Mount Chamberlain?" asked Bounty.

"It's about three hundred miles north of Fairbanks and about the same distance east of Utqiaġvik. The closest community is the oil operation at Deadhorse, about one hundred miles west. Mount Chamberlin is nine thousand feet tall, one of the highest in the Brooks Range. My information is that there's a small landing strip near a research station at Peters Lake, and that's where search teams are likely headed."

"Is it snowbound there?"

"Hard to tell this time of year. Most of the year, yes. I'm told it can get to fifty below in winter, so the snow stays high up the mountain most of the year. We don't know yet how high up the plane may be."

"Any word on the plane's condition?"

"No. And there's not likely to be until crews reach the site or a light plane or helicopter can fly low enough."

"Thank you, Farley. Again, the plane carrying Vice President Sheila Fishburne and members of the Arctic Council, missing for three days in Alaska's rugged Brooks Range, has been located. This is a fast-moving story, and we will return in a moment for full coverage."

Tenny, Carmie, Ben, and Andres stared at the screen. No one had seen the actual wreckage. No one could report yet with any authority whether there were survivors.

Tenny finally broke the silence. "The wait's over," she said.

"Don't give up hope," said Carmie. "Fish grew up in that country. She's resourceful."

"And so are we," said Tenny. On her intercom she buzzed her private secretary, Marcie Friend. "Marcie," she said, "have someone from our communications office come see me right away so we can prepare our statements. After that I want to see Sid Mohamad from the legal counsel's office. Ask Representative Rocker and Senator Keeler to standby for phone calls. And have Secretary Decker over at State arrange personal phone contacts from me with heads of state who had people aboard the flight."

She turned to Ben and Carmie. "We're going to have many busy hours. Please stay and help me," she said.

Tenny didn't need to hear more than what she had heard already. She knew.

CHAPTER 60

T he casket had been quickly assembled by Inupiat craftsmen from Brooks Range white ash. In a band around all four sides, Utqiaġvik artists carved images of whales, walrus, caribou, and eagles, symbolic of the culture in which Sheila Fishburne was born and raised and which she embraced throughout her life. A military aircraft carried the casket to Washington, DC, along with Fish's family and friends. More than one hundred thousand mourners passed through the Capitol rotunda during the twenty-four hours the casket containing Fish's body lay in state. Thousands more crowded the Capitol grounds to watch military pallbearers slowly walk the flag-draped casket down the Capitol's east front steps to the waiting hearse for the twenty-minute drive to the Washington National Cathedral.

Officially, the neo-Gothic cathedral is an Episcopal church, the seat of the church's presiding bishop, and the home of the Washington diocese. Unofficially, it is a nondenominational shrine where presidents and other prominent figures who have made extraordinary contributions to national life are memorialized and honored upon their deaths. The cathedral can seat four thousand. For Fish's service, every seat was occupied.

A week earlier, Fish had charmed the world with her passion and clarity of purpose, urging an international telethon audience to sign the Peace and Security petition. Now, she was again at the center of world attention, eulogized for her accomplishments and her humanity—a compelling spirit the world met and fell in love with yesterday, cruelly taken away today. It was a devastating confluence of events.

When it was her time to speak, Tenny felt frozen in place, physically unable to rise from her front row pew and walk the few steps to the altar, as if every moment of delay might avoid the finality of Fish's loss. She interlocked arms with the military escort who noticed her struggle and unobtrusively lifted her to her feet. As they walked, she quietly asked him to remain with her until she could support herself by holding the podium. Once there, she slid her written speech from its place on a podium shelf and looked at it as if it were written in a foreign language. She simply could not focus. Four thousand mourners remained stone-quiet, waiting for her to speak.

"It is hard, so hard for me," she said, when words finally came. "I've cried so many tears. Many of them today. I may shed many more as I speak of her now. Sheila Fishburne was my friend, the wisest counsel I turned to when important decisions were required. Her loss, for me and for our nation and for the world, is irreplaceable.

"Sheila was the ultimate servant of the public. Devoted to her country and all humanity, with no hidden agenda. Just an unbending commitment to all that's good and right and righteous.

"She loved life. She loved to dance and sing. She was a master storyteller, a worthy heir of the ancient oral tradition of the Inupiat people. Stories came to life in her telling. In full color, 3D, even. I was not alone in being swept up by them, feeling I was living them along with her. Growing up in the Arctic north, she learned to appreciate our good earth and sea and all living things, and humanity's place in the full scheme of the natural world."

Tenny stopped for a moment, tried to speak again, but failed. She drew a tissue from a box stored on the podium and dabbed at tears while those in the cathedral and watching on television waited for her to resume. Emotion swept slowly from the altar like a wave. Audible sobs could be heard throughout the hall.

"I should apologize for my silence," said Tenny when she finally resumed, "but I can't apologize for my tears or my sense of loss. Sheila deserves them, and so much more.

"My heart goes out to her family and friends who loved her, many of whom are here today. Most of Alaska would have come here today if possible. And my condolences to all who were on the plane with her. Their lives, like hers, were devoted to public service, and they died in performance of that service."

She stopped briefly again, then smiled.

"Sheila and I were elected to Congress the very same year. She from Alaska, me from California. Sheila had so much more political experience than I did. She will be my teacher, I quickly decided. We bonded right away and agreed that as two women in the man's world Congress was then, we needed to work together. We recruited other first- and second-term women and formed an alliance we called 'Good Cooks and Tough Cookies.' We had a bloc of votes the men often needed, and that gave us more power than our experience deserved. It was very productive and much fun. A great introduction to the world of politics for me.

"When the vice presidency became vacant last year, Sheila was my first, second, and third choice to fill it. She had my total trust and confidence. I knew that if I could not fill my entire term she would be the best choice to succeed me in this office. She was indeed a star, a brilliant—"

Tenny's voice tightened again. Until now, her words had been extemporaneous. Tenny was a gifted public speaker. For her entire career she had been bringing crowds to their feet with powerful messages, brilliantly timed. But now, she felt she was losing her ability to speak lucidly. She turned to the speech she had written and intended to read from it, then changed her mind. She looked to the audience once again.

"Sheila's last mission, which she performed so brilliantly, was to encourage the peoples of the world to support our plans to achieve peace and security for all and for all time. Let that be her legacy. Billions of us are demanding from our leaders an end to needless, senseless wars. To turn in our weapons. To agree to resolve differences as human beings, not as ravaging animals. This planet is so rich and so beautiful. Life is so precious. Sheila Fishburne devoted her life to keeping it that way and making certain that all God's children share in it. Now, without her, so must we."

OCTOBER

CHAPTER 61

Democrats held a two-vote majority on the House Armed Services Committee, the first committee scheduled to act on Tenny's Peace and Security agenda. Guy Rocker was convinced that if that committee approved the legislation, there would be no other House roadblocks. Passage through the full House would be assured. He also knew that one word from him to Committee Chairman Frank Lipscott would be enough to derail the vote.

Rocker was positioned to make it happen—or not. Publicly, he was one of the program's most important and aggressive cheerleaders. Privately, he was taking his cues from Cal Foley. Their alliance had been sanctified in Gil Adonis's blood earlier in the year. Tenny had her plan; once Rocker allied with Foley, he had his. His prize would be the presidency itself, and that prize was within reach. Tenny would need to nominate a new vice president to replace Fish. Rocker was on everyone's short list of candidates to be that nominee. The calculus now was whether a committee vote for her agenda or against it would increase his chances. If the committee vote fell short, Tenny would need Rocker more than ever to overcome resistance and get her agenda approved by the House. If the committee vote was favorable, he could take credit and she might feel more in his debt. Or possibly the committee vote should be delayed, in effect held hostage to trade for his appointment. Rocker could make a case for any of these strategies, but what really mattered was how Foley and his group weighed the possibilities.

The answer came that afternoon, outside the members' entrance to the House floor. Foley was talking to a group of other lobbyists as Rocker emerged from the day's opening session. Foley turned to him and nodded a greeting. "Mr. Speaker," said Foley, "congratulations on your very moving tribute to Vice President Fishburne at yesterday's memorial service."

Rocker stopped and turned to Foley. "I appreciate that. She was one of a kind. Hard to lose and hard to replace."

Foley moved closer, took Rocker's hand, and gave him what others in the hall perceived to be a hug of condolence. "I know that must have been hard for you, given how close you and the vice president were." And during that hug he whispered, "I understand she's going to appoint you. Pass it."

Rocker patted Foley on the shoulder and continued walking to his office. No one else heard the last few words of that message, so artfully had Foley delivered them. He's so impressive at this, thought Rocker. So often during the past few months Foley had surprised him with his finesse at handling their relationship. It was never obvious to others. Foley and his group were masters of stealth. Although his role in Gil Adonis's murder still weighed heavily on his conscience, the way they managed it, penetrating Adonis's fortress without leaving a trail was brilliant.

As he nursed this thought, another floated into his mind. A dark and troublesome thought. If they could do that to Adonis, could "they," Foley's people, the same group who managed the Adonis murder, also have arranged Fish's death?

CHAPTER 62

For the first time in three months, the Symfonia met on its virtual private network. Malik also was invited to participate in this meeting, the first time such an invitation had been extended to him.

"As is our custom for maximum protection," said Three, "the meeting will last for no more than five minutes. This may be the most important meeting we've ever had; that's why I've invited Malik. You will understand in a moment. Richfield?"

"Thank you, Three," said Richfield. "The illness and hospitalization of the United States president, as all of you are aware, elevated the importance of the vice president. Now the death of the vice president opens the possibility one of our own may replace her. That may occur within the next few days. Many believe the president will not live out her term. With our person as vice president, I believe it is imperative to accelerate the timing of the president's death in a manner that we can do so without calling attention to ourselves, given the highly public nature of the president's failing health. I've called this meeting to ask for approval of that plan."

"What's your confidence level in the vice presidential appointment?" asked Thirty-Nine.

"High confidence," said Richfield.

"Do I understand correctly that we were involved in the accident that took the life of the vice president?" asked Fifty-One.

"We were alert to opportunities, and when one arose requiring immediate action, I did that on my authority, yes," said Richfield.

"That was beyond your authority and very disturbing to me," said Fifty-One. "We have survived because we do not make instant judgments about such important matters. Too many variables. Everything must be considered with greater context than a single operation. Particularly one of such exceptional visibility."

"I apologize," said Richfield. "I admit it was a hasty decision, but it was a rare opportunity and required an immediate go or no go answer. As you can see, there's been no mention other than that it was a typical accident in a dangerous area known for its high incidence of fatal accidents. And from a cost-benefit standpoint, the value will place us one small step from ultimate success."

"I, for one, congratulate you for that decision," said Three. "Brilliantly conceived and executed. But with the president, a similar operation requires unanimous consent of the Symfonia. Do we have it?"

"Not as a blank check," said Fifty-One. "I want to see the plan in detail, with every possibility for failure considered."

"I agree," said Thirty-Nine. "And I want your commitment that neither you nor Malik will act without our express consent. We have survived and grown through the years using stealth and subtlety. Our very existence was a mystery to authorities until last year. To have impulsively killed the vice president of the United States without Symfonia approval and now planning to kill the president herself is totally contrary to the strategies that have brought us this far. Time is on our side. Nature may do the job for us."

"You have your answer, Richfield," said Three.

"As you wish," said Richfield. "But my assessment stands. We are very near the endgame. I asked Malik to be on this call so that he understands what's at stake and where we will be focusing our attention. I will develop our plan with Malik and submit for your approval. Meanwhile, there are other operations that require his attention immediately. So, Malik, go to Washington, order most of your team there, and await further instructions."

"Understood," said Malik.

"Our five minutes have elapsed. Meeting adjourned," said Three.

CHAPTER 63

Neither Tenny nor Carmie could remember their last meal together, just the two of them. It hadn't been during the frantic months of last year's reelection campaign, nor during the equally frantic months of this year's effort to win approval of the Peace and Security plan, Tenny's hospitalization, or events since.

Tonight, though, they were together at the White House. Andres was in California visiting his family. Ben was in New York, meeting with network executives about the complex advertising campaign he had planned for the next two months.

Tenny always found comfort with Carmie. It wasn't only their lifelong friendship that bound them. Carmie's counsel had helped Tenny through a bout of depression after her divorce from Andres decades ago. Carmie had steered Tenny into numerous career choices, including her social work on the streets of Los Angeles. Tonight, though, Tenny had more on her mind than a pleasant evening with an old friend.

"I met with Guy Rocker today," she said. "I may not have told you, but before I got sick, Fish warned me that Guy was getting shaky on the House vote, especially the Armed Services Committee vote."

"Guy?" asked Carmie, genuinely surprised. "He's been part of the team from the beginning. Do you think that was true?"

Tenny sipped her Chablis and nodded. "I had my doubts, but Fish served too many years in the House not to know how to count votes. She still had many friends there." She refilled her glass. "So I asked him straight out, and he kind of admitted it. He said the pressure from the industry was enormous. He wasn't sure our people would stay with us. That he personally wasn't getting soft on the issue, but was reconsidering strategy so we didn't lose both the vote and the majority in the next election."

"Do you think that was true?" asked Carmie.

"I want to believe it," Tenny replied. "At any rate, he said events of the past weeks have stiffened backbones and that when the committee votes later this week, it will pass.

"'Guaranteed?' I asked him.

"'Guaranteed,' he answered."

"Well, that's good news. Getting past that committee will be a big message to everyone else."

The White House stewards arrived with dinner.

"I had another reason for seeing Rocker today," said Tenny after the stewards departed. "I hate to even think about it, but you know I've got to replace Fish."

"And you're thinking about appointing Rocker?"

"He's an obvious choice. He's already next in line to be president if something happens to me before a new vice president's confirmed. He's got more government experience than anyone else I might consider. He helped me a lot when I was a member of the House. He's pushed our plan and would likely keep doing it if I'm not able to. He's from a big swing state, Michigan, so the politics would be good. And he'd have no trouble getting confirmed."

"All that makes sense," said Carmie, "but do I hear a bit of hesitation in your voice?"

"I suppose you do," said Tenny. "And maybe it would be there for anyone. Fish is irreplaceable, except for only one other person I know. You."

Carmie could not contain her laugh. "Don't hesitate with that idea," she said. "Run from it as fast as you can. Trust me, that is not a good idea."

"Trust you is the best reason for that idea," said Tenny. "There's no one on earth I trust more. With your reputation, the finance community would be excited by the appointment. You've done a great job at Commerce. You've got more common sense than anyone I know, including me. Think of all the times you've saved me from myself."

"Well," said Carmie, "I'm going to save you again, from this one. Don't get me wrong, I'm flattered and I love you for it, but let's get to the dumbness of this. First, I'm not a politician. I never have been, never wanted to be, and would be absolutely awful at it if I had to be a candidate and give political speeches. Next, I can't help you with Congress. I only know the people on committees I work with. Third, it would be one messy confirmation fight. My Wall Street background would become a big negative in your own party. My lack of government experience would embarrass you once the opposition began working me over. Your political people would see whoever you appoint as someone they would need to run with at the next election. That wouldn't be me, and it would begin a civil war that would ruin your power for the next three years. Finally, Tenny, I'm your girlfriend. How would that look to voters? It would be worse than naming your own sister if you had one. If you're having doubts about Rocker, find someone else. Not me."

"Oh, I suppose you're right," said Tenny. "I'm just so unsure. I need more time, I guess."

"What's bothering you about Rocker?" asked Carmie.

"I don't know. Maybe it's some of the people who've been pushing for him. Some of the guys from the weapons lobby, for example. Why would they do that?"

"Maybe they're convinced you will win and they want to be on the winning side so they retain influence."

"Retain influence with Guy Rocker?" said Tenny. "That doesn't make much sense to me. If it makes sense to them, that concerns me."

"So what are you going to do?"

"While Rocker was here, I asked him if he would accept the vice presidency if I offered it to him. He tried to be humble, but his eyes lit up like a string of lights at Christmas. No offense to him. Politicians are ambitious, and everyone wants to be president."

"Are you going to offer it to him?"

"I told him he was on my short list and I'd let him know soon."

"Who else is on your short list?"

"You. Or at least you were until you just talked me out of it."

CHAPTER 64

Renetta Chance waited impatiently in her hotel room at the Bethesda, Maryland, Hyatt. The US National Institutes of Health had asked her to travel from London to Washington to meet with their virology experts about a new Ebola outbreak on the Ivory Coast. When she arrived, Chance discovered that sixteen other authorities in the field also had been summoned, including biostatistician Bauman Kabiri. She considered that a stroke of good fortune. At the meeting she signaled him she wanted to meet later, at her hotel. Now he was an hour late for their agreed-upon time, and she was anxious and frustrated.

She found a small bottle of vodka in the room's minibar, poured it into a glass, and drank it quickly. Chance was not a daytime drinker, but today she felt had to be an exception if there ever was one. She was sipping her second drink more slowly when Kabiri called from the lobby to say, "Here."

"Room 416," she replied.

He found her highly agitated and noticed the empty vodka bottles. This was not the Renetta Chance he knew, or others knew. Her reputation was that of a buttoned-up, highly disciplined academic in a field that demanded an unusual level of analysis. Seeing her like this was startling. Given the secrets they shared, it was chilling.

"What is it?" Kabiri asked, bypassing pleasantries.

"The Project killed Vice President Fishburne," she exclaimed.

Kabiri was alarmed, both at the statement and how loudly she had delivered it.

He moved toward her, put his arm around her shoulders, and steered her to the only sofa in the room.

"Renetta," he admonished her. "Get yourself under control. Here, sit, lower your voice and tell me what you know."

It was impossible for her to say the words without emotion, but she did as Kabiri asked. In a more whispered tone, she said, "A number of people from British intelligence are Project operatives. One of them went to Alaska on a trip just before the plane crash. He had no official business in Alaska. He went with no notice, returned quickly, and refused to say a word about it."

Tears threaded their way down Chance's cheeks, pooling into salty formations above her lips. Kabiri grabbed some tissues and handed them to her. He said nothing and urged her to continue with a simple nod.

"I know this because the person who recruited me, a woman who handles files in MI5, told me, and she's as upset about it as I am. She works in the same science-based MI5 unit as the person who went to Alaska."

"That doesn't prove he had anything to do with the crash," said Kabiri. "People in that business I imagine get assignments to move quickly and are sworn to secrecy."

"My friend knows that, understands that. She said this one was off the charts. Unauthorized. A surprise to the unit chief. Personal business, personal emergency, the agent said. There's nothing in his files about his having any family or contacts in Alaska."

Chance was sobbing now and motioned for more tissue. Quietly, she said, "I could think of nothing else on the flight from London and just felt it was my duty to get word to American authorities. That's what I did before even checking into the hotel."

Kabiri was stunned. He fought to keep his composure.

"My God," he said. "You've given us all up? We'd better hope we all get arrested before the Project's death squad comes looking for us."

Chance continued as if she hadn't heard Kabiri. "If I could resign from the Project, I would, but if I tried, they would likely kill me. No, the whole Project must be crushed. What they did was unspeakably evil."

"Why didn't you report this at home, to British authorities?"

"Ha," she sneered. "Old boys' club. School chums. I wouldn't have known who to trust."

Kabiri scanned his surroundings. Was this room bugged? He knew that on many occasions when he traveled, he was under surveillance. Had he been seen in the lobby? Had his previous meetings with Chance put them on alert? Surely, they must have watched her when she arrived in the United States and possibly tracked where she went. Renetta would be in danger, and because of his association with her, he could be as well. He agreed with her, even about the dissolution of the Project, but there were ways to achieve change without being as direct as she had been. Who had she told? Would they take her seriously? His mind swirled with questions that could make the difference between life and death. His and hers.

"Renetta," he said, "who was your point of contact in the American government?"

"An old friend and classmate of mine at the London School of Economics, a woman by the name of Carmen Sanchez. And I think they'll take this seriously, since she's very close to the president."

CHAPTER 65

K abiri convinced Chance that she was in immediate danger and quickly developed a plan to help her. As a professor at University of Virginia, he lived in university housing off grounds in Charlottesville, a three-hour drive south of Washington, DC. He told Chance to pack for a quick departure, and then, checking frequently to assure himself he was not being followed, he entered an AT&T store near the hotel's lobby. Using a false identity, he purchased a phone, set it up with a new phone number, and called his sister who lived nearby. Then he went to a women's wear store on the same block and bought several articles of clothing. And waited. Within thirty minutes, his sister arrived and parked nearby. Kabiri gave her the clothing and Chance's room number. And waited. He didn't have to wait long. Within minutes, Renetta Chance, dressed in new clothing that carefully hid her identity, walked by him with his sister. Both were carrying packages, as if they were two friends enjoying a shopping outing. They entered his sister's car unhurriedly and drove away.

Now, Kabiri needed to consider his own situation. He likely would not be under surveillance yet, but when they discovered that Chance was off their network, his association with her would quickly lead to him because they had last been seen together at the same meeting.

Leaving his own car in the parking lot, he disposed of both his old and new cell phones in a commercial dumpster and rode the escalator to the underground Bethesda Metro subway station attached to the hotel. He had to think fast and move fast. Were any of their assassins in Washington? Likely. It would not be long before they came for her, and for him, and probably for Sanchez too.

He rode the Metro for twenty minutes to Amtrak's Union Station near Capitol Hill and lost himself in the terminal crowds. Where to next? Continuing to watch for anyone who might be following, he reentered the subway station, this time riding back into downtown Washington. It was late afternoon. He would not be alone. Commuting crowds and tourists would be his allies. That was helpful.

Think, Bauman, think. Sit in a side seat so you can look both left and right to see who might be coming into this car. Be conscious of needles. Malik had been known to give lethal injections to those in crowds—when he wasn't pushing victims off subway platforms. With each new station stop, each new group entering his car, Kabiri's anxiety took another leap,. He'd been on this train long enough. Just before the doors closed at the DuPont Circle station he slid out of the car and onto the platform. He quickly looked around. No one followed him off. On the next track another train was loading, heading back to where he had first boarded. He was the last person to get in the car. If anyone had been following him, now they weren't.

Okay, safe for a few minutes. Think. Did Secretary Sanchez take Chance's warning seriously? Did she share it with US intelligence and other authorities? He needed to see her too. But how could he, a total stranger, get an appointment with a cabinet officer in the US government?

The subway car pulled into the Farragut North downtown station, one of the line's busiest. A scrum of riders boarded through both of the car's doors, too many for Kabiri to size up with a quick glance. All the seats were taken. Many were standing in the aisle. The car pulled away heading to the Metro Center station. Then, deep in the tunnel, it stopped. Why? He knew these things happened. Dispatchers held cars at times for scheduling. Power problems, trouble on the track. Could be anything. Stuck in this box, shoulder to shoulder with people he didn't know, only raised Kabiri's sense of panic.

Now they were moving again, to Metro Center, the largest station on the line. The doors opened and Kabiri bolted out.

This is stupid, he told himself. He had nowhere to go. He couldn't return to his home. He couldn't keep riding the subway like this. He couldn't keep running. They would find him eventually. A train appeared, headed for a stop near the US Department of Commerce. His next step became clear to him. He had to go there and somehow get to Sanchez.

Ten minutes later, after a brief ride and a short walk, he was at the Commerce Department's entrance and encountered a uniformed guard requesting his federal ID.

"I need to meet someone in the secretary's office," said Kabiri.

"Do you have an appointment?" asked the guard.

"No," said Kabiri, "but it's urgent."

"Here's the office phone number," said the guard. "Call there to see if someone will see you."

"I've lost my phone," said Kabiri.

"Sorry," said the guard.

"Do you have a phone I can use?"

"No, we don't have one here."

"Can I go inside to use one?"

"Sorry," said the guard.

Kabiri stood at the door, considering his options. Every moment he was on the streets was a moment closer to being found by someone with orders to kill him. It was only a matter of time, a very short matter of time, before both he and Renetta Chance would be relentlessly hunted by professionals who seldom missed their targets. He had been on the Project's Executive Committee long enough to know that with certainty.

Without a word, he rushed toward the front entrance, getting just five steps inside before two uniformed guards grabbed him and shoved him hard against a wall. He was too stunned to say a word.

"Spread them," yelled one of the guards as a small crowd formed to watch.

Kabiri shook his head, trying to process what was happening.

"I said spread them," the guard yelled, louder.

Kabiri put his hands on the wall and spread his feet while someone roughly inspected his body for weapons. They quickly placed restraints on his wrists and led him to a security room not far from the entrance.

As his head cleared, Kabiri took stock of his situation. His wallet was gone, so they were checking his ID. The workday was ending, and he could hear activity in the halls as employees headed for the exits. How late did Sanchez work? Was she in this building? Was she even in the city? What would he do if she wasn't here or wouldn't see him? At least he was in the hands of the law, not a likely place to be executed by the Project. Jail? He could tolerate it for a while.

Finally, a man dressed in civilian clothes entered the cubicle-size room where he was being held.

"Detective Carlisle, DC police," said the man. "What is this, Professor Kabiri? Are you writing a paper on what it's like to be arrested in Washington? What's a nice statistics professor like you doing in a place like this?"

How much to tell him? The full story is far too improbable to be believed.

"I have an urgent message for Secretary Sanchez," he said.

"Hmm," said Carlisle. "Wouldn't it have been easier to send her an email or call her office? Busting through a police checkpoint could get you killed, you know. We're touchy here about these things."

"I know this sounds bizarre, but something just happened that I know about that puts her in danger."

"Well, that's what law enforcement is for. Tell me and I've got a whole department of trained people who can deal with it."

"I can't," said Kabiri. "It has to do with national security."

"National security!" said Carlisle, seemingly amused. "Are you a fed? You have a badge? Which agency are you with?"

Kabiri struggled with what to say and how to say it. How to get past this routine interrogation to Sanchez without sounding as if he'd lost his mind.

"Can you please call her office and tell her it has to do with Renetta Chance? She'll understand," said Kabiri. Would she? Not if Renetta hadn't made clear what a threat the Project was. Not if she didn't know Renetta could pay with her life for telling her.

Carlisle sat silently for a moment. Kabiri was a puzzle. Totally atypical of the ordinary gate-crasher. Most seemed half nuts. Not this one.

"Well, you get one phone call before we arrest you," said Carlisle. "If this is the one you want, I'll see if anyone's still upstairs."

The wait seemed interminable. Kabiri needed to use the toilet but dared not ask. There was an equilibrium here he felt he could not disturb. They may or may not be calling Sanchez. There may or may not be anyone in her office to take the call. She may or may not be too busy to be disturbed, if she was even there. All he could do was wait.

Finally, Carlisle reappeared. "Come with me," he said, and led Kabiri to a larger office. In the room were three people, two of them obviously part of the building's security force. The third was an attractive woman in a business suit. She was standing, leaning against a desk.

"I understand you want to see me," she said. "What about Renetta Chance?"

"She told me she spoke to you about the Salvation Project," said Kabiri.

Carmie nodded, trying not to convey her surprise.

"She's a member."

"That's what she told me, yes," said Carmie.

"So am I," said Bauman Kabiri. "Because she talked with you, her life is in danger. Because she spoke with me, so is mine. And because you now know about us, so is yours."

CHAPTER 66

During her Wall Street career, Carmen Sanchez was known for her meticulous research and analysis, a trusted resource when major decisions were required. Carmie's nod of approval moved billions of dollars in loans and deal money.

So it was in character that immediately following her conversation with Renetta Chance, Carmie retired to her office, wrote an extensive memo on all that she had been told while it was still fresh in her mind, and appended documents that Chance had given her. The story of the Salvation Project was not new to Carmie. Tenny had revealed it to her months earlier. But that her old friend Renetta Chance was part of it? That was unsettling. She had never known Renetta to be political in any way. How many others had fallen into this trap through naivete and misinformation?

She was just completing her report when the call came about a gate-crasher who also invoked Renetta's name. This could hardly be coincidence. She had to see for herself. What he told her was stunning and too urgent to take time appending to her written report. Carmie called Tenny's office and asked for an immediate appointment.

After Carmie shared her information with Tenny, FBI Director Sam Vellman and CIA Director Kyle Christian were summoned to the Situation Room for a late-night meeting.

Could Fish's plane crash have been a murderous act, as Renetta Chance had learned? Vellman replied that the accident investigation team had just completed its fieldwork and the wreckage had been moved to a hangar at Eielson Air Force Base for a nose-to-tail analysis. The investigators were puzzled, he said, as to why the gauges showed plenty of fuel left in the gas tanks when the plane had apparently behaved as if it were out of fuel. Nothing like that in the long history of Twin Otter flight had ever been reported.

"Luckily the plane didn't burn when it hit the trees," said Vellman. "We never would have known this otherwise."

"Does MI5 know it has Salvation Project people in its organization?" Tenny asked, turning to Kyle Christian.

"Yes, they do," said Christian. "We had them too. We may still have, even after we cleaned out a few in last year's purge. But this new information will help them identify more trouble spots. Especially their agent who made the trip to Alaska."

"If I may, Madam President," said Vellman, "with the new information from Chance and Kabiri, we've got a lot more to go on to find the moles in our operations. And I believe we have a much better handle on how to pick up Executive Committee communications and track them back to the individuals. That is, if it all checks out. What are the odds your informant has given us misinformation to throw us false leads or that she herself was misinformed?"

"None," said Carmie. "I've known Renetta for years. She's one of the smartest, most precise people I've ever met. No one can deceive her for long. That's why she's turned on them. The Project isn't what it seemed, and she's figured that out now."

"Well, why did she sign up for it in the first place?" asked Vellman.

"Because like many scientifically informed people, apparently, she's fearful of how things are spinning out of control and outraged that government leaders aren't responding," said Carmie. "She turned away not because she disagrees with their goals, but with their methods. Just like Gil Adonis. Just like Lester Bowles."

"Is Chance secure, Sam?" asked Tenny.

"Our people picked her up an hour ago. Kabiri, of course, is in DC's jail for breaking into a federal building. We'll get him moved in the morning after we talk to the DC people."

"Madam Secretary," said Christian, turning to Carmie, "about your written memo, how many copies of it exist?"

"Just those at this table," said Carmie.

"And how did you make copies?" asked Vellman.

"Why, on my office copy machine. I made the copies myself. Was that a mistake?"

"If the Project has anyone planted in your office, they can capture residual images from copies," said Vellman. "It's a sophisticated process and takes specialized equipment, but it's done frequently. We do it ourselves. Also, printers are on wireless networks. If anyone is tapped into the network, they could grab the signal."

Carmie shook her head. "Sorry, I had no idea. But everyone in my office has security clearance."

"Top secret?" asked Christian.

"Well, no. Confidential."

Christian turned to the FBI director. "Sam, you'd better do a check on personnel—anyone who might have access to that copier."

"Right," said Vellman. "I'll also have our guys take a look at the wireless network for any usual activity."

"I can't believe anyone I've hired would be spying for an organization like this," said Carmie.

"Believe it," said Vellman. "A lot of the people we've already turned had no idea what they were signing up for. Until we've screened your office, you need to be particularly cautious yourself."

That raised Tenny's fear antenna.

"You think they'll really come after Carmie?"

"Kabiri thinks so. He says they come after anyone who knows about them, and they don't trust," said Vellman. "Secretary Sanchez and Ben Sage live in the same location. We must assume that apartment is on their radar screen because of Sage. If they learn of this breach, I will guess it becomes an even bigger target."

"Great," said Carmie. "Ben already spends most of his days with hair standing straight up on the back of his neck."

CHAPTER 67

Since her hospitalization, Tenny was more conscious of her health than at any time since her body was racked by the assassins' bomb. With Fish gone, her Peace and Security agenda relied on her survival—not just to remain alive, but to maintain a sharp political edge. Yes, more than a billion people worldwide had signed the petition, and her efforts to secure the most significant disarmament treaty in world history was edging toward success. Nevertheless, neither house of Congress had yet passed her legislation. The treaty talks would collapse if she did not maintain firm personal rein on negotiations. She had to survive to see these efforts through to success, to manage them through the inevitable legal fights that would follow, to nurse them along in their infant years and navigate them past whatever unforeseeable roadblocks arose.

After Fish's death she radically changed her daily routine. No longer awake before dawn. No more late-night office meetings. Travel only when travel could not be avoided. A firm 6:00 p.m. end to routine office days. To bed no later than ten o'clock. For everything that fell by the wayside with that schedule, delegate—more delegation of authority to others than she had ever before felt comfort with.

But just before she was preparing to go to bed, two nights after the meeting with the Chance and Kabiri revelations, the FBI director called requesting an immediate meeting.

"It can't wait until morning, Sam?" she asked.

The urgency in his voice convinced her that it could not.

Vellman hurried to the White House from the FBI headquarters, a ten-minute walk away. With him was an aide tightly holding a small file. They met in the private residence, Tenny in nightgown and robe.

"Agent Morris Jenkins, Madam President," said Vellman. "I'll let him describe the information we've just received. He's an expert on aviation matters and can answer any questions you have better than I can."

"Proceed, Agent Jenkins," said Tenny.

Jenkins opened his folder and read from a memo.

"At thirteen hundred hours today, Alaska Standard Time, National Safety Board inspectors discovered that a fuel tank on the de Havilland Twin Otter that crashed in the Brooks Range was obstructed to such an extent that when the pilots routinely switched to it in midflight, fuel could not pass sufficiently through the obstruction to keep the aircraft aloft. The inspectors' preliminary judgment is that this condition caused the aircraft to have insufficient fuel to maintain flight and to quickly lose altitude in an area where there was no available clearing for it to safely land. Upon examination of the obstructing material, the inspectors found an unusual quantity of material, in particular, dead insects such as flies, mosquitos, and spiders. Among these insects were remains of monarch butterflies. Monarch butterflies are not known to be in Alaska. Preliminary indications are that this collection of insects was purposely dropped into the fuel line and gas tank by a person or persons unknown before the aircraft was fueled for this flight. The pilots would have no indication of this problem until they switched to the blocked fuel tank while in flight, at which point they would have had no recourse to prevent the accident. These judgments are preliminary. The inspection is continuing."

Tenny listened to this report with increasing outrage.

"It's true then!" she said. "What we were told the other day. Fish and the others were murdered!"

"It appears so, Madam President," said Vellman.

"You should also know, Madam President," he continued, "that we followed up on that lead about the British MI5 agent going to Alaska. MI5 ID'd him right away. He's an entomologist, an expert in the study of insects. Also, about the reason I felt you should have this information right away: I'm told that a reporter for the *Anchorage Daily News* inadvertently learned about the sabotage of the fuel line and that you can expect calls from the media at any time asking for comment. The story will likely be widespread by tomorrow."

"Does the media know about the MI5 agent's involvement?"

"No. At least I've had no indication. The Brits are unsettled about the leak. They intended to keep their suspect under surveillance, hoping he would lead them to others. Instead, they had to pick him up. He's undergoing questioning now. But they will keep their side of this under wraps. I suggest your press people refer all media calls to the FBI. We will confirm the findings and say we are investigating."

After Vellman and Jenkins left, Tenny sat at her bedroom desk, her thoughts churning with the implications of what she had just been told. Fish murdered, and in such a cunning way that if the plane had burned on impact, no one ever would have known about the blocked fuel tank. All the insects would have burned, all the evidence been destroyed. These were clever, evil people. Capable of anything. Why would they kill Fish? Obviously to get someone else installed as vice president, someone working with the Salvation Project. Four candidates had been actively seeking the appointment, not directly, but through intermediaries. One of them had to be the Project's candidate. Which one? *If I guess wrong*, she thought, *it would only be a matter of time before they kill me too. Then they would be free to do what I stopped them from doing in last year's election: taking control of the United States government. Taking control, and never giving it back.*

CHAPTER 68

It was not unusual to learn that authorities had apprehended an Executive Committee member. In a few cases they died while being tortured. Unfortunate, but that only justified why the Project insisted that members remain unaware of each other's identity. Each had his or her own assignments, siloed so that their capture would not expose others or reveal more than their own activities.

Now, for the first time in Richfield's memory, two members had gone missing at the same time and at the same location. Number Thirty-Five had been captured by Washington, DC, authorities. That was surprising. Almost always when someone was captured it occurred during the performance of an assignment. Thirty-Five was a veteran Executive Committee member, trusted to a level that he was once considered for a Symfonia vacancy, but his portfolio had been inactive for two years. He was engaged in no way, had no assignments. Why would authorities find him now? Forty-Six was relatively new to the committee, selected because of a recommendation by someone in British intelligence and because of her academic prominence. But she had never had an assignment and therefore never been tested. Why would authorities have an interest in her? And why would she evade all of the Project's attempts to contact her?

Troublesome. Very troublesome. Particularly because both were last seen in Washington, DC, at the same academic meeting. It was a situation that never should have occurred. A serious miscalculation on the part of the Project selection committee. Malik had been notified, of course, and he had a full team operating in Washington. Until he reported in, nothing more could be done. But it was troublesome.

Nevertheless, urgent business was at hand and could not be postponed. A meeting of the full Executive Committee had been called to weigh in on the campaign to place their operative in the White House as vice president.

"Welcome, everyone," Richfield began. "We have just one item and one item only on today's agenda. Eighteen, please describe the situation."

"Thank you, Richfield. As you all know, the vice president of the United States died in an aircraft accident. The position is now vacant. One of ours is the leading candidate to replace her. I don't need to tell you what an opportunity this presents to control the government of the United States, since the president is very ill and likely will not survive much longer. And so I am asking all of you to press your in-country contacts to urge the president to appoint our person, the Speaker of the House of Representatives, Guy Rocker, to the position. Contact any head of state or foreign minister or personage of importance you may know. The president will value the respect Mr. Rocker has internationally, and that will solidify his reputation with her. This appointment will be made any day now, so it is urgent you attend to this at the close of this meeting."

"Questions or comments?" asked Richfield.

"Yes, did we kill the vice president?"

"Who is this?" asked Richfield.

"Twenty," answered a voice in English, with an obvious Canadian accent. "I have just seen a news article that says the plane crashed because someone tampered with the aircraft's fuel tank. Did we kill her?"

"That question is out of order for this meeting," said Richfield. "We are meeting to discuss only the matter described by Eighteen."

"My question is very much in order," Twenty persisted. "If we, the Project, killed her, we are all complicit in one of the most heinous crimes of the century."

For years the Project's Executive Committee meetings had been pro forma information sessions, with the Project Control advising its national and regional leaders of progress and issuing assignments. A challenge such as this was unheard of.

"Three here," said a British voice. "You are most certainly out of order to question decisions made by me and other members of the Symfonia. Don't be naive, Twenty. We are engaged in the final battle of our long struggle to save humanity. What the president is doing sounds so good on paper, but it's nothing more than a glorified photo opportunity. The so-called disarmament treaty she advocates would never result in the armies and weapons of the world standing down. The world will never overcome the power of the monied classes to make weapons and war. They will never allow us all to do what must be done to prevent climate catastrophe. If we allow the president to win with her program, it will falsely appear that democratic government can succeed. That would set back our efforts indefinitely. They must fail so that people will turn to us. The only way to make this happen is to take control and make it happen, over the dead bodies of those who would stop it, if need be."

"Dead bodies. That's all we think about anymore. This is Fifty-Three. Kill. Kill. Kill. Who's next? The president of the United States herself? Eighteen says the president is ill and won't survive much longer. We all know what that means—"

"We're not here to debate the plan," Richfield interrupted harshly. "We're here to implement it. You will all get your instructions. The new situation in the United States means different approaches and timelines in many of your areas. Please do as required and be aware, very aware, of the penalty for unauthorized disclosure. Meeting adjourned."

Richfield shut down all communications and turned to consideration of what to do about Twenty and Fifty-Three. Malik already had instructions about the Sanchez woman and that fellow Sage. Now he had concerns about his two missing members, Thirty-Five and Forty-Six. Had they also learned what had happened in Alaska? Forty-Six, the committee member who went mysteriously missing, was British. Just like the operative he had sent to Alaska.

CHAPTER 69

There is no constitutional deadline for a president to replace a vice president, but there is an expectation that when the office becomes vacant, the appointment will be made with little delay. Continuity of government requires it. Tenny particularly was under pressure to name a successor to Fish because of the upcoming votes on the Peace and Security agenda. The Senate vote would be close. In fact, it could end in a fifty-fifty tie. If it did, the vice president could provide the fifty-first vote to pass it.

Two weeks had gone by since the memorial service for Fish, little time for the FBI and CIA to complete background checks, but all the leading candidates already held public office. Most had undergone extensive investigations prior to receiving their current security clearances. Updates were ordered days after Fish's death. Today, Sam Vellman and Kyle Christian were in the Oval Office to discuss them with the president.

"Let's do this quickly," said Tenny. "Just tell me if you've found out anything about any of the candidates that would disqualify them. And let's not forget the politics. We don't want to make an appointment that would blow up on us politically."

Christian looked knowingly at Vellman. "Sam, clearances are your baby."

"But you've got the goods."

"Please," said Tenny. "What kind of game are you playing? Let me in on it."

"It's hardly a game," said Christian. "Remember when Gil Adonis died? A mysterious phone call was made to his number the night before he was murdered. A message left on his voice mail."

"Yes, I remember. The NSA was going to try to unscramble whatever distortion there was to identify the caller."

"Well, they succeeded, months ago. Then they neglected to let us know. Chain of command, red tape things. It's not usual for NSA to be involved in a domestic murder case. The CIA either," said Christian.

"But now you have the answer?" asked Tenny.

"Yes. When we requested files on the four candidates you're considering for vice president, we discovered that the call to set up Guy Adonis for the murder came from one of them. NSA converted the scrambled signal to a voice in the clear. I have the recording and will play it for you."

Christian reached into his inside jacket pocket and removed a small voice recorder, placed it on Tenny's desk, and pressed play.

The recording began with Gil Adonis's voice: "I can't talk now. Leave a message."

Then, the incoming caller's voice: "Gil. Guy Rocker. Sorry to disturb you, but this can't wait. This comes directly from the president. Early tomorrow a White House courier will arrive at your office with important information. It's so sensitive, it must be delivered orally and in person. She says you should tell no one about this call and meet the courier alone, with no one near enough to overhear the conversation. The reason for secrecy will be explained by the courier. I would not have called you on this number at this hour except for the urgency. Good night, Gil."

Tenny looked across her desk at Christian and Vellman with an expression of disbelief.

Neither of the men felt they should break the silence while Tenny absorbed the full meaning of what she had heard. In fact, they both had gone through similar emotions. Both had worked with Rocker for years. They had no doubt that it was his voice. NSA assured them that it was not a digital alteration, a combination of words Rocker had spoken in other contexts, rearranged to create this damning message.

"I assume you would not have brought this to me if there was any question of authenticity," said Tenny.

"None," said Vellman. "Guy Rocker set up Gil Adonis to be murdered."

"Any motive?" she asked. "Anything personal between them?"

"We checked personal lives, financial interests, any prior disputes. None. We're confident that it was Rocker. And if you have any doubts, we have another recording for you."

Christian pressed the play button again. On this recording, the voices were electronically distorted, but the words were clear enough to understand.

"Thank you, Richfield. As you all know, the vice president of the United States died in an aircraft accident. The position is now vacant. One of ours is the leading candidate to replace her. I don't need to tell you what an opportunity this presents to control the government of the United States, since the president is very ill and likely will not survive much longer. And so I am asking all of you to press your in-country contacts to urge the president to appoint our person, the Speaker of the House of Representatives, Guy Rocker, to the position. Contact any head of state or foreign minister or personage of importance you may know. The president will value the respect Mr. Rocker has internationally, and that will solidify his reputation with her. This appointment will be made within the next week, so it is urgent you attend to this at the close of this meeting."

"Questions or comments?"

"Yes, did we kill the vice president?"

"Who is this?"

"Twenty. I have just seen a news article that says the plane crashed because someone tampered with the aircraft's fuel tank. Did we kill her?"

"That question is out of order for this meeting. We are meeting to discuss only the matter described by Eighteen."

"My question is very much in order. If we, the Project, killed her, we are all complicit in one of the most heinous crimes of the century."

Christian stopped the recording. "Thanks to that fellow Kabiri, we were able to tap into what Kabiri says is a meeting of the Salvation Project's Executive Committee. That recording was from a meeting yesterday. Very clearly, Rocker's their candidate."

"Good God," said Tenny. "And he was my first choice for vice president."

"And with that appointment," said Christian, "you would have been the Project's first choice for their next victim."

CHAPTER 70

As Speaker, Guy Rocker's domain in the US Capitol Building included a luxurious office across the hall from the House floor and smaller hideaways where he could hold smaller meetings or isolate himself to work alone or rest. This morning he was absent from all of them. Rocker had moved his car from its assigned space in the underground House garage and parked it on a residential street three blocks from the Capitol Building. From there he called Cal Foley, insisting they meet immediately.

That had been an hour earlier. Rocker waited with growing impatience. The longer he was gone from his office, out of touch from even his closest staff, the more curious and suspicious his absence would be. His staff knew Rocker was in line for the vice presidential appointment. He did nothing to discourage that possibility. In fact, he called in once to say he'd been away longer than he expected and conveyed the impression that he was at the White House. His staff would buy that for a while.

He had indeed been called to the White House that morning, just after an unannounced visit to his home from Sam Vellman and three accompanying FBI agents. Immediately following his conversation with Vellman, Rocker went to his office and met with staff to arrange the day's activities. Then he announced to his secretary that he would be out for a while. Where? He couldn't say. But he gave her a knowing wink.

He was about to call Foley again, despite the risk, when a car pulled up beside his, Foley alone at the wheel. Foley motioned for Rocker to get in. Rocker quickly undid his necktie, shed his suit jacket, and opened his shirt collar, better not to appear a person of importance, and slid into the passenger seat of Foley's car.

"What's up?" asked Foley. "Did you get the call?"

"I got the call, all right," said Rocker. "A call from the FBI. That other call, you know, the one you had me make to Adonis the night before he was killed. The one you assured me was untraceable. Well, they've traced it right back to me. Vellman and his guys played it back to me this morning, at my house, with my wife home!"

Foley started driving, meandering through the neighborhoods around the Capitol. "You denied it was you?"

"I couldn't deny it was me. They had my voice clear as a bell, just like I'm talking to you."

"So what did you say?"

"They caught me totally off guard. I thought they were there to interview me for vice president. I said the first thing that came to mind. The only thing I could say. I told him yes, it was true. That the president herself asked me to make the call. I didn't know why."

"Did they buy that?"

"Not for a minute. In fact, Vellman said he personally had told Tenny about the call. She said she knew nothing about it."

"Well, stay with that story. She's the one who must have been lying to him, not you."

"Are you nuts? With her speech, that telethon, and her eulogy for Fishburne, the world has just anointed her to sainthood. Who's going to believe me? No, Cal, they're going to arrest me as an accessory to the Adonis murder. I know that. And I know another thing: I'm not going down alone."

I didn't like it when you asked me to make the call. I had never done anything like it before in my life. I'm going to tell them why I did it, tell them I was duped and hope I can avoid jail time. It will cost me my House seat, my political career, maybe even my marriage. But I'm not going to jail over it."

Foley continued to drive aimlessly around the Capitol. Finally, he said, "So you're warning me to save myself."

"Exactly," said Rocker. "Whoever's behind this should pay for it. I didn't kill Adonis. Neither did you. You can get out of it by using the same defense. You were told the messenger was really sent to talk to Adonis, not kill him. We can put our stories together. We can get past it if we're on the same page."

"You're right," said Foley. "How did you leave it with them?"

"Well, they said the president would want to see me about it and probably to kick my ass out the door. After meeting with the president, they said they wanted me to come to their office for a full so-called interview. I've avoided White House calls all morning."

"Guy, I can't believe I got you into this," said Foley. "Let's keep our stories together. People will think we were fools, but not murderers. I've got a long military record. You've been Mr. Clean in the House. We may survive better than it looks. Don't say anything to anyone just yet. Hold off on the White House; give your story to the FBI. That'll give me time to arrange things on my end. Thank you for letting me know and not getting sandbagged like you did."

"I hoped you'd see it that way, Cal. Take me back to my car now. I've been out of sight too long already."

"So have I. I've got people waiting for me," said Foley. "Look, my office is just a block away. I'll let myself off and have someone from my staff drive you to your car."

Foley pulled into a parking lot next to his office and made a call. Within minutes, a man quickly emerged and replaced Foley in the driver's seat.

"Guy, meet Juan. He'll take you where you need to go."

CHAPTER 71

Guy Rocker had slipped away from his security detail before. On numerous occasions he would do it just so that he could have a private lunch with his wife or drinks with friends. His security people were aware of this tendency to "go dark" now and then. They gave him space when he felt the need for it.

This was no ordinary day, though. The media expected the president to announce her choice for vice president, and the smart money said that choice would be Guy Rocker. Rocker, though, most definitely was not at the White House. In fact, the president had been trying without success to reach him by telephone. As Speaker, he almost always was on hand to review the day's schedule with his leadership team and to be present for the day's opening House session. This morning, except for a brief stop in his office, Rocker had been nowhere to be found for any of it.

By 2:00 p.m., the Capitol Police became involved. So did the Metropolitan Police of the District of Columbia. And, very quietly, without informing other law enforcement agencies, so did the FBI. Director Vellman had considered reading Rocker his rights and bringing him back to FBI headquarters when he met with Rocker at his home earlier in the morning, but Rocker was a powerful political figure and, until now, one of the country's most respected leaders. Surely, Vellman decided, Rocker could be trusted to come in when summoned. Vellman assumed Rocker would arrange for legal counsel before turning himself in to the FBI. He already had admitted his involvement and expressed a willingness to cooperate. Now, Vellman realized that netting Rocker would require more than his cooperation. Vellman dispatched teams of agents to all the area's airports, the train station, and bus terminal. Other agents were posted at Rocker's office and home.

By late afternoon, the news of Rocker's disappearance was actively buzzing through the city's political grapevine. Why would he vanish on what was expected to be the most important day of his long political career?

The answer came from a District of Columbia parking meter worker. While writing a ticket for a car overparked on a residential street near the Capitol, she noticed a man slumped behind the steering wheel. Nearly hidden by the car's tinted windows, she did not see him until she placed the citation on the driver's side windshield. She rapped on the car's window, assuming he was asleep. When that didn't rouse him, she tried the door handle. It was unlocked. She opened the door and asked if he needed help. His body fell into her arms.

EMT workers were called, but there was nothing for them to do but remove the body. The license plate number was called in, and dispatch quickly matched it to the car law enforcement had been searching for all afternoon.

The story quickly burst onto the news. HOUSE SPEAKER FOUND DEAD! First appearances said suicide. Coatless, tieless, alone in the car, wallet still in his pocket, no signs of injury. But suicide? Today of all days?

Vellman had no doubts about what had happened.

"As soon as I left him this morning, Rocker obviously told a confederate, someone connected to the Adonis murder," he told Tenny. "A person he obviously trusted. Someone who didn't want Rocker to reveal how he got involved."

"Unbelievable," said Tenny. "Guy Rocker mixed up with his murderous group. If they're that deep into this government, what next?"

CHAPTER 72

The prospect that the death of Vice President Sheila Fishburne was a cunningly planned murder, not caused by an unfortunate accident, dominated media reports for days. Now, House Speaker Guy Rocker had also died a mysterious death. Although official sources were not linking the two events, the *New York Times*, *Washington Post*, and The Associated Press all had. The media's investigative teams found British intelligence sources willing to surmise, off the record, their suspicion that an international conspiracy known as the "Salvation Project" was responsible for both killings. The story reopened the still unsolved questions surrounding the deaths of Ohio Governor Lester Bowles and New York financier Gilbert Adonis.

The Salvation Project? Media files turned up scant prior reports about it. The name was linked to the death of a Kenyan opposition leader two years earlier. There were reports of its involvement in the Argentina coup earlier this year. One article, from a Tokyo newspaper ten years ago, mentioned the formation of such a group to press for climate change action. Could this be the same Salvation Project? Who were they? No individuals ever were linked to it. No press releases were ever distributed under its name. Could it be possible that a group powerful enough to murder high-ranking American leaders had been operating so stealthily for years that it had never drawn public attention?

For Richfield, all this attention was disastrous. The Project's chief asset was its secrecy. Now that was irreparably gone. True, intelligence agencies knew of the Project and had since last year's unfortunate breach. But the agencies' embarrassment that they had failed to uncover the Project sooner meant that they were not disposed to publicize its existence. Now, with all this attention, the Project would find it impossible to recruit talent. Defections were likely. Every government would review and tighten its security. Enterprising journalists would relentlessly pursue leads for newspaper and magazine exposés.

The Project would be forced to disappear, at least for a while. All current operations would have to be cancelled, all existing tracks erased. The storm eventually would pass. Other sensational stories would replace it over time. Even if the Peace and Security agenda was enacted, it would be difficult to implement. The public would be distressed. The possibility could even exist for the Project to reemerge openly, as an attractive alternative. It was time for one last Executive Committee meeting, with instructions to destroy all incriminating evidence.

And one last instruction to Malik.

CHAPTER 73

Malik parked his car at an elevated point on the street where he had a clear view of the Wharf, a newly developed area of restaurants, hotels, and entertainment venues in southwest Washington, DC. Small ships plied the Anacostia River, some belonging to those who moored them at the Wharf's marina, others on nightly dinner and sightseeing cruises. It was an attractive and popular scene, one that regularly drew crowds to the river walkway for its nightlife. In the car with Malik were two members of his team, Serge Bronson and Andre Siderov, both formerly of Brooklyn's Russian Mafia. Bronson and Siderov had summoned Malik here after covertly following Renata Chance and Bauman Kabiri to one of the Wharf's restaurants.

"It's the only outdoor restaurant in this area open to both the river and the street," said Bronson.

Malik removed a pair of high-powered binoculars from the car's glove compartment. "And our targets are the ones at the third table from the left?"

"Yes," confirmed Bronson. "They are the targets, and the woman seated alone at the table to the right of them is one of their guards. A second guard is at the bar. He's that large man in a brown sports jacket."

"There are only two guarding them?" asked Malik.

"One of the guards, the man, drove them here. The woman accompanied. They were the only guards in the car."

"And they met no other security people when they arrived?"

"We've been watching them every moment," said Bronson. "No others appear to be involved."

"Odd," said Malik, "that they would select an outdoor restaurant. It's almost too easy for us."

For many years Malik had been in the service of British intelligence. Then, the Cold War with the Russians ended, and British public opinion became more sensitive about death squads, particularly their own. The Salvation Project proved a more satisfactory client. It kept him far busier than the British ever had. Much less bureaucracy. Many more targets.

Malik valued careful planning and patience. Most assignments required creativity to avoid capture and deflect suspicion. These things could not be hurried. Opportunities would come to you if you had the patience to wait for them. This assignment would permit neither careful planning nor patience. The order from Richfield was to dispose of these people now. The Project was temporarily closing. All tracks that could lead to it must be erased. These two were a danger to everyone—to Richfield, to the Symfonia, even to Malik himself.

Malik weighed the risk against the current opportunity. Until now, the targets had been carefully confined and guarded. Why would they suddenly appear in public? Did they think two FBI protectors, or whoever was guarding them, would be enough? Against him? The man who had performed the impossible on every continent except Antarctica? Maybe they didn't know him. Maybe, despite him having walked calmly from the Adonis office and that congressman's car and all the other scenes where he had personally dispatched victims, they still didn't have a good identification of him. Maybe they believed the Project had already disbanded because of all the unwanted publicity. Or maybe it was a trap. All possibilities needed to be considered.

Under most circumstances he would have waited for another opportunity, but the victims were right here, easily identified, and easy to kill. And this was a time like no other. The Project was folding. Everyone involved, including Malik, would need to disappear quickly for their own safety. Besides, Malik had never failed. His reputation and his pride were at stake.

Finally, he settled on what he believed would be a low-risk plan.

"Serge," he said, breaking a long silence, "is our car switch lot near the ballpark still operational?"

"It is," replied Serge. "We have four cars there, all with keys under the floor mats."

"Okay then. Here's the plan. Both of you go to the bar. Arrive separately. You don't know each other. Serge, make sure you stand or sit next to the guy at the bar guarding our targets. I'll drive down to Maine Avenue. When I'm in position, I'll signal to both of you on my cell phone. Andre, on my signal, begin flirting with the woman guard at the table. Ask her if the other seat at the table is available. You know what to do. Distract her. Serge, when you see Andre make his move, get into an argument with the other guard, the one at the bar. Pretend you're drunk. Maybe even act like you want to fight him. When they are both distracted, I'll drive up next to the restaurant, shoot and kill our targets with my silencer. It will take a moment for people to realize what's happened. Both of you can look as afraid as everyone else. Yell, 'Shooter!' Everyone will run or hide under tables. You run too. Get away in the confusion before anyone suspects you. I'll drive to the car switch lot. Make sure you're parked in an easy place to clear the area before the police come. We'll all meet in an hour at our Virginia house. Then we will drive together, south to Richmond, and take planes from there. This is our last assignment. No need to return to our apartments. All understood?"

Risky, thought Malik as he moved his car into position on Maine Avenue, where he could clearly see Serge and Andre. Risky, but not as dangerous as some other jobs he had escaped from. If it was a trap and Serge and Andre were spotted, he would merely blend into the line of street traffic and wait for another opportunity.

Malik observed Serge ordering a beer and starting to converse with the bartender. Serge was a large man, nearly three hundred pounds. His size and weight often made strangers near him uncomfortable. That obviously was the case with the woman at his left, who slipped off her barstool to make more room for him. Then he turned his attention to the man seated to his right, the targets' guard. At first Serge was friendly, but even from a distance Malik could see the guard did his best to ignore him. At Malik's signal, Andre, who entered the bar separately, walked to the table where the other guard was seated. As he engaged her in conversation, Serge eyed the exchange, moved off his barstool and began threatening the man next to him. Perfect. Both guards were distracted.

Malik slowly rolled his car to a curb space directly in front of the restaurant, rolled down his car window, and picked up his AK-45 from the passenger seat. The targets seemed oblivious to their danger. But before he could place the muzzle completely out the window, two other diners seated next to the targets jumped up, turned their guns toward Malik, and yelled, "FBI. Drop it!" From the other side of Maine Avenue, two men, weapons drawn, were running toward him.

Serge saw the trap instantly, unholstered a gun concealed beneath his jacket, and began to run. The agent next to him at the bar did likewise. Instinctively, Serge fired. Another FBI agent stationed nearby killed Serge with a bullet to the heart. Two other agents grabbed Andre before he could draw a weapon or run.

With the gunfire came bedlam in the outdoor restaurant. Tables were kicked over for protection. Some diners threw themselves flat to the floor. Malik tried to escape from the agents coming toward him from the restaurant and across the avenue. He quickly pulled his car away from the curb only to see a police roadblock at the corner. Malik accelerated. A police vehicle with flashing lights wheeled onto the street, directly into his path. He pressed harder. By smashing into the rear of the police car and spinning it, Malik created a path for his own car to get through. He was about to accelerate again when a volley of shots rang out, deflating his rear tires.

The car's momentum took him into the next street. Malik rolled to the passenger seat and out the door. His only chance for escape now was to return enough fire to gain him a minute of time. Time to shed his shirt to his tee, remove his pants for the khaki shorts he always wore beneath them, his slip—on shoes for sandals he always carried. A different hairpiece and other disguises were part of his toolkit. If he could just buy one minute, he could change his appearance, blend in with the crowd of terrified spectators on the busy street. He had had close calls before. That time in Rio. That afternoon in London, where they even had dogs on his trail. He needed to stay cool, stay in control. Arrest was not an option. Too many bodies. Too many police agencies bidding to question him, torture him. Too many judges all too willing to hang him.

Using his AK-45 he began spraying shots indiscriminately, remaining carefully hidden behind his car door while ripping off his clothes and changing his facial features. His attackers were pinned down. He needed just a minute.

Now ready to flee, Malik spun his head to the right, looking for an escape route. He saw where he could run. An alleyway. A door into a busy bar. Perfect. The crowd was thick, hunched behind cars, hiding in doorways. He could be like them. A frightened bystander. Then he turned his head left, just for an instant, just time enough to see an armed man no more than three feet in front of him, with a weapon just like his, pointed at his head.

"Drop it," yelled the man.

Malik swung his own weapon around to defend himself. But for the first time in all his years as a paid assassin, his timing was late.

CHAPTER 74

Two men were killed, and six law enforcement officers were wounded, two seriously, during a gun battle that erupted last night before hundreds of terrified onlookers in the District of Columbia's popular Wharf area.

According to the FBI, both men killed were extremely dangerous members of the shadowy group calling itself 'the Salvation Project,' which has been linked to the recent deaths of Vice President Sheila Fishburne and House Speaker Guy Rocker.

At a press conference after the shootings, FBI agent Resa Parvaz, who heads the agency's DC office, said that his agents responded to information that suspects were planning a terrorist attack at the popular Riverhead Restaurant. When the suspects arrived, said Parvaz, an agent attempted to make an arrest, and one of the suspects resisted and displayed a weapon. In an exchange of gunfire, the suspect was killed and the agent was wounded.

A second suspect was in a car facing the restaurant and attempted to flee, said Parvaz. A DC Metropolitan Police roadblock stopped him. The trapped suspect began spraying bullets at law enforcement agents. The gunman was killed and five others were wounded in a gun battle that took place over the span of two blocks on Maine Avenue.

The action took place amid a large Saturday night crowd patronizing the area's popular restaurants and entertainment venues. Hundreds huddled behind *cars and ran for other cover. Four people were taken to an area hospital for minor injuries suffered during the melee. According to Parvaz, a third suspect was captured and is in FBI custody. (Story continues on page 7.)*

Tenny, still in her bathrobe, still nursing the day's first cup of coffee, stopped reading the newspaper article and pressed a number on her secure cell phone's speed dial.

"Madam President?" answered FBI Director Vellman.

"Tell me about it, Sam," she said.

"It happened late last night. I didn't want to wake you. A tipster identified one of the Project's killers as a Russian expat by the name of Siderov. We knew about Siderov from some action he was involved in up north, in Brooklyn, but we didn't know he was working for the Salvation Project. After the tip, we found him here in Washington. Before we moved in to arrest him, our tap into the Project's communications network uncovered an urgent order to their hit team to kill the two Project people who had turned themselves in: Kabiri and Chance. We talked about it with Kabiri and Chance, and they both agreed to be bait to trap the killers. So we arranged for Kabiri and Chance to have dinner together at a restaurant where they'd be vulnerable. When we removed Kabiri and Chance from their safe houses, sure enough, Siderov and another guy on the hit squad followed them. Our hope was that the head of the team, a killer known only as 'Malik,' would also get drawn in like a moth to the flame. And he was. We quickly flooded the restaurant and the entire area with our people and asked the DC police to set up a couple of roadblocks. It was a textbook operation."

"And they didn't even realize you had set up a trap."

"You know, Madam President, that guy Malik had literally been getting away with murder for years. He was on wanted lists all over Europe and Asia. He probably considered himself invincible. And everyone in the

Project was feeling extra pressure because of all the media exposure. It would only get harder as everyone tightened security."

"Great work, Sam. Congratulations to you and all your people. I hope the wounded agents are okay."

"One of them took a pretty serious stomach shot. He'll survive, but he's in for a long rehab."

"Very heroic of all of them. Give me their contact information, and I'll let everyone involved know how much I personally appreciate them. Does this mean, Sam, that the siege is over? Can we come out of hiding?"

"Very likely," said Vellman. "With Malik and the others gone, and MI5's cleanup work in London, I'm fairly certain we've at least disabled their death squad. As an extra bonus, we positively identified Malik as Adonis's killer. Perfect facial match with the building video we had of him."

"Let's make sure that becomes public. But Sam, let's not link Guy Rocker to them. Guy made a terrible mistake, and he died because of it. Let's not give his family any more pain since there's nothing to be gained by it. Identify Rocker as someone the Project people killed, which appears to be true. They were on a mission to kill all the leaders of the US government. Fish, Rocker, even me. Okay?"

"Certainly. Anything else, Madam President?"

"Yes. Out of curiosity, who tipped you off to that man Siderov, the one who gave you the chance to set the trap? We should reward that person too."

Vellman was silent for a moment. Then, with hesitation, he said, "I'm sorry, Madam President; I can't tell you. I promised him no one would ever know."

"You promised him personally? The tip came directly to you? Now I am curious. Who was it, Sam?"

"I'm sorry, Madam President."

"Sam?"

There was silence.

"Sam?"

"It was your husband, Dr. Navarro."

Now it was Tenny who was speechless. Andres?

"He told me everything, Madam President. Why he made contact with you during the campaign. The order he received from the Project to inject you, kill you if necessary. Everything that happened next. How you've been protecting him from being arrested ever since. He came to me after it became clear the Project had killed the vice president. He said he realized that divulging this to me meant he would likely face serious charges and go to jail, but he couldn't deny it any longer, knowing he had information that could help bring down the Salvation Project. The person who told him that his daughter had been kidnapped and would be killed if he didn't play ball with them was Siderov."

"You have Siderov in custody?" asked Tenny.

"Yes, Madam President, we do," said Vellman.

"Have you questioned him about his contact with Andres?"

"I have, Madam President. I've handled this personally. He confirmed Dr. Navarro's account in every detail."

Tenny wanted to respond, but her voice wouldn't obey. A tsunami of emotion raced through her mind and body.

Vellman filled the silence. "On my official report I've listed this information as coming from an anonymous tip. I don't see a need to tell anyone else if you don't."

CHAPTER 75

Most nights when she wasn't traveling Tenny and Andres would share a private dinner in the White House's second-floor dining room. Those dinners became more frequent with Tenny's limited post-hospitalization schedule.

Tonight's conversation was unusually subdued. Tenny had eaten only half her green salad and a small corner of her broiled halibut. Andres, respectful of the multiple pressures weighing on Tenny's mind, seldom broke long silences. Tonight's silence, though, felt different than others. Did she hear the few words that had passed between them? Her thoughts seemed elsewhere, her eyes not on Andres but on her plate of food.

"Particularly hard day?" he asked.

Tenny didn't immediately reply. Andres became concerned that her distraction was related to something physical.

"Tenny?" he asked again. "Are you feeling okay?"

She turned her eyes toward him. "Do you recall the night we first met? Your fraternity's party?"

"How could I forget?" He smiled. "You were so beautiful. I asked my sister who you were. Were you with anyone? Would she introduce me to you?"

"We shook hands," said Tenny. "You looked at me. Directly into my eyes. With that look and that touch, my entire body felt a jolt. It was physical. Like nothing I had ever experienced. My mind was too muddled to think."

"Like electricity? An electric shock?"

"Exactly. Like I imagine what happens to you if you accidently put two battery cables together. Meeting you, seeing you, touching you. That shock ended a young me. Whoever I was then, a flighty girl thinking only of herself and her own daily pleasures, that girl disappeared. For the first time, I understood love. What it really meant. The future became more important than the present. From that night on, I wanted us. Us to be together. To live together. Raise a family together. Share life's experiences together. I haven't the words to describe it, but it happened that night, when we met, when we had sex, when we held each other long and close and desperately didn't want to say good night. I felt that a new me was born then."

Andre began to respond.

"No, no," said Tenny. "Let me finish. The new me born then didn't die through our divorce or all the years since or even with your reappearance in my life and our remarriage. But it died today."

Andres sat back in his chair, uncertain how to react.

"I was thrilled when you came to my hotel asking to see me during last year's campaign," Tenny continued. "My love for you had been dormant for decades. I vaguely knew it was there. I didn't realize how near the surface it remained. Then, suddenly, you no longer were an aging memory I could recall fondly. You were right there in the hotel lobby, and honestly, those battery cables connected again. I was jolted again. And despite everything that's happened since that day, I've realized my love for you was too strong to die, to hide, to drive back into the box where I had packed it many years ago."

A steward appeared to remove the dinner plates. Keeping her eyes fixed on Andres, she signaled the steward to leave.

"Love, though, is not trust," she continued, "and I have to confess, Andres, that many times this year I've wondered whether my trust in you was again misplaced. Not because of anything you've done this year, but because of what's past. As people I knew and trusted were exposed as part of the Salvation Project, it made me wonder: If them, why not you? Did they really kidnap your daughter, or was that just a cover story so you could explain your behavior? Did you really intend to inject me or kill me, but lose your nerve at the last moment? Would you try again, this time with more courage? If they took another member of your family hostage and gave you another kill-or-be-killed choice, how would you react this time? Could I trust you with my medications? Would you do something in the White House infirmary or at the hospital to make my death appear natural?

"That night in bed last year. In that dark room. My crazy, wild passion for you. And you responding to it with that hypodermic needle. My bare leg. The vulnerability. The shock of moving from uncontrollable lust to mortal danger in the space of a single second."

Andres reached across the table for her hand. "Tenny, oh my God . . . What happened today to bring on all of this?"

She pulled away. "Today the old Tenny died. Actually, the Tenny who fell in love with you at that fraternity party and who has been living that love ever since died."

She let silence fill the space between them, as if transitioning from one life to another.

"A new Tenny was born today, Andres. When Sam Vellman told me that you gave him the information that brought down the Salvation Project death squad, I realized that my decision to protect you from arrest, from jail time, was really a decision to protect myself, protect myself from accepting the reality that our old life was over. I told no one what you did that night because if I had, my young dream would have ended. And so I preserved it, despite the risks, the continuing doubts. What I learned today lifted that veil for me. The veil of mistrust. Now I know the story you told me about your daughter's kidnapping was true. I know the name of the man who made the threat and has confessed to doing it. I no longer need to doubt you, protect you, or protect myself.

"When I say the old Tenny died, I say it with relief, not anger, not sadness. And when I say a new me's been born, it's with a clear-eyed understanding of who we are at this moment in our lives, not who we were at twenty-one or where we've been since. I've been living a fantasy. That's over. This, today, what we feel for one another at this place in our lives, is where I want to be. With you, now and for every remaining hour of every day we have left to be together."

NOVEMBER

CHAPTER 76

Air Force One was four hours into its thirteen-hour flight from
Beijing to Washington, DC, before Tenny emerged from her
sleeping quarters. Andres insisted that she nap immediately after
takeoff. She needed little encouragement. The past four days had been the
hardest days of negotiations she had ever experienced.

Other nations would move forward on disarmament only if the
Chinese agreed, and so she decided to join her negotiating team in Beijing
to answer every difficult question immediately, to make yes-no decisions
firsthand, to surmount obstacles as they arose and keep the discussions
moving toward a finish line. Questions remained as she boarded her flight
home, but Tenny was confident that after the Beijing agreements, it would
be more difficult for negotiators to backslide than to go forward. She left
Beijing with a sense of relief—and weariness from the hours of unrelieved
tension.

Now, awake from her nap, Tenny felt refreshed. Andres had made the
right call; sleep was the correct prescription. Until this flight, Andres had
seldom accompanied her on official trips. But from that night a week earlier
when she declared she wanted to be together with him "for every remaining
hour of every day we have left together," they had been. For Tenny, these
were more than words of love. Andres was mental comfort, physical

assurance, a sense of closeness and caring that had eluded her during her political years.

Kyle Christian read Tenny's buoyancy the moment he joined her for lunch. Christian seldom was invited on Air Force One. The sight of the CIA director traveling with the president activated the media's speculation sensors, but Tenny had insisted on his presence in Beijing in the event she faced questions on intelligence matters beyond her knowledge. Now, on the return flight, he was the first person she asked to see.

"Hungry?" she asked. "They somehow come up with amazingly good food from that small galley. I'm not sure what they serve others, but they treat me well. Enjoy it."

"Thanks for inviting me," said Christian. "You certainly appear effusive for someone carrying the weight of the world. Reminds me of our days in Congress together."

"Oh yes!" said Tenny. "Weren't hey great days? We were a bunch of energetic young people who didn't know any better, taking on the old fossils who ran the committees. Now look at us; we're the old fossils."

"But we're not fossilized," said Christian. "There's a lot more to do before they cart us off to the old politicians' home."

"A lot more," Tenny agreed. "And we're so close to delivering some big wins. I'm told we're just two votes short of passing the disarmament treaty. It looks like I'll be able to make it part of my next State of the Union package. And the Senate will pass the other bills in our agenda before Christmas."

"Truly remarkable," said Christian. "Coming to Beijing was the right thing to do . My contacts in Chinese intelligence say it was a test. If you're serious about this, the Chinese leadership thought, you will come personally. If not, it would be considered a charade. Looks like you passed the test."

"That was my instinct. The last thing I wanted to do was make this long flight with so much happening back in Washington. The last obstacle I had to knock down was what to do with North Korea; the idea that if the rest of us drew down our arsenals and the North Koreans didn't China would be pretty vulnerable. But I assured them that the US, and the NATO countries wouldn't let that happen. We got the Russians to confirm they were aboard, too. North Korea can't fight the world, nor for that matter, can Iran. We'll pull their fangs before we disarm ourselves."

"And how did you wind up on the human rights questions?"

"I told them that we have fundamental disagreements with them on the whole package—freedom of speech, their judicial system, how they brutalize their political opposition, their treatment of the Tibetans and the Uyghurs. The whole package. I said I would continue to speak out against it. Nothing in our negotiations will affect that. But we're not going to go to war with them over it. This isn't about their political system or economic system. It's about removing the means of mutual destruction. I know a lot of our own people will disagree, but we can't work for human rights in China if we're all turned into nuclear ash.

A steward emerged from the galley with two dishes of spinach lasagna, freshly baked rolls, and coffee.

"See what I mean?" asked Tenny. "Just like dining at a fine hotel in New York. I'd offer you wine, but I need a full deck for what's waiting for me after our lunch. Can't take any chances. Do you use cream or sugar?"

"No, just black, and this lasagna looks just perfect."

"Okay then," she said, "I have two other questions for you. First question: Let's say our Peace and Security program passes. Our disarmament treaty gets signed. What comes next?"

"How do you implement it?" asked Christian.

"Exactly. I don't expect the opposition to go away. There will be suits filed hoping to make it all unconstitutional. Even people inside our own military will try to sabotage it. Old ways die hard. What would you do?"

"Well, the first action I would advise would be a bold stroke to demonstrate your determination to make it work. Announce the immediate disarmament of fifty percent of our nuclear force. Unilaterally. Without requiring anyone else to do it immediately."

"That's what I consider bold," said Tenny. "Then what?"

"Even with the fifty percent cut, we still would have more than enough weapons to blow up the world and more operable nuclear weapons than the Russians and Chinese. Taking a strong first step would be like we used to say on our Oklahoma farm, priming the pump. Once the action's flowing, it would be hard for the others to not join Step Two: phased disarmament, on say a five-year timetable, full inspection so we can all verify that no one's cheating. And with each cutback in military spending, immediate transfer of that money to keep workers who would lose their jobs employed. That's key politically. There can't be big employment gaps. It wouldn't take much of a job loss to turn the public against us."

"You agree with what I'm doing?"

"It should have happened long ago. Remember, before you appointed me to the CIA job, I chaired the Intelligence Committee. We talked about the need for disarmament there, but no one had the guts to take on the whole military-industrial world. It took you to do it."

Tenny was quiet for a few moments. She ate a forkful of lasagna and sipped some coffee. Christian wondered whether she approved or disapproved of his suggestion.

Finally, she looked up from her meal.

"Kyle, I said that I had two matters I wanted to discuss with you. The second matter is that I would like to nominate you to be my vice president."

Christian laid his utensils on the table and pushed back his chair.

"Whoa, Tenny!" He exhaled loudly. "Oh, I'm so sorry, I should have said, 'Whoa, Madam President!' You can't be serious. I haven't even considered it. I hope no friends of mine have been advocating for me."

"No, they haven't," said Tenny. "That's one of the reasons I trust you. If you were in any way connected with the Salvation Project, others would be campaigning on your behalf the way they were for Guy Rocker. No one has. Another reason I trust you is that last year, when Chinese intelligence discovered the documents that allowed us to defeat Gil Adonis, they gave them to you to act on. They wouldn't have done that without believing you would play it straight with them and get those documents to me. That's important going into our new Peace and Security world. So much hinges on trust. Trust will be the most effective substitute for weapons. I trusted Fish. You and I have worked together well for years, and I trust you. More than that, you think strategically. I need that."

"Tenny," said Christian, "this is so unexpected. Are you certain?"

"Of course," she replied. "For all the reasons I just mentioned, and two more. Kyle, four times you were elected to Congress in Oklahoma. If you can do that in Oklahoma, where Democrats seldom win, I know you can keep the White House for four or eight more years. We need time, Kyle. Time. That's the only way we will keep this flame alive. And one more thing. As CIA director you have dossiers on every world leader and files on everyone with power and authority in their countries. With you as president or vice president, they will be much more wary about dealing with you and not crossing you. No one, no matter how authoritarian they are, wants embarrassing public disclosures."

"I haven't looked at as many dossiers as you might think, Tenny," said Christian.

"They don't know that. They all have things to hide, and they all believe the CIA knows where to look. Just act like you know more than you do. They'll believe it."

DECEMBER

CHAPTER 77

Vice President Kyle Christian rapped the United States Senate to order from the presiding officer's chair. "The clerk will call the roll," he announced. Occasionally there are surprise outcomes when the US Senate votes, but this was not likely to be one of those times. All one hundred members had declared in advance where they stood on the Peace and Security Act, and there were more than enough "ayes" to approve it. Christian, as presiding officer, could cast the deciding vote if the roll call ended in a tie, just in case.

Tenny, Andres, Ben, Carmie, and Lee watched the roll call on C-Span from the private residence. In anticipation of their success, a victory party was in progress downstairs, in the East Room. Diplomats from most major countries, members of Congress, heads of government departments, campaign staff workers, and celebrities who had participated in those campaigns were either there already or would be before the night ended. Senators would make their way to the White House once their votes were cast.

"I've just realized," said Tenny. "It's almost a year to the day that I had dinner here with Gil Adonis. A year since I had my eyes opened to the risk his group was to all of us. Until then, I didn't realize they were so powerful."

"Quite a lot to get done in just a year," said Carmie. "Especially when so many people believed it couldn't get done at all."

The electronic tally showed thirty-six votes for, twenty-three opposed. The vote count changed slowly as senators continued to arrive on the Senate floor and answer to their names.

"A billion and a half dollars helped," said Ben.

"Is that the final cost?" asked Tenny.

"No," said Lee, "just what we know about so far. It may get closer to two billion."

"Money well spent," said Tenny.

"I can give you a loan if you're tapped out," said Carmie.

"Here's the thing about having a lot of money," said Tenny, "it just keeps making money for you. During the year, my investments probably made me two billion. I doubt the campaign lowered my assets at all. But as long as we're talking about money, I want to tell you what I plan to do with the rest of it. Ben, please mute the sound on the TV for a moment."

As Ben did that, the screen showed the vote count at forty-one in favor, thirty-three opposed.

"This is just step one in a fight that's likely to go on for a dozen years or more," said Tenny. "It's really a battle for minds, to change mindsets, to get people to stop thinking of war as an option for anything. So here's what I'm doing. What I've done, actually. I've set up a nonprofit Peace and Security Foundation and endowed it with just about my entire fortune. That's close to twenty billion dollars. If democracy is going to survive, people who vote need to know what their choices are. Not just which party or ideology to vote for, but real choices that affect their lives. That's hard to do when self-interests with big war chests can buy advertising and influence and others can't. I want our Foundation to be a peoples' lobby. Every issue we care about starting with disarmament, having the same resources to educate, advertise, lobby and even work to elect people as whoever's on the other side. We don't have to be adversaries. The idea is to make sure voters really know what's at stake and what their choices are. You know, real democracy, not a government responding just to those who have the money to buy it."

"Tenny!" said Carmie. "That's amazing. What a project."

"And," added Tenny, "I want you and Ben to run it. That is, if you two are still able to work together after being roommates all year and if you, Ben, aren't planning to leave us again."

"You know the answer to what's happened to us already," said Carmie. "And you knew it would happen if Ben came to live with me."

Tenny shrugged. "You think I purposely played matchmaker?"

"Would you rather I say you played the politics of romance? Whatever it is, Ben and I are very happy together. I know I am. Ben?"

"I'm not going anywhere. We've had people with guns chasing us all year. But the scariest thing for me is how happy Carmie and I are together."

"Great," said Tenny. "Ben, Lee, you've got a huge campaign to keep running. Carmie, you've got a twenty-billion-dollar enterprise to manage."

"The vote count just passed fifty-two," said Andres. "Congratulations to all of you."

"Time to go downstairs and take a bow," said Tenny.

The group made its way downstairs with Secret Service escorts. As they approached the entrance of the East Room, a man who had been standing by the door, apparently waiting for Tenny's arrival, stepped forward.

"Remarkable achievement, Madam President," he said. "Truly remarkable. Whatever I can do to help, just call on me."

As they walked into the party, Carmie whispered to Tenny, "That man's so familiar. Who is he?"

"A retired army general who headed their nuclear program. Very knowledgeable and well connected. He can be very helpful to the new foundation. Maybe add him to the board. His name's Cal Foley."

A Guide to Characters In This Story

MAIN CHARACTERS

Gilbert "Gil" Adonis. Billionaire hedge fund manager based in New York. Close friend of Lester Bowles.

Lester "Les" Bowles Jr. Ohio's governor. Former Republican vice-presidential nominee.

Renetta Chance. Salvation Project manager. Holds a seat in the statistical department of the London School of Economics.

Kyle Christian. Director of the CIA. Former Congressman. Democrat from Oklahoma.

Sheila "Fish" Fishburne. Tenny's vice president.

General Cal Foley. Retired army general. Member of the National Intelligence Review Board and former head of the US Army's missile program.

Bauman Kabiri. Salvation Project manager. Professor of biostatistics at the University of Virginia.

Malik. The head of the Salvation Project's enforcement team.

Dr. Andres Navarro. Tenny's ex-husband.

Project Manager Three. The only surviving founder of Salvation Project.

Project Manager Eighteen. The U.S. member of the Salvation Project Executive Committee.

Richfield. Salvation Project Executive Director.

Guy Rocker. Speaker of the U.S. House of Representatives.

Ben Sage. President Tennyson's long-time political consultant.

Carmen "Carmie" Sanchez. Tenny's best friend and U.S. Secretary of Commerce.

Lee Searer. Ben Sage's consulting partner.

Isabel "Tenny" Aragon Tennyson. President of the United States.

Sam Vellman. Director of the FBI

OTHER CHARACTERS

Lois Adkins. Gil Adonis's secretary.

Garrett Baumgartner. Secretary of Defense.

Carla Bounty. A news anchor at CNN.

Ann Bowles. Lester Bowles's daughter.

Craig Bowles. Lester Bowles's oldest son.

June Bowles. Lester Bowles's wife.

Lester Bowles Sr. Former US senator. Lester Bowles Jr.'s father.

Zach Bowman. Former Republican presidential nominee.

Serge Bronson. Salvation Project hitman.

Farley Caragin. A reporter for CNN.

Detective Carlisle. A detective with the Washington, DC, metropolitan police.

Henry "Deac" Deacon. Tenny's chief of staff.

Stanley "Stan" Decker. Secretary of State.

DuWayne. Owner of the Green Light Diner, Poulsbo, Washington.

General Carter Edsell. Commander of Eielson AFB, Alaska.

Horst England. Raytheon's CEO.

Alicee Fishburne. Sheila's mother.

Reed Fishburne. Sheila's father.

Darren Fitzgerald. Medical expert for CNN.

Marcie Friend. Tenny's secretary.

Janice Gainsboro. A friend of Renetta Chance.

Charlotte Gambel. A reporter for CNN.

George Hernandez. U.S. House Majority Leader.

Hughes. Gil's regular driver.

Morris Jenkins. An agent with the FBI.

Juan. Malik in disguise.

Lane Juliano. Senate Majority Leader.

Karen. One of Fish's aides.

James Lazarre. One of Adonis's bodyguards.

Marianna Lee. Former Executive Director of the Salvation Project.

Hank Leidimeier. Alaska bush pilot.

Frank Lipscott. Chairman of the House Armed Services Committee.

Claire Liston. The White House press secretary.

Josef Lorenz. An anchor for CNN.

Louellen. Tenny and Andres's wedding coordinator.

Sid Mohamad. White House legal counsel.

Kellen Monroe. A well-known actor.

Father Bennett Morgan. Priest for Tenny and Andres's remarriage.

Grace Navarro. One of Andres's daughters.

Karen Navarro. One of Andres's daughters.

Lucille Nobel. Chair of the U.S. House Energy Committee.

Resa Parvaz. FBI agent in charge of the bureau's DC office.

Pete Quist. U.S. Senator from Washington State.

Carla Redbone. Assistant House majority leader.

LaVenna Seraphin. George Washington University Hospital assistant administrator.

Andre Siderov. Salvation Project hitman.

Simon. A Secret Service agent.

Gillian Stockwell. CEO of Lockheed Martin.

Ingrid Stolski. Chair of the U.S. House Foreign Affairs Committee.

Angel Suarez. A legislative assistant in the White House.

Tulak. Fish's uncle. Alaska whaling boat captain.

Chief Valdez. Chief, Metropolitan Police Department of the District of Columbia.

Carol Vincent. Alaska bush pilot

Anatoly Voronin. President of Russia.

Dr. Lucille Walker. The official doctor at the White House.

Wong Ho. Premier of China.

AUTHOR'S NOTES

Here's a bit of background on why I wrote this story.

A century ago, those who lived in the United States and other economically developed countries experienced an unprecedented wave of technological change. Electricity lit their homes. Telephones and radio revolutionized their communications. Automobiles replaced their horses. Airplanes created a whole new form of transportation for commerce and personal travel.

If you were alive then you did not need to know anything about electricity or the internal combustion engine or why heavier than air vehicles didn't fall from the sky. You just knew that they worked and that you could light your home without candles. You could buy a car. You could make a telephone call. You could learn things you never knew and be entertained by radio. The changes were revolutionary, but you could understand them.

There also was a dark side to those changes. Airplanes could carry bombs as well as the mail. Radio could be used by power-hungry dictators to control their publics. The same technology that made automobiles possible could be used to build tanks. And failure to contain the dark side resulted in dreadful consequences. Multiple wars. Tens of millions dead. Destruction of cities and countries on a scale never experienced.

In our own time we are experiencing an even more profound wave of change. Science has made it possible to manipulate the very building blocks of life. Artificial intelligence is creating a digital world well beyond the human brain's capacity to perform. Robots are assuming ever more jobs we always considered part of the human domain. Quantum computing promises to move all of this and more into an even faster dimension of life-changing development.

Unlike a century ago, few of us understand any of this. DNA and RNA? Rewiring of brains? Hypersonic weapons? The singularity? The meta universe? Cryptocurrencies? Designer babies?

In their most positive applications, these discoveries offer the prospect for making life infinitely better for all humanity. Hunger and homelessness and many diseases may be eliminated. Longevity may be increased. Tedious and unrewarding work may be a thing of the past.

But the potential dark side is far darker than humanity has ever known because through lack of awareness, or experimental error, or technical glitch, or malign intent, weapons could be launched without human intervention that would make the planet inhabitable; creatures could be created through DNA manipulation that would be far different and more dangerous than any we've known; quantum computers could take on a life of their own. These are not my doomsday fantasies. A large and growing body of scientists have waved red flags about such dangers.

How does society reap the benefits of scientific and technical advancement without suffering the consequences? It's a question seldom asked, but one that needs immediate attention. Can democratic government provide the answers? That's the question at the core of "Menace."

Three decades ago, a meeting at Kyoto, Japan confirmed the threat of a warming planet and produced a plan for dealing with it. Three decades later, with unprecedented heat, fire, storm, flood, drought, and climate-related migration accelerating even beyond the Kyoto forecasts, governments still have not responded in a manner equal to the threat.

Six decades ago, nuclear bombs were used in warfare. The risk of their use again in much more deadly form has not receded. More nations have them stockpiled. Delivery systems remain trigger-ready and could launch without human intervention at hypersonic levels.

Even a technology seemingly as benign as the Internet has been transformed into the beating heart of social turmoil and political repression.

I wrote *The Moment of Menace* and its prequel, *The Salvation Project* to imagine these threats in the context of fiction. But the question addressed is very much our reality. How does democracy survive in this age of advanced science? Where are the elected representatives who understand how to manage the 21st century world of scientific discovery? How can the public that selects those representatives make rationale choices if the knowledge gap is so vast?

Humanity is on the knife's edge of a potential golden age—better, longer lives for all who come after us. Far from being bleak, the future can be glorious. Can it be both glorious and remain the democratic system most of us cherish? That's the question *The Moment of Menace* addresses.

***

More than a million books are published each year. From all those choices, I am grateful to you for selecting mine. Thank you. I hope you found reading *The Moment of Menace* worth your time. I would appreciate any comments or suggestions you may have, posted on the book site of your choice, or sent to me directly at jrothstein@rothstein.net

It did not take a village to write *The Moment of Menace*, but it required much research, editing and advice. I am grateful for the legion of the friends, family and acquaintances who provided it.

--Joe Rothstein, 2022

ABOUT JOE ROTHSTEIN

I sat down to write my first book when I was in my 20s. It didn't take long for me to realize that I could not write a book because I had nothing useful to say. I'd have to live my life first.

In between then and now:

--I was the advance man for a traveling automobile stunt show. In the act I was "Suicide Saunders." (That's my next book).

--I sat at the side of the governor of Alaska as his staff aide, in the private quarters of the top military commander in Alaska, while the general clutched a red telephone expecting a call telling him we were at nuclear war with Russia over the Cuban missile crisis.

--I experienced the most powerful earthquake in U.S. history, in Alaska, and worked on rebuilding in the aftermath.

--I became editor of a daily newspaper, The Anchorage Daily News, before I was 30.

--I flew as a passenger with the Navy's Blue Angels (and have the photo to prove it).

--I managed a successful U.S. Senate campaign and moved to Washington, DC as the new senator's chief of staff.

--I was deeply immersed in the revelations of the Pentagon Papers.

--I was political consultant to Congressman Peter Rodino of New Jersey as he presided over Richard Nixon's impeachment.

--I worked as strategist and media producer to help elect and re-elect nine U.S. Senators, dozens of members of Congress, and countless other candidates.

--I've started five businesses, one which went public, and another that's become an important Internet news distribution service.

--Also, I've had the experience of raising four sons and, among other things, coaching their Little League baseball team, which was one of the most intense political experiences of my life.

And now, in my 80s, I've written three novels with two more in progress.

Having something to say no longer is an obstacle.

THE LATINA PRESIDENT

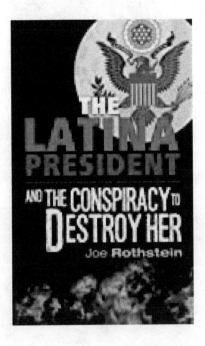

"If John Grisham wrote political thrillers instead of legal ones, they'd feel like this!"

"An unusually deep plot for a political thriller...An enthralling protagonist at the heart of a gripping tale. A suspenseful--and topical--tale of White House intrigue." --- *Kirkus Reviews*

"For intrigue and suspense, The Latina President rivals anything I've ever read about campaign politics." -- *U.S. Senator Tom Daschle, former Senate Majority Leader.*

"Joe Rothstein spent decades living in the real world of political drama. Now he's packed all of that experience into a riveting political work of fiction that is a guaranteed page turner." -- *U.S. Senator Byron Dorgan, former chairman, Senate Democratic Policy Committee and best-selling N.Y. Times author.*

"Powerful fiction, directly relevant to growing risks now facing us as individuals and the stability of our entire global financial system." -- *U.S. Senator Don Riegle, former Chairman, Senate Banking Committee."*

"A gripping tale about our country's first Latina president and her unbelievable rise and fall. Couldn't put it down. How does one say 'spell-binding' in Spanish?" -- *Dick Lobo, award-winning journalist and broadcast executive.*

THE SALVATION PROJECT

Political Thriller of the Year Finalist

"Joe Rothstein's The Salvation Project is fashioned as a novel that conjures positive memories of great political thrillers of the past such as Richard Condon's The Manchurian Candidate or Steven King's The Dead Zone. Far from simply imitating those books however, Rothstein takes high stakes political espionage to a very contemporary, credibly scary, and absolutely addictive level with his opus, The Salvation Project."
–Pacific Reviews

"Picks up neatly from Latina, very sophisticated take on business as well as politics, intriguing plot."

"More than enough shots from left field to keep me hooked!"

"I enjoyed reading about strong women who also help each other and encourage growth in others."

"I felt as though I was a part of the action!"

"I could apply 'thought provoking' to so much of the book, that I'm not satisfied with one-time reading."

"Love the worldwide conspiracy, the Vatican and the Israelis. What a mix!"

"I love the pace, a lot going on but not so much that it is hard to track."

"The intricacies of the Project—are unusual and memorable."

—BookLife by Publishers Weekly

"Be forewarned: there's a lot of juicy action to digest here…and just when it seems like a tidy ending will evolve, yet another unexpected twist emerges."

—Midwest Reviews

RATE THIS NOVEL

How would you rate The Moment of Menace?

1,2,3,4, or 5 stars?

Let us (and other readers) know by posting a grade and short review on your book store's web site.

BOOK CLUB
DISCUSSION GUIDE

In addition to its entertainment value, *The Moment of Menace* deals with important real-life issues. The novel lends itself to Book Club discussion. Here are a few suggested discussion questions.

1. Do you agree with the premise that democratic governments are struggling to manage new science and technology?
2. Would you have signed the petition for worldwide total disarmament?
3. Were Tenny's speech and arguments for her agenda convincing?
4. Did the story hold your interest throughout?
5. Were you satisfied or disappointed in how the story finally resolved?
6. If you were making a movie of this book, who would you cast?
7. Have you read other books by this author? How do they compare?
8. If you had a chance to ask the author of this book one question, what would it be?
9. Was the book's title an accurate description of the story inside?
10. Have you read other books with similar messages?
11. Does the story feel as if it could actually be real?
12. Do you have personal knowledge or experience pertinent to the subject of the story?
13. Do you feel you learned anything important from this story?
14. Are you motivated to take any action because of this story?

If you have a question or message you would like to discuss with the author, his email address is jrothstein@rothstein.net.